Cherbourg Peninsula 1942

In the silence of the dark pine wood the crack of a broken twig sounded like a rifle shot.

Geoffrey froze. The burly Commando in front of him slowly turned his head, grimacing. They waited, senses straining. Beyond the quiet trees the two men could hear a faint hum of activity coming from the airfield, half a mile ahead.

Heart hammering against his ribs, Geoffrey wondered, not for the first time, how in God's name he had ever managed to get himself into this situation. Five o'clock in the morning in enemy-held territory and creeping forward to attempt something so audacious it was verging on suicidal yet, if successful, might just change the course of the war…

OPERATION AIRTHIEF

A Dolman Scott Book

Book Design: Alison Wills

ISBN 978-1-905553-43-3

Published and Printed by
Dolman Scott Ltd
www.dolmanscott.com

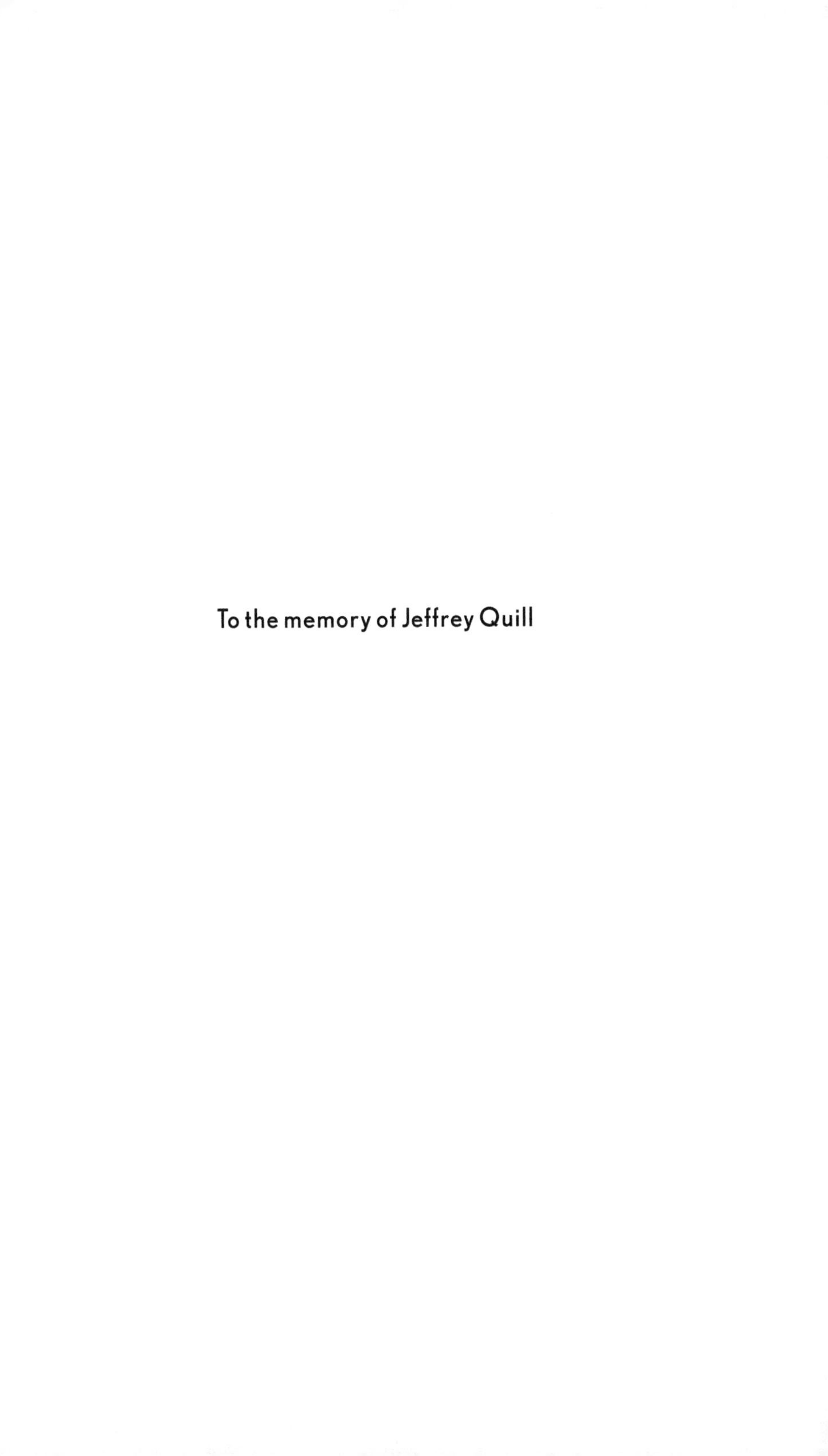

To the memory of Jeffrey Quill

ONE

Geoffrey Penn eased back lightly on the throttle of the de Havilland, banked slightly to the left and looked down upon a frost-covered, hedgerow-littered English landscape. The sun was just rising over the east coast, casting long shadows from the dark green hedges across the white fields. There is no place lovelier than England when the weather is right, he mused, and this was one of those all too rare moments. On days such as this he never ceased to marvel at how far he could see.

Geoffrey had always known that he wanted to fly, at least as far back as he could remember. His favourite early toys were model planes, many of which he laboriously stuck together with glue, balsa wood and paper, then dutifully rebuilt after they inevitably crashed. As these little planes had no pilots it never occurred to Geoffrey that one might have to 're-glue' the pilot as well in these circumstances. Bright at school and good at sports, his parents had held high hopes of his going to Oxford or Cambridge, but Geoffrey suspected that his father, while a little upset, wasn't too surprised when he announced that he wished to become a pilot. No-one knew how a pilot could make a living in those days. The Army took a few, but the airlines didn't need many and most of the flying clubs already had some would-be instructors hanging around looking for pupils. None of this concerned Geoffrey. He simply wanted to fly.

Grantham, the institution where he ultimately went, had been a boy's dream too, with plenty of sports along with lessons on flying theory followed by actually going up in a Tiger Moth, a bi-wing open cockpit trainer aircraft which could be looped and rolled by instructors and advanced students. The planes were of such light construction, Geoffrey recalled, that when grounded they had to be tethered at each wingtip to avoid becoming airborne in a really stiff wind. He remembered seeing one landing into a forty mile an hour headwind and someone walking alongside holding one wingtip steady before the wheels finally found and held the ground. He was convinced that no boy could have asked for a better life and his glowing letters home convinced his parents that, even though they'd been given little option, their son had at least found the right place for himself.

The day eventually arrived when Geoffrey had to leave Grantham and face earning a living. There were a few jobs available for the better students, and Geoffrey's ability, rated by his teachers as exceptional, made him fervently hope that exceptional actually meant exceptionally good. Apparently it did, and he took the offered commission in the Royal Air Force. Life there was, according to Geoffrey, 'bloody good', with plenty of flying in Avro Tudors and then in what was considered to be a real fighter, the Armstrong Whitworth Siskin.

It was 1934 and nearly everyone in the RAF considered that France was the most probable enemy in any military confrontation. After all, Britain and France had been foes for centuries, hadn't they? And many in the forces thought that the Bristol Bulldog fighter plane, with its two 303 calibre machineguns would be enough to keep the 'Frogs' on their own side of the pond. The Bulldog was a lively, fully aerobatic plane which, despite having no brakes, no oxygen and no heater, managed to keep Geoffrey amused for a while. Life in the service, as is usually the case in peacetime, eventually became a bit tiresome, although there were glamorous interludes such as the parties frequently given by Sir Philip Sassoon, himself a pilot. Sir Philip used to invite young airmen to these events at his estate in order to liven up the proceedings, something they could be relied upon to do.

It was during one of these gatherings that two events occurred which changed the course of Geoffrey's life. He was strolling across the lawn with Dudley Whitchurch, one of his best flying and carousing pals, when Dudley surprised him with a question.

"Geoffrey, old boy, how do you feel about getting out of this life? I'll admit it *is* pretty good, but don't you feel it's getting just a teeny bit tedious?"

"Frankly, suicide's a long way from my mind, old chap, but what's bothering you?"

"Nothing that drastic, I can assure you," Dudley laughed, "but having watched your acrobatics I'm not so sure you're being quite straight with me! No, I've in mind putting in for a transfer to the Met Service. They're looking for two idiots to fly in any weather who, if they survive, can tell everybody about the conditions, though it does seem to me that if it's too shitty to fly you hardly need to tell anyone about it! Anyway, I'm going for it and you're the most likely other idiot that comes to mind, so how about it?"

"Hadn't heard about this," replied Geoffrey, looking thoughtful, "but it would be a welcome bloody change. Where would we be stationed?"

"Cambridgeshire, I believe. Probably Duxford, not so far from London that your old Morris Cowley wouldn't get us there, or here for that matter, if we're invited again. Frankly, I'm surprised we're here at all after your bare-arsed somersault from the high board last month!"

"Oh, I think Sir Philip likes a bit of bad behaviour to liven things up. It gives some of those chaps something to talk about besides the stock market. Duxford, you say?" asked Geoffrey, returning to Dudley's proposal. "To whom would we report, and where?"

"The way I understand it," replied Dudley, frowning at his empty glass, "we'd be practically our own bosses, reporting now and again back to RAF headquarters but daily to the Met Service in London. Sounds just right, especially as we can make our own decisions about whether to fly or not."

Geoffrey, stopping in his tracks, exclaimed, "Dudley, old boy, let's do it! I'm your man, but before we go rushing off, what do these meteorological eyes see before me on the tennis court? What a beauty!"

"Forget her, old man, and to her you *would* be an old man; I believe she's only about sixteen. She's called Clarissa. Her father is Sir Archibald Smythe who would probably get you posted to the Arctic if you even tried to get near her. I do agree, though, that she's the most attractive bit of crumpet

I've ever seen. I suspect we'll have to join rather a long queue waiting for her to reach her prime and cut loose."

By now the two young airmen had joined several others around the court, all ostensibly watching the game of tennis but actually admiring the remarkably beautiful and well-formed Clarissa. A badly hit tennis ball flew over the wire and landed at Geoffrey's feet. Clarissa turned towards him and smiled with the confidence that much admired young ladies seem to possess.

"Sir, would you be kind enough to toss that back?"

"Only if you'll sign it for me and include your address," he blurted in reply, appalled by the 'Sir' which had promptly relegated him to another era.

This riposte was rewarded with a dazzling smile which, Geoffrey decided, was reward enough. He realized that from that moment on the bar for his standard of femininity had been raised. For years afterwards, as he emerged from steamed up cars and well-used hotel rooms, his mind would drift back to the lovely Clarissa Smythe. He felt sure that he would meet her again, somehow, somewhere. What he didn't realize at the time was that his forthcoming transfer to the Met Service would, in fact, be the catalyst.

TWO

Sir Archibald Smythe had been knighted for his services to British industry. Coal and steel had been the main recipients of his shrewd mind and tough leadership, but many thought that he should rather have been honoured by the state for fathering one of the most delightful and attractive teenage daughters anyone knew. Yes, he also had a fine son, but his daughter Clarissa seemed, in most people's opinion, to be so exceptionally sweet and beautiful as to merit an award of some sort to her progenitor. Sir Archibald's wife had died only a few years after Clarissa's birth and the bereft widower had never really recovered from the loss. Accordingly he lavished too much love and attention on his children, particularly Clarissa. Somehow she weathered the attention, which would have smothered the personality of most young girls, and emerged as not merely startlingly beautiful, but also an enchantingly modest young lady.

Sir Archibald, well aware of his daughter's charms, protected her fiercely. Few young men were permitted to cross the threshold of their Eaton Square home, so Clarissa found herself drawn more and more frequently to the Hurlingham, a club where a crowd of hormonally active young men would be certain to gather at the sight of her on the tennis court. She wasn't a particularly accomplished player, but she displayed great poise as she parried their verbal approaches as easily as one would expect her to be soon parrying their more physical advances. Sir Archibald felt rather pleased that he'd kept her incarcerated down at Roedean School for the past several years. He did realize however, and the thought caused him some anxious moments, that one couldn't keep the lid on boiling water indefinitely. In fact these thoughts worried him more than the rumblings and rumours he'd heard from his steel industry counterparts in Prague who seemed, to his mind, to be overly concerned by the political movements in Germany on one side of their country, and a nervous and rapidly developing Russia on the other.

This week, Sir Archibald decided, he was not going to worry about anything in Europe. It was nearing Christmas, his beloved Clarissa was home from school for a few weeks and she'd agreed to go shooting with him. He'd have loved it even more if his son Robert was here too, but he was skiing in Scotland with several of his friends from Eton and wouldn't be returning until Christmas. Actually, if he was honest with himself, he preferred Clarissa's company as she generally paid more attention to him, laughed more at his jokes and, rather than wanting to shoot herself, was quite happy to load for him when the pheasants flew in great quantity over his stand. A good quick loader could make quite a difference to the bag, for nothing was more frustrating than having an unloaded gun just as another flush of birds broke cover and presented themselves as challenging shots.

"Clarissa, darling, please be ready to leave tomorrow morning at seven o'clock. We've nearly a two hour drive ahead of us and we simply must not be late."

"Where are you shooting, Daddy? Any place I've been before?"

"Nicholas Farringdon's place. Lovely shoot with some hills and valleys which make for some splendid high birds. Highest right and left I ever shot happened there a few years ago. I expect they'll bring that up, they always do. They like to claim that the back gun behind me shot the second, always hoping to get a rise out of me."

"Does Sir Nicholas have any nice sons?" ventured Clarissa, thinking that some young men might brighten things up for her a bit. Usually these shoots made for pretty dull dinner parties, unless you liked to talk guns, dogs or politics. She also knew that her father could be counted upon to rise like a trout to the bait of her question.

"No, thank God," he duly thundered as Clarissa grinned. "Allows me to concentrate on shooting and not keeping my eye on you, young lady."

"Now, Daddy, be fair. I'm nearly sixteen and we hardly ever see a useful boy at school. You know how few dances we have and they're always so supervised. Oh well," she continued, trying to get another rise out of him, "I'll just have to cast my eye over the beaters. Some of them can be quite dishy, you know."

Unfortunately for her this time he refused the bait, so she gave up and stood watching him lay out the clothes he would need, shooting tweeds and black tie gear for the dinner.

Always said old Nicholas had a lot of style, thought Sir Archibald, shooting mid-week as he does. Bloody shame I wasn't able to get away tonight though. I hate arriving just as the shooting starts; never feel properly settled with all that dashing about from London to car to standing in a field. Much too abrupt.

Clarissa, in common with most young people of her age, was not very keen on early rising, realizing that leaving at seven meant, for her, having to get up at the latest an hour beforehand and most likely having to make do with a rushed tea and toast breakfast. Perhaps she'd make something to eat in the car. The back of the Rolls had a lovely walnut bar, but never anything to eat in it. She knew that there would be a sherry-laced cup of hot soup served at the end of the first drive, but until then she'd be pretty starved and more than likely wet and frozen as well.

As she drifted upstairs to start gathering her things together for the journey she found herself remembering the last time she had accompanied her father shooting. It had been at Lord Alvingham's estate, somewhere near Reading she seemed to recall. It was a beautiful place and, most interesting of all to her mind, Alvingham's son and heir was tall and rather attractive. Her father was always jokingly reminding her to make sure that when she did eventually marry it would be to the owner of a decent shoot. Oh well, she thought, no point worrying too much about what to wear this time if there were to be no nice sons on offer. She stood in front of the long mirror in her bedroom, staring absently at a long dress held up to her body, remembering how Lord Alvingham was such a stickler for doing everything the proper way.

He often amused himself, and his other English guests, by taking it upon himself to rectify the bad shooting habits of his occasional American visitors. He particularly enjoyed telling them the embarrassing story about the Yank who purportedly had jumped into the back of the shooting brake, there to carry the guns to the next stand, and had banged his gun on the floor of the vehicle causing the gun to go off, blowing a great hole in the roof. There had, of course, been a deathly hush as everyone knew that at the end of each drive, signaled by a horn or whistle, all the guns were 'broken' and unloaded. In the midst of the appalled silence the American realized that he had better say something.

'That's damn funny.'

'Exactly what is so funny?' retorted one shaken Englishman.

'Well,' replied the Yank, 'same thing happened last week!'

Probably just another of his Lordship's stories, thought Clarissa, but he loves telling it and, quite honestly, even though some of those Americans on various shoots are good shots, they really do need a bit of education about the rituals of a pukka English shoot. And none, she thought, dropping the dress on the bed and holding up another, is more pukka than Lord Alvingham's.

There was always hot coffee or tea for the eight 'guns', as the actual participants were called. Eight always seemed to be the number and most shoots were organized so that any birds driven by the beaters towards the guns and fortunate enough to get past them unscathed would land in an area destined to become a later drive. Each gun would be given a number corresponding to a stand, a practice which would, in theory, ensure that over the course of the shoot no one gun always got the best position. Clarissa was always amused to note how many captains of industry forgot their number, even if they were only to move up two numbers each drive. The placement of the stands was designed to maximize the amount of shooting each gun in the line would get and quite often to ensure the birds were as high as possible. Seasoned good shots were loath to shoot low birds and even more loath to be seen doing so. Lord Alvingham loved to humble his sometimes cocky guests by presenting birds over their heads so high they resembled sparrows and had, in the words of some, snow on their wings. Rather than manning a stand himself, Alvingham often took a back gun position where he could 'wipe the eye' of a guest trying to hit an impossibly high pheasant. He was a renowned shot and Clarissa knew that any gun, aware of his presence a few yards behind, would feel enormous pressure not to let any birds get past or risk hearing that familiar croaky laugh as his eye was wiped by the unerring shot of his host.

Men and their games, thought Clarissa. How competitive they are, and how they seem to somehow equate good shooting with masculinity. Perhaps it was some innate characteristic but, in her experience, most men hated being considered a poor shot whereas they would quite happily admit to being mediocre at golf. Anyway, she mused, dangling an earring from a finger, waiting for the first flush of birds to break in each drive is exciting enough and gets everyone's adrenaline going.

On a well-managed drive the beaters would slowly and steadily work the birds towards the waiting guns. If they bunched up and suddenly all flushed at once, usually over just one or two guns, the drive was generally considered to be a failure, although terribly exciting for the guns underneath. This had happened once or twice when Clarissa was loading for her father and she prided herself that her nimble fingers were gaining her a bit of a reputation, although she still hadn't completely mastered the skill of loading a second gun and passing it to him as he handed his empty gun to her. Rather balletic, she considered, although definitely more dangerous.

The guns used were always doubles or side by sides so that only two shots could be fired before a reload, although occasionally a foreigner, usually American or French and ignorant of British shooting customs, would show up with an automatic. The locals would happily mutter about this but allow them to shoot anyway presuming, Clarissa imagined, that they couldn't hit anything anyway.

The thought of the shoot lunch at Lord Alvingham's brought a smile to her face. At many shoots it consisted of soup, sandwiches and something to drink in a fairly basic lodge or shelter somewhere in the midst of the estate, but at Alvingham's it was a proper affair served by staff in his great dining room. On rainy days he was obliged to become almost abusive in order to prise the guns away from his fine wine supply and back out into the miserable weather. After the final drive of the afternoon the day's bag would be laid out on the lawn or hung in the game wagon, and a card given to each gun showing the total number of brace taken of pheasant, woodcock, rabbits, hares or 'other'. 'Other' sometimes included fox, which were shot but never discussed, a fact that struck Clarissa as remarkably silly. Everyone knew that the keeper shot as many as he could, possibly more on one estate than all the hunts in the country killed together. It was another of those peculiar English things, she supposed, the guns pretending not to spoil the sport for the huntsmen who might, or might not, ever actually ride on an estate. She didn't believe that either Lord Alvingham or Nicholas Farringdon had had a hunt on their land due to the terrain being too wooded and hilly; marvellous for shooting but not necessarily riding.

With her clothes and accessories chosen and her mind dwelling on past shooting days, Clarissa decided that she was rather looking forward to the next day's possibilities. Certainly there would be some more stories to come out of it which would entertain her friends at Roedean. The best part of going back to school was relating and hearing all the adventures the girls had had. She hoped that some of their adventures would have included boys, as being at Roedean was, in her opinion, only one step up from being in a nunnery and with about as much hope of excitement.

THREE

Geoffrey Penn still thought life was pretty bloody fine. Here he was, only twenty-three years old and already a fully qualified pilot with a job that enabled him to fly every single day. Some days, it was true, the weather was so bad that many thought only a lunatic would fly, but he was what was called a weather pilot. More exactly, he conducted meteorological surveys for the Met Service, who in turn provided weather forecasts for the various airports in Britain as well as general information for the BBC. Geoffrey's job each day, that is to say, each day the weather made it possible, was to take off from the Cambridgeshire aerodrome, fly up to various prescribed altitudes and record the conditions which he then carried or telephoned back to base which, in turn, relayed the information to London. The decision on whether to fly or not was Geoffrey's. He could choose to stay on the ground if the weather was simply too awful to take off or, much worse, get back down again but, true to his sometimes perverse nature, he had yet to miss a day and was determined to see if he could keep it that way for an entire year.

To most of his friends and fellow airmen he was regarded as reckless, bordering on suicidal. On many days at the crack of dawn the runway could scarcely be seen through the ground fog and even if take off were possible, the chances of getting back to base depended entirely on the fog clearing or lifting within a couple of hours. It was highly likely that there was no other pilot alive who would even consider flying on many days when Geoffrey cheerfully rolled down the grass strip, pulled back on the stick and instantly disappeared into the grey.

Normally he would expect to break out into startling sunshine at about three thousand feet, but on occasion he had to head upwards to ten thousand feet or more to find clear air. His reports of such conditions left those on the ground wondering how, when and where he would return, if he returned at all. But Geoffrey seemed to have an extraordinary sixth sense of where he was in relation to where he'd come from. Even when the cloud or fog failed to lift he usually got back to base, often by recognizing church spires and steeple tops sticking up through the mist, much as a sailor might navigate by known lighthouses. Frequently, however, when low on fuel and all he could spot was a break in the overcast through which he could dive, he found himself landing on large estate lawns or golf courses. Actually, he quite enjoyed landing on the lawn of some great house.

'It's a bit like masturbation,' he was quoted as having said, 'you meet the nicest people!'

In fact, having an aeroplane land on your lawn, provided it hadn't knocked over any specimen tree or bush, was an exciting event and almost invariably Geoffrey would be welcomed in, given a stiff drink and even occasionally a bed for the night if there was no possibility of taking off again. The fact that he was young, exceptionally handsome and equally charming didn't go down badly either and it was suspected that a number of English gentlemen with young wives or pretty daughters were relieved to see this romantic figure, who had literally dropped from the sky, depart again.

Today, as he rolled the plane gently from left to right and duly recorded the rare and incredible weather, his mind drifted back to how he had got into this strange business in the first place. By his reckoning he had the world's best job. He was pretty much his own boss doing what he most liked doing, well, almost, and meeting all kinds of important people who might one day offer him a job if he were forced to find what his father waspishly referred to as 'a real job'.

Geoffrey's eyes quickly scanned the basic instruments. There was the compass for direction, fuel gauge for available time aloft, altimeter showing how high the plane was and lastly the air speed indicator to see how fast he was traveling relative to the air around him. This would differ from the speed relative to the ground beneath him due to any head or tail winds. Flying into a forty mile an hour headwind with the airspeed indicator registering one hundred and fifty mph he would actually only be covering one hundred and ten miles in an hour on the ground, and vice versa with a tail wind. This could be pretty confusing if the pilot wasn't quite sure what the wind speeds were and their direction at different altitudes, but Geoffrey, according to his instructors at Grantham, was a natural flyer, almost as much at home in the sky as his early morning avian companions.

Any clouds gathering over Europe, across that great barrier the English Channel, were not going to disturb this young British pilot enthusiastically pursuing one of his favourite pastimes. The only clouds of which Geoffrey was aware were those that he joyfully flew through each day.

The following day, however, was another matter altogether. The weather looked as hairy as he had ever seen it and it was definitely a morning when he should stay in bed rather than take off into that low, dark cloud. Conscious that his self-imposed goal of never missing a day's flying in a year would very likely be the cause of his demise, he amused himself composing suitable epitaphs for his headstone.

He liked to fly but not to die!

When he should have stayed in bed
He flew regardless, just instead,
And now the bloody fool is dead!

Why did he choose to fly this day?
Only so the charts would say
He never missed a day of toil
And now he's deep within the soil.

Watching only his instruments Geoffrey kept the plane climbing in a gentle turn which he thought would bring him out into clear air somewhere about the centre of England. However, at three thousand feet the weather was, if anything, getting worse. At least keeping record was easy, it was terrible at each check point. At last he caught a glimmer of sunshine and turning instinctively towards the brief shaft of light Geoffrey felt his spirits lifting. He had made his notes and now his only thought was how to get back down through this mass of dreadful weather.

Damnation, I think I may be lost, he thought, looking around for a familiar marker. The bloody winds up here must be blowing me west, but at least they're breaking up the cloud a bit, and with that thought he dived towards a break that had given him a swift but welcome glimpse of mother earth. He pushed the nose of the Avro down as hard as he dared, hearing the strut wires shrieking in protest. When he finally broke out into clearer air he found himself at only about five hundred feet elevation and surrounded by hills extending up into the cloud all around him. Thanking his lucky stars that the opening in the cloud had been over such a natural bowl, he realized that he wouldn't be able to get out of there that day and so started looking around for somewhere to land, and fast.

At that height the land was going past pretty quickly. Geoffrey had limited forward vision and was flying as slowly as he could, at about seventy miles an hour but, even so, he was almost dodging trees. Suddenly on the left he saw a large stretch of park-like lawn and without further thought Geoffrey went straight for the longest piece he could see, full flaps down and prop to fine pitch, downwind, crosswind or whatever wind, he was going to grab the first two hundred yard piece of green he saw. Every nerve in his body concentrated on the landing while he fervently hoped it wasn't his last. The Avro hit hard, bounced back into the air and was nearly flipped forward on end by the tail wind element, but Geoffrey had the stick back hard the instant he felt the lift and the plane straightened out as it finally held down.

For the first time since taking off from Duxford Geoffrey had time to look around casually and to his delight saw a large house not far to his right. He noted that although it wasn't a pretty house it was certainly imposing and, best of all, lights were shining through the long windows onto the lawn in front. He turned the plane and taxied towards what he hoped would be an entertaining evening, assuming with the blithe confidence of young airmen that he would be welcomed. At least he could sing for his supper: people seemed to be endlessly fascinated by aeroplanes and the crazy men who flew them. He parked the plane into the wind, hoping that he'd placed it off the lawn itself, and tied down the wings to the spiral land grabs that he always carried. By the time he'd finished there were already people on the loggia, drinks in hand and waving him in. A good ending to a bad day, thought Geoffrey as he walked towards the welcoming group.

"Good evening young man, and do come in. I'm Nicholas Farringdon and, given this weather, I'm delighted that my park was available for your impromptu arrival."

"Thank you, sir. Geoffrey Penn's the name and I do apologize for interrupting your evening but, as you correctly surmised, I didn't have too many options. I'm terribly grateful that you haven't more trees than there already are in your park! Would it be all right if I used your telephone to ring Duxford, my home base, and then perhaps a taxi to take me to a pub for the night?"

"Nonsense, young man. Wouldn't dream of it. Absolutely do use the telephone, there's one in the hall, but we have loads of beds and dinner will be ready in about an hour. I insist you stay the night, it's the least we can do for our marvelous Air Force. I take it you *are* in the Air Force, from what I can make out of the plane's markings?"

Dinner turned out to be a shooting party affair and Geoffrey's uniform was in stark contrast to the black tie dress code of the other men. He was a welcome addition to the gathering and clearly this particular evening's entertainment. Fair enough, he thought, surveying the group which included a couple of very attractive women, and by the way some of these ladies are looking at me I may just leave my door unlocked tonight, although on second thoughts, perhaps not; all these buggers have guns!

His host seemed very interested in the Air Force, wondering if the British planes were up to the competition. He had heard that the Germans were building up an air force, despite the Versailles Treaty, and of course the French were always open to question. The general opinion around the table was that war was inevitable. Nobody seemed sure who they would be at war with, probably the bloody Hun again, with perhaps France on the German side.

Having talked this over and exhausted the subject of what the Met Service actually provided, Geoffrey realized that the exertions of the day, coupled with plenty of wine from the excellent cellar, had caught up with him. Pleading tiredness, he excused himself to let the group return to their talk of birds, feathered and otherwise, and their brandy. As he settled himself into a warm bed up on the third floor, having regarded his unlocked door with a hopeful grin, he again thought to himself that life was pretty damn good.

Breakfast the next morning was an early affair as the first drive would be at nine o'clock. Shooting was a sport that Geoffrey loved and he wished he could have stayed, even to watch, but he had to grab the opportunity that the slightly improved weather gave him and get back to Duxford. He was rather impressed that they were shooting on a Wednesday and thoroughly enjoyed the explanation that they did so in order that it wouldn't interfere with the weekend. As he tucked into his plate of bacon, eggs, fried bread and black pudding, listening to the jovial banter at the table, he mused that this was a life well worth having and a far cry from the usual solitary tea and biscuits taken back in his digs.

Reluctantly making his grateful farewells, he set off down the wide steps towards the park and his waiting plane, but was forced to pause as a magnificent Rolls Royce crunched up the gravel drive and stopped in front of him. A heavy door clicked open and from the plush interior of the car a large man clad in tweed plus-fours emerged, followed by a similarly clad but smaller and much more attractively shaped figure.

"Strange shooting kit you're wearing, young man," bellowed Sir

Archibald Smythe, arriving nearly too late for the first drive, but assuming that as usual the world would wait for him. Geoffrey was well aware that shooting drives wait for no man, not even the king. The beaters, flankers and pickers-up had to start moving at a set time and had to assume that the guns were in their butts or at their posts otherwise the drive would be wasted.

"Yes, sir," replied Geoffrey, unable to take his eyes away from Clarissa who appeared as lovely as when he had first sighted her. "I'm afraid I'm simply 'shooting' off home but, had I known you were bringing along such an eye-catching loader I'm sure I would have found a way to stay."

"On your way then, lad. I'd love to chat but I'm running a bit late myself," was the fairly dusty response to Geoffrey's attempt at gallantry. Clarissa had heard, though, and rewarded Geoffrey with another dazzling smile and charmingly pink cheeks as she followed her father up the stone steps to where the other guns were gathering to await their transport to the first stand.

With his spirits high Geoffrey left the classic British scene behind him and turned his attention to his plane. After a short ground inspection he started the engine and taxied towards the point where he would be able to turn the plane and get the longest run into the wind. Thinking more of Clarissa than flying he was nevertheless soon airborne and seriously considering a few acrobatics over the shoot which he thought might impress her. He knew, however, that the guns would take a very dim view of such behaviour, especially Sir Archibald who probably already regarded him with suspicion. Heaving a sigh he reluctantly headed back towards Duxford, flying just above the green countryside and just below the leaden skies, skies that were soon to turn darker over Europe.

FOUR

Clarissa, back at Roedean and wearing what she considered to be her singularly unattractive school uniform, was hugely enjoying relating her weekend adventures to a rapt group of friends.

"Well, you know, shooting parties can be such a bore, all those old men and their dogs, mind you the dogs are rather sweet except when they're all smelly and wet and they whack you with their tails and get your clothes all dirty. Anyway, all the men ever seem to talk about is pheasants and dogs and all the wives look as though they're going to die of boredom, even though they're thoroughly dreary themselves. But, guess what, this weekend I saw a really super young man for the *second* time! Actually he's not that young, but at least he's not ancient like all the others."

Her friends set up an excited chorus of questions, wanting to know who he was, how had she met him, what did he look like, had she managed to be alone with him, had he kissed her, and so on, while Clarissa sat and smiled, loving being the centre of such interest. She was beginning to revel in the attention given to her by men who made no secret of the fact that they found her extremely attractive, and being able to confirm her desirability by describing her adventures to her friends was a boost to her self-esteem.

"No, not even close I'm afraid," she said in answer to one of the questions. "Dads was with me and you know how fierce he can be! The man I met, well, saw is perhaps more accurate, is the same chap I saw at the Sassoons' house party when I hit a tennis ball at him."

"On purpose? How wonderfully devious."

"No, actually by accident, but he picked it up and said he'd only give it back if I autographed it with my address on it too! Frightfully smooth I thought, but I couldn't think of anything clever to say in return so I embarrassed myself by just going bright red. He's terribly handsome, even if he is a bit old, some-where in his twenties I suppose."

To girls cooped up in an English public school, adventures such as this were magical. From the age of fourteen they all dreamed of and talked about little else but boys. Hockey and rounders got some time too, but not much from the group of pretty, sociable girls of whom Clarissa was the undisputed and popular leader. She was lucky in that her father was a widower who sought the company of his daughter more than most fathers might, resulting in her being able to get away from school more often and have some adventures.

Clarissa continued, enjoying the attention and the reliving of her weekend.

"Well, the first meeting was a few months ago, in the summer. I think I did tell you, Debbie, that I had seen a really smashing man who was quite cheeky. Anyway, would you believe it, this weekend I went on this shoot with Daddy and, just as we arrived, late as usual, this same chap came walking down the steps in one of those flying costumes, really glam. I'm sure he recognized me. He said something to Dads about bringing along a pretty loader and, typically, Dads bundled me right past before I could even say hello again.

"Apparently he had dropped out of the sky the evening before and had spent the night at the house. I only wish we'd gone up the night before too! We all watched him take off. He looked frightfully brave flying right through the park trees."

To the assembled girls this sounded about as romantic as things could get. There followed much discussion along the lines of 'what if' and 'what next' and other girls related their own weekend experiences, but it was generally agreed that Clarissa's adventure was the most thrilling and provided the most fuel for their overheated imaginations.

Back in her room Clarissa wondered if she would ever see this aviator again and if he would consider her to be too young for him. Such a man seemed so much more exciting than the Eton and Harrow boys who seemed to cross her path most often. She also fell to wondering what she might do after she left Roedean. Her father thought that she should go to university, but Clarissa preferred the idea of something she considered more glamorous, like modelling, an idea which absolutely horrified Sir Archibald. He regarded advertising as an occupation to be contemplated only if one was not qualified or able to do anything else, although he would grudgingly admit that banking was also a profession that required no credentials whatsoever. In any case, he had no wish for his daughter to pursue either line. Little did he know that the looming conflict across the Channel would help resolve this dilemma.

FIVE

By the late autumn of 1935 Geoffrey and Dudley Whitchurch had successfully completed more than one year of flying and producing weather reports each day. It was a source of satisfaction to them both, a feeling of a unique job well done, but it left them wondering what next to do with their lives. Quite frankly, other than coping with the occasional terrifying weather in which they flew, they were beginning to run out of the adrenaline charges that young men seem to need. This time it was Geoffrey who initiated the idea of change as he had heard of an interesting job.

"Dudley, much as I hate the thought of leaving the RAF, I don't fancy my promotion chances too highly. Up here in lovely old Cambridgeshire we've been out of the limelight for too long and there are simply too many old pilots ahead of us. I know that there's all that talk of war on the Continent going around, but it doesn't look to me like we'd be in it even if it does start. So I'm rather tempted to take up a job I've been offered as it might well give me even more flying."

"What job could possibly be better than this one, old boy?"

"I know, I know, it is a fantastic job, but there's a position going at Supermarine, down near Southampton. Assistant to Mutt Summers, their chief test pilot."

Dudley snorted. "Don't they just make seaplanes? You might as well shift over to the Navy!"

"No bloody way the Navy, old chap, but you're almost right about seaplanes. They won the Schneider Trophy *and* set a world speed record with one, over three hundred and fifty miles per hour! Just compare that with what we can get out of our Bulldog. They've got a really terrific designer there called Mitchell who did most of the work on the Schneider planes and I was told that he's working on an Air Force fighter too. Now, I could quite fancy getting involved in *that* development. I've always had lots of ideas that no-one in the RAF seems remotely interested in listening to."

"Doesn't sound bad, Geoffrey, I grant you, but I'm going to stick it out up here a bit longer, if it's all the same to you. Fact of the matter is, I've met a rather lovely lass. You should get a bit more serious yourself and stop dreaming about that Smythe girl, though to be fair I can't say I entirely blame you."

"Well, maybe I'll be a lot closer to her down at Eastleigh, which is where I believe I'd be doing most of my flying. Should really build up the hours with test flying every day and it would be fantastic to fly some *new* planes and not these antiques!"

"Can't agree with you there, I quite like antique aeroplanes. It means they've been put together well enough to last. Don't think I'd like going up each day and wondering if all the bits were screwed on right. Just up your alley though, I should imagine!"

Geoffrey parted company with Dudley, Duxford and the RAF with some real regret, for he'd had, as he stated, a good innings. However, buoyed by the greatly increased salary of a test pilot he lashed out on a 1926 supercharged 4.5 litre Bentley and motored off south to present himself to the reputedly formidable chief executive of Supermarine, Sir Robert McLean. McLean had a reputation as a possibly humourless and definitely no-nonsense sort of man, but he was also regarded as a highly capable executive and, thought Geoffrey, worth putting up with for the experience of working for him. Their first meeting went well, though McLean wasted no time on small talk.

"Picked you out from several candidates for two reasons really. One, you have an exceptional rating as a pilot from your old school and the RAF. Well, so do a few others, but the difference to me, and the second reason you're here, is your Met service. Anyone prepared to fly in that dreadful weather up north has to be either barmy or bloody good. We can use some of that down here, because a lot of time is wasted by us not testing in bad weather. Now, old Mutt Summers will fly anything in just about any weather, but we're starting to turn out more planes than he can test alone, so he'll be delighted to have your help. Have you found digs yet?"

Without waiting for an answer he grasped Geoffrey's upper arm and marched him off to meet the well known and highly respected Mutt Summers and, before Geoffrey knew it, he found himself deeply caught up in the programme which involved both sea and land planes and even some multi-engine bombers. Within a very short space of time he had decided that his new job was a great improvement on the old one, despite no longer being his own boss.

It was only some time later that Geoffrey began to feel that perhaps he should have stayed in the Air Force as he, in common with many, saw unpleasant signs of war looming across the Channel. At Supermarine, however, most minds were on a new and exciting aeroplane. Mitchell had come up with a quite revolutionary design for a single seat fighter which looked to everyone at Supermarine as the plane which could put Britain in a position of air supremacy, should they ever need it.

The government was less enthusiastic and just keeping Supermarine's order book warm, let alone getting a firm order, was driving McLean wild with frustration. His awesome temper was now directed towards the powers-that-be in Whitehall, and work continued at Eastleigh in the hope that his energy, fury or pure salesmanship would prevail. The fear was that the government would decide to place their orders with a competitor of Supermarine, Hawker, who also appeared to have a fine aeroplane on the verge of completion.

On the fifth of March, 1936 the new plane was finally ready for testing. Mutt Summers ordered it to be rolled out of the hanger. Powered by a Rolls Royce engine it appeared to desperately want to take off as Mutt took it through a number of high speed taxi-runs. Geoffrey, watching with Mitchell, McLean and others, was thrilled when Mutt eventually pulled back on the stick and the long slim aircraft lifted her elegantly tapered elliptical wings into the air.

"Don't touch a thing," Mutt said when he landed. Many interpreted this as meaning the plane was perfect as it was, but Mutt actually wanted no changes made until he'd had time to note and verify all the details that the inaugural flight had told him. It was indeed a fine plane but, like all thorough-breds, was going to take some training and refining. Geoffrey knew that this was where his job started and felt delighted to be the second person to fly this beautifully designed aircraft.

By 1938 Mutt, Geoffrey and others had ironed out any serious problems with the plane, now dubbed the 'Spitfire' by Sir Robert McLean. Mitchell regarded the name as silly, but it stuck. It flew beautifully, even when equipped with eight Browning 303 machine guns, whose added weight slowed it down. Meanwhile Hawker, who had won in the race to gain government orders, had been producing ever more Hurricanes, which were also excellent aeroplanes.

Thank God Westminster finally pulled their finger out, thought Geoffrey, as the dreaded but expected news came through that Britain was at war. Listening to Neville Chamberlain's solemn voice, Geoffrey sensed that the Prime Minister thought the great dark cloud cast by the Third Reich over most of Europe would soon overshadow, if not envelop, Britain too. With this sobering thought, Geoffrey approached Sir Robert McLean with the first of several requests to be allowed to quit his job at Supermarine and get back into the RAF where he was sure he could do some good.

"Geoffrey," replied McLean, "I've been wondering how long it would be before you came up with this idea. I can tell you right now, it's not going to work. Your flying *here* is far more important."

"But, sir, I'm still in the Reserve and they may well call me up."

"No chance, Geoffrey. I've already checked out that possibility and, thank God, I still have some pull up at Whitehall. They are now really desperate for those planes we had so much trouble convincing them to order and we are going to expand your team, not decrease it, and you'll be in charge now that Mutt's retired."

A mixed bag, thought Geoffrey, promotion and frustration. Yet it was only after the Germans began bombing London that Geoffrey's desire to see some action prompted him to again broach the subject with McLean.

"You know, Sir Robert," began Geoffrey, "we aren't getting much good information back from the lads flying the Spits: they're so busy trying to stay alive they haven't much time to be objective analysts of the planes' performance in combat. We know they like its turn circle and its speed versus the Messerschmitt, but they complain from time to time about other problems and I've an idea about how to solve them."

"How's that then?" asked Sir Robert suspiciously. "What other problems?"

"Well, misting over in a dive, for example. Rearward vision and momentary stall at the onset of a dive is another. We're getting more and more reports of these."

"And just how do you propose to sort them out? Come on, give me your idea. I've got a hunch what it is and I'll probably still say no."

"Well you might be right, sir. I propose to join up again. Only for a while, mind you, but think how useful it would be to have a qualified test pilot actually sending back reports. And you've plenty of good men here now to cover for me."

"How long then?"

Geoffrey had hoped that McLean would see that his idea had merit and wasn't just another romantic idea about saving the country, and, by God, he had!

"Only a few months, but enough to really fly the plane in action. I know you have the power to get me back when you want me, but I do believe you'll be getting back a better test pilot than you have right now. I'm pretty sure I can keep out of trouble if their pilots are as inexperienced as most of ours."

"Oh all right, I'll go for it, if only to stop you pestering me. As it happens, I heard from Dowding last month that the bombers are getting through more and more often and are accompanied by more and more Messerschmitts. He thinks we're in for a really big showdown before long."

On the fifth of August, 1940, Geoffrey found himself back in uniform and, more importantly, back at Hornchurch with his old 65 Squadron. His homecoming was muted, however, when he learned how many of his old friends had already been killed. He was also justifiably alarmed at how few hours most pilots, far younger than he, had accumulated in Spitfires before taking to the skies to face German pilots, some of whom were veterans of the Spanish War. Although the Spitfire V seemed the better plane, generally the German pilots were more skilful and in many dogfights the young British, Polish and Canadian pilots felt lucky to escape. They were delighted to have Geoffrey with them and he could at least tell them how fast they could dive before the wings buckled. He even put on a remarkable aerobatic show over the field one quiet morning, not to show off, but to reassure the pilots about what could be done in a Spit.

By this time the Battle of Britain had begun in earnest and Geoffrey was thrilled to at last be in the thick of it, with 'scrambles' every day, often more than one, and dogfights with an enemy he was sure he could shake off. He also knew, however, that it was usually the one you never saw who shot you down. He learned to rubberneck, constantly turning to look back at both sides, to look upwards and to check the rear. It was exhausting as well as clearly dangerous, but he felt he was helping to protect the country he loved so well, and he knew that, back at Supermarine, his reports were being carefully scrutinized.

For his part, McLean knew that he would never get Geoffrey back until he had a few swastikas painted on his plane. Once that had occurred, he pulled his Whitehall strings and retrieved his most valuable test pilot.

SIX

Ninety-six, ninety-seven, ninety-eight, ninety-nine, one bloody hundred! *Why* do I do this? I'd a hell of a lot rather be reading a good book. If there is a God somewhere up there I wish he'd blessed me with either a good body or a fair brain, but not both!

Philip Quigley was doing his daily and much hated one hundred push-ups, something the rugby coach at Cambridge thought his best prop forward ought to do, in or out of season, just to stay in shape. Philip suspected the coach knew that Philip far preferred a glass of wine and a soft body or two to getting in shape for another season of head-bashing rugby. Not that Philip didn't enjoy the head-bashing, but training was another matter. What neither the coach nor the rest of the squad knew was that Philip's idea of a *really* good time was an intense, intelligent argument with a bright and lovely girl about ancient literature, followed by an intense afternoon of mending fences in bed, followed by a serious attack on nearly any sort of drinkable wine, followed by, with any luck, more intense atonement for past sins and arguments. But, for God's sake, push-ups, and those not even over a warm body, that was too much. Perhaps he'd give up rugby and try tennis, maybe even chess. The image of his sixteen-plus stone cavorting around a tennis court or even his massive hands moving chess pieces brought a smile to his lips. He sighed, reluctantly acknowledging that he was probably destined to shove men around rather than anything else.

An outstanding athlete at both his schools, St. Neots and Eton, Philip had found no difficulty obtaining a place at Cambridge. He would have preferred to have been admitted, even sought after, for his intellectual abilities but, in the end, it didn't really matter. He was ensconced in a stimulating city with access to an endless supply of all the old books he so loved to read. From time to time he could enjoy a great physical game of rugby, or wrestle or even box if the coaches could find anyone willing to have a go at his formidable frame and frequently glowering countenance.

Philip envied those of his counterparts who seemed to know exactly what they wanted in life, whether it was to be a doctor, solicitor, barrister, even a vet. He hadn't a clue what he wanted to do except play sports, read books, drink and sleep with women as often as possible. That wasn't a bad list, he realized, but he also knew it couldn't last. He would have to do something else eventually. Someone had suggested a commission in the army, but having to obey and even salute someone he might consider an arrogant fool didn't appeal to him in the slightest. On the other hand, being what might be the world's strongest librarian did not hold much appeal either. Well, he thought, at least he had another couple of years ahead of him before he had to consider the future seriously.

In fact, Philip spent most of his first year at Trinity College not in the library, but on the fens shooting birds, watching birds and dating 'birds'. This began to pall after about a year, so in 1930 he left to join his father's tea importing business. However, despite a fun-filled social life centered around his shared flat on Primrose Hill in London, he soon departed for India, ostensibly to work.

India fascinated Philip and he spent a great deal of time in the Himalayas and even visited Tibet, but his restless spirit drove him back to London where his powerful form was often seen in small shops, browsing for old books. It didn't seem to make sense to people that such a large and rough looking man should be interested in rare books. But then, Philip had always been a study in contrasts, seemingly waiting for whatever the world had specifically in mind for him. He was not going to have to wait much longer.

While in Iceland, salmon fishing with his old flat-mate Stephen Johnson, the news came through on a scratchy-sounding radio that Hitler had finally pushed the reluctant Chamberlain too far and war had been declared.

"This is it, Stephen, old boy. We've got to get our arses back to Blighty pdq before all the good jobs get taken."

"Why don't we just wait up here until we're called? There are a great many blonde bombshells up here that need defusing before we get down to the serious stuff," Stephen retorted indignantly.

"No way, old man. I know that the Berkshire Yeomanry is looking for lads: found that out before we left home, 'cause I had a bad feeling about that nasty piece of work Hitler, but why don't we see how many bombs we can handle up here in the next two days and then leave. To hell with the fish, there's a war on! Here we go!"

Within months Philip had finished his basic training with the Berkshire Yeomanry and was given an officer's commission, but upon learning of something that seemed to him far more romantic and exciting, he promptly resigned and joined up as a private in the Finnish Expeditionary Force, a small elite group that was going to be sent to help the Finns fight the Russians.

"Oh bugger," complained Philip to a fellow soldier shortly afterwards, "why on earth have the blasted Finns signed a truce with the Russians? Now the whole caper's been called off. Well, I suppose we've at least had some bloody good skiing training in France, and a good chance to update my French with the local girls too. Not too bad a war really, but so far I haven't been able to do a damned thing to even annoy the Germans. Nonetheless," he continued with a grin, "I've got a plan. A chap I know called Henriques is looking for troop commanders to set up some Commando units. Sounds just right for us, old thing. How about it?"

"Just what are the Commandos supposed to do that's going to be as good as what we're already doing here in the French Alps?"

"Basically, I understand the intention is to harass the Germans all along the French and other coastlines, just pissing them off and keeping them off balance. That's got to be fun! Can even pick my own lads, Henriques says, and the old Berkshire group has a few nasty chaps who would love this."

Once again Philip was off, this time to Northern Ireland to train and where, before long, his section gained a reputation for not only being the toughest and meanest bunch of men, but also the scruffiest. Philip became nearly as well known for his dress, or lack of it, as for his fierce discipline of his men.

"I don't give a bugger how they look," he roared, "but show me a better bunch of fighters and I'll buy you dinner for a year."

Even Philip's dog, Cool, was scruffy: an Irish Spaniel who seemed able to locate and intensively explore every mud puddle in Ireland.

By 1941 'Peachy' Harrison, the commanding officer of 12 Commando, was getting frustrated by the lack of action. Well-planned operations were being cancelled at the very last minute for no apparent good reason and Peachy knew that trying to keep the lid on a group of highly trained fighters was next to impossible: they had to do something soon or he would be facing a revolt.

Operation Barbaric, a test raid on the heavily fortified Pas de Calais coast, had been the first to be cancelled, followed by Operation Cheetah, a raid on the Canary Islands which was supposed to take place in May of 1941. After these disappointments the forces in charge started up Operation Chess, which consisted of a series of small raids on the French coast, designed to see how seriously the Germans would defend it. This was right up Philip's alley and at two o'clock one morning he led his party of ten ashore at Ambleteuse, just north of Boulogne. Unfortunately, despite the early hour they were spotted and Philip was lucky to escape with the loss of only two men. Saddened by the death of such good team members, Philip was nonetheless elated that at last he had seen some action. Further raids took place against the Isle of Sark, using only five men, then a short invasion of the Lofoten Islands off Norway, which nearly resulted in Philip and his cohort Captain Jefferies landing in a British military prison.

"Jesus Christ," bellowed Philip, while being questioned by the naval captain of HMS Prince Albert, "I know that we should be grateful to you for getting us up here to the Lofotens and now away again, but old Jeffers and I are not going to let your idiotic photographer make a film showing how much these islanders hate the Germans and how much they welcomed us. I know it would make a good show for the public and boost morale back home and all that, but these people here have to live with these bastards; we're the ones leaving. If the German spies in England see those films these people will never have a day's peace."

"Understood, Captain, but no need to grab the man's camera and throw the film overboard. Navy property in the first place, I may say."

"Cheeky bastard is damned lucky I didn't throw him overboard too: he wasn't about to give up the film and didn't seem to give a bugger about the islanders. Of course his fat backside was here on the ship watching most of the time, can't expect him to be too sympathetic."

"Captain, I don't need a lecture on politics from you. If you were in the Navy I'd see that you spent time in a less pleasant place than where I am putting you now, which is under close arrest. I suppose we need madmen like you, so you'll probably only get a slap on the wrist. However, if I ever again have the dubious pleasure of dropping you off in some inhospitable place, I shall take great pleasure in leaving you there, understood?"

"Yes, sir," replied Philip, "I do understand that I am on your patch and thanks for the lift anyhow."

A few months later Philip wondered if his inactive posting to a base at Bursledon, on the mouth of Southampton harbour where the Itchen meets the sea, had anything to do with his naval confrontation. In any event, he was thirsting for more action and just training and re-training his rough company of lads fell far short of satisfying his needs.

SEVEN

Geoffrey Penn eased back on the throttle and felt the Spitfire settle slightly, much as a good racehorse might if you gave it a chance to catch its wind. He was doing his usual check flight of a new plane, fifteen thousand feet over Southampton which lay shrouded in mist and fog, occasional church spires appearing through the gloom. Geoffrey kept an eye on these spires for, on days like this, they helped him to find his way back to the Supermarine airstrip at Eastleigh.

"Too many bloody days like this," he mumbled, half out loud and half into the dangling oxygen mask. Regulations dictated he should have been wearing it at this altitude, but he found it an inhibiting pain in the rear most of the time. After all, he'd spent a lot of hours on high weather flights before this war started without the help of oxygen or fancy instruments to assist his return to base.

More out of habit than any expectation of trouble, he glanced in the overhead mirror and rolled left and right, scanning for any German marauder who might be returning from a mission or perhaps just on a fast hunting incursion over the Channel with the hope of catching a pilot off guard.

I doubt the Hun would expect even the mad Brits to be flying in this weather, he mused, but I'm up here, so maybe one of those other blokes is just as insane. All was quiet, however, as the plane droned through the sky. At one point he suddenly found himself between two layers of cloud , hurtling as though through a low tunnel of endless width; a situation which made one as aware of speed as one was unaware when in cloudless skies. He occasionally put the Spit through various mechanical or instrument checks to confirm its fitness to fly, shoot and get shot at while God only knew where around the world. Lots of the Allies are using these beauties when we can spare them, he thought, patting the instrument panel with a mixture of reverence and affection.

Suddenly he jammed the throttle full forward with his left hand and simultaneously pulled hard on the stick. The Rolls Merlin engine, ever faithful, roared and the Spit shot up out of sight into the cloud bank above. Shaken out of his reverie by a sudden shaft of light that had startlingly but beautifully leaked through a break in the cloud, he flew by his battle pilot's instinct into a violent evasive manoeuvre.

God, I'm getting jumpy, but better to run and hide than play tag when you've got no guns on board, he thought, while levelling out the plane. He was sure, though, from previous experience that without the extra weight of the eight magazines, he could out-fly anything the Germans might produce. Or could he, he wondered, actually out-turn or out-climb the plane that had been troubling his mind all week; this mysterious new fighter that had so alarmed the Spitfire pilots accompanying British bombers in the Northern France area.

Up until now no-one had a plane to touch this version of the Mark V Spitfire and Geoffrey had tested every captured German plane to date. He had even advised Joe Smith, Mitchell's successor, to incorporate modifications that had kept his marvellous machine the envy of all air forces, even the Yanks. But now, just the previous week in fact, stories were coming back from various squadrons suggesting that the Germans had leapfrogged the Allies by building an astonishing plane capable of incredible performance.

I'm sitting in the latest model of the Spitfire, thought Geoffrey, that together with the Hurricane probably saved us from an actual invasion last year, and yet there are pilots, good experienced pilots, telling me that in missions over France in particular, they have come up against a plane that can out-climb, roll faster and even out-dive this. Christ, I can't believe it. It could set us right back to defending ourselves again with fear and fury, but I'm not sure we could stand another Battle of Britain. We barely scraped by the last one.

Gloomily he rolled the Spit over, cut the power and by some sixth sense headed directly towards the test field, dropping about a thousand feet a minute and occasionally blipping the engine to keep it warm and thereby avoid a carburettor freeze-up. All this he did mechanically, without thinking, just as he still constantly scanned the increasingly foggy skies for any intruders.

Maybe I should have breathed a bit of oxygen, he thought glumly. I might not feel so bloody depressed. To hell with it, this is still the sweetest thing flying, I'm damned sure. I wonder if the new Boche bird can do *this?* With that, Geoffrey shoved the nose down further and gave the plane full throttle as he sighted two landmarks steeples that told him where he was in relation to the runway. In this weather they were invaluable for, at two thousand feet, he could not see a single piece of the ground or any buildings at all in Southampton.

The Spit roared that wonderful noise, so beloved by the war-weary Brits and so recognizable by all, as it came streaking out of the murky sky, breaking cloud at three hundred feet above and off the end of the runway. As he started descending to the runway at over three hundred miles an hour he glanced at the two faces staring out through the window of the lit-up control tower. He knew that there would always be at least one person there, waiting to see if it was necessary to talk him down. Without further thought he cut the engine, rolled the Spit on its back and, as it hurtled along, just above the runway, he started to extend the wheels, knowing they wouldn't and shouldn't emerge, at least not until his speed was way down. Then, still inverted, he pushed the stick forward and shot up into the fog in a great outside loop, engine still nearly silent as he lost speed. Suddenly, out of the fog he appeared at the original end of the runway, silently performing a slow roll, wheels extended and flaps down, before gracefully settling to the ground.

"Bloody hell!" a white-faced Sergeant Davis exclaimed as he turned to the control tower master, Clive Donovan. "Who in the hell is that? I've never seen anything like it."

"No, and you probably never will again," replied Donovan. "What you have just witnessed was our chief test pilot, Geoffrey Penn, a man who's considered possibly the greatest aerobatic pilot ever. Frankly, for me, he is the best test pilot who ever lived and I just hope he keeps on living. Something must really be up his nose for him to pull a stunt like that in this weather. I wonder if it's a girl, or perhaps the lack of one. He hasn't had a lot of time to play lately, though I gather that he likes all that as much as flying. Rumour has it he's had more women than I've had hot dinners."

Sergeant Davis was still too awestruck by the totally unexpected flying exhibition he had just witnessed to be able to reply. Penn taxied the Spit past a row of identical planes. These were all waiting to be ferried, usually by WAACS, to eagerly waiting bases, most of which were desperately short of anything resembling the latest state-of-the-art model Mark V Spitfire.

As the hatch slipped back, the handsome head of a young man appeared. Supermarine's living legend, thought Sergeant Davis enviously. Not only can he fly like nobody I've ever seen, but the swine is good-looking too.

Geoffrey climbed down from the Spit as two Vickers mechanics emerged from the hanger to put the plane in one of two rows; those checked out for armour fitting and those needing some minor or major tweaking to get right. Seeing Geoffrey's slight frame step wearily out of the plane they assumed it was a 'bummer' destined for some more work, but a simple wave of the hand and thumbs-up from Penn suggested the plane was serviceable.

This same sequence of events occurred day after day, even in this kind of weather, for Penn insisted in flying nearly all the time, in spite of the local Naval station commander's rules on weather and 'minimums' for flying.

"I'm not in the RAF anymore," Penn had said, "and I certainly don't have to take orders from some bloody Navy captain. I'm damned sure the Germans aren't this fussy about what weather they test their planes in. The bloody barrage balloons all around the works don't help a hell of a lot either. Yesterday one of my pilots nearly hit one that they'd moved and not told us about. And what's more they probably attract more Jerries to our works than they scare away."

Not a lot of love was lost between the people at Vickers Supermarine at Eastleigh and the commander of the Southampton area who, of course, was a Navy man. To the commander himself, and to the powers at

Whitehall, Southampton port was far and away the most important part of the war effort in that area, or at least it seemed that way to the Supermarine group.

While Geoffrey was talking or indicating to the ground crew and reflecting on other gloomy subjects such as 'naval flying regulations', which in any case he largely ignored, barrage balloon attractions to German flyers and the possibility of air attacks on his beloved grounded Spits, Clive Donovan and Sergeant Davis descended from the tower, which had been blacked out again. They met Penn as he came into the lower room.

"Bloody hell, Geoffrey," said Clive, neglecting to introduce Sgt. Davis. "I don't much care if you kill yourself, but we can't afford to have you break up any more planes."

Penn managed a rueful smile. He remembered rather too well having to put a dead-engined Spit down in a field near Eastleigh, three days previously. He thought he'd done it perfectly, in spite of a frozen prop, when he'd seen a dyke he'd failed to spot on his first dead stick pass. Wheels up, the plane slid along easily. Minimum damage, he thought, then the dyke and, wham, a totally messed up plane with only a few bits salvageable. At least he was unhurt and flying again that afternoon.

"Clive, old chap, I was merely making sure this plane was better than the one you gave me last week."

"Bollocks," said Clive. "You're barmy, which is why they pulled you out of the RAF and sent you down here. Chaps as daft as you are apt to shoot down our own planes just for the hell of it. As a matter of fact I heard you got bored with shooting up 109s and were chasing Hurricanes around, just to prove you could out-turn and out-dive them."

This was typical banter after flights, and indulged in particularly when Clive sensed that Geoffrey was tired or tense. God knows, he thought, testing brand new planes day after day and never knowing how well they had been put together was enough to make anyone twitchy.

"Oh," Clive continued, suddenly remembering the man standing at his side, "by the way, this is Sgt. Davis. The RAF has assigned him here to help me count the planes to make sure we don't lose any. He'll take your flight check notes and put them in the record sheets. I take it this girl's OK, in spite of you trying to break her?"

"Nice to meet you, son," said Penn, shaking Davis's hand and thinking how young the lad appeared to be.

"Where to tonight, Geoffrey?" asked Clive. "I'm surprised you've got any strength to fly, the way you screw around every night."

"Off to London. I hope this blasted fog will lift a bit. It's going to take me about an hour and a half, even in the Green Bomb. There's a deb dance on at the Hyde Park Hotel and I think because I'm an ex-officer I got invited. Either that or somebody knew I owned a dinner jacket and thought it would be a nice contrast to all the uniforms and medals. Is there any of that spilt petrol of yours lying around, Clive? The old Bentley is fast but it does rather eat the stuff."

"Strangely enough, some fell into a can about an hour ago. I hope you don't get stopped and asked for coupons, especially dressed in a civvie suit!"

Penn vanished into the gloom, heading for his office where he'd change and start for London, curious about what the night would bring. No twopenny uprights in a crowd like that, he thought, using the current phrase for a quickie against a wall in blacked-out London.

"So that's the famous Penn," said Davis, staring after him. "How did he end up down here if he's such an ace? Wouldn't some air wing be a better place for him than here, just testing aeroplanes?"

"Son," Clive explained, "it's quite a story. Basically he's already done his bit; RAF before the war, ended up flying weather flights when nobody else would go up; seemed to have a sixth sense of how to get back. Got bored and Vickers Supermarine offered him a job as test pilot. He arrived just about the same time as Mitchell's first Mark I Spit and has been testing them ever since, except for a stint when he talked his way back into active service to see, first hand, what the Spit could and couldn't do against the Messerschmitt 109.

He fought in the Battle of Britain, shot a few down, after which he got called back here to help develop the Spit further. It's a bit more than just testing aeroplanes, though God knows that's dangerous enough. We've actually got a captured 109 up at Farnborough, and Geoffrey's flown it. Not as good as our current Mark V, he told me, but faster than our Mark I; dived better and flew higher and now he says he wouldn't have been half as worried fighting against it if he'd been able to fly one first!

"Do you know," he continued, " that crazy sod took one of our new Spits up into a dog fight near Southampton, with no guns or ammo on board because he said he would like to see if it really could out-manoeuvre the 109s and the new twin-engine 110s. Said it could and that's the reason he got back! I thought McLean was going to kill *him* instead of the Germans. I happened to be in his office after Geoffrey had landed. Air traffic control had told him where Geoffrey had gone. McLean called him in and really hauled him over; didn't give a damn about losing a Spit or two, but God-damned if he could afford to lose his top test pilot and everything he was contributing to the evolution and development of the plane.

"Meek as a lamb, Penn said he was sure he was safe because the plane was so good and with no ammo and guns he was so light he could actually turn inside anybody. Besides, he'd learnt a lot that would help further development of the plane. That was, so he said, the only way to get practical experience since they wouldn't let him fight anymore. Actually, I think the old boy regards him more like a son than an employee anyhow and finally let him off, but only after all sorts of threats!"

EIGHT

As Geoffrey's 4.5 litre 'blown' Bentley left the security gate at the test field, a meeting was in progress at the Air Ministry in London. Air Vice-Marshal Sir Sholto Douglas, head of Fighter Command, and Sir Cyril Newall, Marshal of the Royal Air Force, were engaged in a tense debate in the presence of a few other very highly cleared staff members.

"First of all," declared Newall, "there is this damn memo of yours expressing 'grave concern' about Fighter Command's ability with Spitfire Vs to maintain air superiority through the spring of '42. Just what the hell does that mean? Have we stopped making them or what? The Beaver tells me we're up to five hundred per month now. Are we losing them faster than that? If so, I'd like to know why. And now," he continued, raising his hand to forestall the Air Vice-Marshal's reply, "I have another bloody memo from Sir Archibald Sinclair saying we are being left behind. Look, I've got it right here." He stabbed a finger at the page. "It says our 'mastery of daylight air is being threatened'. You've just replaced Dowding as head of Fighter Command, Douglas. You're supposed to solve these problems but I'm still getting harassed from every side. I thought we had proved our air superiority beyond doubt last summer. I was told that now we're even sending fighters on rhubarb missions over France in addition to providing bomber cover. What the hell are all these memos about if we've got enough planes to do that sort of playing around?"

Finally given the chance to speak, Sholto Douglas took a deep breath and responded.

"Well, sir, the fact is that the Spit and the Hurricane proved that they could and did out-fight the Messerschmitts, both the BF109 and the later BF110, but we think the Germans have taken a great leap forward. They've got a new fighter that's knocking hell out of us over France, particularly the northern part of France. We're not even sure if the Mark IX, which as you know is the next version of the Spit, will be as good. It *is* serious, even critical, because we *must* maintain control of the air, at least over the British Isles. If we can't also support our bombers over France and Germany we are going to be in very deep merde, as our French friends would say. Incidentally, those Frogs lost damned near every one of the fighters we sent over there to support them; over three hundred of them, which we could ill afford to give them in the first place."

"Let's not fight that battle again, Douglas," said Newall, furrowing his brow, "that's behind us, but what you've just said is very worrying indeed. Have we any more information on what this plane is or where it's made?"

"Not much, I'm afraid. Here's all we have," said Douglas, signalling an aide to come forward with some notes.

"First of all, early reports thought it was a variant of, or improvement on, the American Curtis Hawk fighter that the Germans obtained before the war in Spain, or perhaps captured in France. But then flight reports coming in from the chaps running incursions around the coast near Cherbourg say that these jobs are completely new planes. Here are some blow-ups from gun photos. These planes can out-climb and certainly out-dive even the latest Mark V Spit, and easily knock hell out of the earlier Mark I, *and* the Hurricanes. Their radar seems to be as good as ours and, when they pick up our bombers coming into their area, they have time to get airborne and above our boys before they cross the coast. The usual tactic is to dive from the sun and there's often a damned sight more of that in France than there is here! They dive right through our bombers, then turn and climb back towards our now scattered fighter escort which, of course, is beginning to run out of fuel at this point and ready to turn home anyhow.

"They now show no reluctance at all to mix it with the Spits. As you know the 109s used to get quite windy and abandon the fight when one of us showed up with the latest Spit. Now the reverse seems to be the case. In short, we're getting pasted."

Newall sighed heavily.

"What a bloody tragedy Reginald Mitchell died so young; he never even saw his plane fight, but I'm damned sure he could have kept us ahead were he still here. What are the other boffins down at Vickers doing? Sitting on their arses, polishing their laurels, thinking the Battle of Britain was all we had to win, hmm? Don't they know about this new Hun plane?"

"This may be only one of the usual Air Force rumours, sir, and they're usually exaggerated, but this plane *is* scaring the hell out of everyone," offered up one attending officer. "Apparently this plane has cannon and, as you know, we only have Brownings in the Spit, so the Germans will have a range advantage also."

"Tell me more about our own development," demanded Newall, bringing the subject back to facts rather than rumour. "I read a report the other day, written by Vickers' chief pilot, I believe, saying he'd flown a BF109 at Farnborough, one we'd captured, and in his eyes it wasn't a patch on the Spit V. Hard to see out of, limited range, poor rear vision, poor aileron control over four hundred mph, and no rudder trim. Said he wouldn't have been half as impressed or worried about them if he'd flown one before he fought against them. Are you sure we haven't got another 'grass is greener' situation on our hands?"

Surprised and deeply impressed by Sir Cyril's up-to-the-minute knowledge about what was happening at development level, Douglas was even more sure than when he'd entered the room that he shouldn't try to flannel this man by giving him the impression he simply wanted better and more of it, the usual complaint, hoping to frighten him into providing more support. This was the last thing Douglas wanted, because he was utterly convinced that his precious fighter resource was gravely threatened and he needed all the top level help he could muster.

"Does the Old Man know about this problem?" asked Newall.

"I think so," Douglas replied. "I was told that the minister of aircraft production had sent a memo via Lord Cherwell to Churchill, discussing the relative performance of this new German plane versus the Spitfire. All conjecture at this stage, of course, but backed up by a lot of actual bad experiences. We've lost too many damn good pilots in this past month."

"I'm sure I'll hear more about this," stated Newell. "You know how the Old Man loves this sort of detail. He appears to even love a crisis, so I'm sure he'll have Beaverbrook on this, if he hasn't already. Thank you for this, gentlemen, even if it is bad news, but before you go, can you tell me something positive that I can report? Something we can do, or are doing, to the Spit for the development of the new Mark IX?"

"Well," replied Douglas, "the chaps at Vickers are, in fact, straining all their resources to keep up. Some of the Spits have now got two Hispano-Suiza 20mm cannon, plus four 303 machine guns. There's some detail he might like. The Merlin engine is being tweaked to get more horse-power and we're now nearly completely rid of the fabric ailerons which limited the dive speed and were also terribly heavy and difficult to control. That Vickers chap you mentioned is ex-RAF, named Penn. We pulled him back into service. As a matter of fact, he insisted, so he could see for himself what we needed to do. A lot of ideas emerged which are now being acted upon."

"For example?"

"Well," continued Douglas, using his fingers to tick off items as he spoke, "aileron control, as mentioned; misting-over problems with the windscreen; side panel opticals are poor so we need to change from perspex to optical glass and our rear vision is about as bad as a Messerschmitt; plus, and this is serious, they have injection systems which solve the problem that we have of our carburettors cutting out in a negative-G situation, sudden dives for example."

Sir Cyril snorted. "I do know what negative-G means."

"Sorry, sir. Usually when I come to these exalted halls I expect to have to explain everything. My apologies."

"Incidentally," said Sir Cyril, again exhibiting a remarkable awareness of what was going on, "didn't some lady at Farnborough solve most of that carburettor problem with a hole in the float, somewhat ungallantly called Miss Schilling's Hole?"

"Quite right, sir, and on that somewhat more pleasant note I'll leave you, but hopefully you can impress Winston and he can impress the Beaver that we must give the people at Vickers every possible support, or we may be in big trouble. We can't afford to fight another Battle of Britain, especially if we're liable to lose it."

God, what a gloomy place, thought Douglas as he left. An especially gloomy place to bring gloomy news. A place full of grey people, but I suppose they're just as necessary as we are. I just hope the Germans have as many obstructionists in their own headquarters. Thank God for Sir Cyril though; I do think he'll put a poker up someone's arse. Just hope it's not mine!

NINE

The dark green Bentley purred as Geoffrey made his way up the A30 to Winchester and on towards London. Sounds as sweet as a Merlin, he thought, then laughed as he reminded himself why it should. Christ, it was made by the same people!

Rationing being in full swing meant there were few cars on the road. Geoffrey figured he could explain the petrol for the thirsty car as being his last splurge of coupons to get to this dance. He actually didn't feel particularly guilty about his private fuel supply, calculating that he'd already saved thousands of gallons by improving the efficiency of the test procedures. His biggest worry was whether the 100 octane they used in the planes had been cut back enough not to burn the valves in the old Bentley. She was, after all, a gracious old lady of sixteen years.

It was still full light at six o'clock and he felt sure that he would be parked in London well before dark. This thought reminded him of the many times he'd landed planes in unlit fields as late as ten at night in June and early July, possible because England lay so far north. He pondered again on the fact that London was, interestingly, further north than any part of the United States. This led him to wondering if any Yanks would be at the dance: he enjoyed meeting them, especially if they were fliers and he always hoped he might learn of any new developments in aircraft over there. Though from what he had heard so far, the Spit and especially its Merlin engine, was still streets ahead of anything the Yanks flew. He felt certain he'd have heard if the situation were otherwise as they didn't seem able to resist boasting of their achievements whenever they had the chance.

One or two army convoys heading south passed him, presumably still en route to bolster the southern coast against possible invasion. Reconnaissance planes still reported lots of activity on the French coast, but Geoffrey thought it unlikely they'd invade if they couldn't control the air over England.

These thoughts brought him full circle again, wondering how much truth there was in all the chatter he'd heard about Spits getting mauled over France. Apparently, whatever the Germans had over there they were keeping over there and not risking losing over England. That meant, he thought, that this new plane must either be very short ranged or, and he thought this far more likely, just highly secret.

In spite of its age the Bentley roared along through the particularly lovely countryside of this part of Britain. Far too lovely to be in a bloody war, he thought, as he enjoyed the green lawns and blossoming rhododendron and azalea that framed picturesque cottages and village greens. He could see very few signs of war in the area, though he knew that Guildford, nearby on the A3 road, had taken a few hits, possibly from bombers bounced before they got to London and anxious to unload their explosive cargo. He didn't think there was a lot in Guildford to really pique Jerry's interest. Once past the city he continued towards the Robin Hood roundabout at the bottom of Roehampton Hill. Only another half hour or so, he thought, and I'll be chatting up some of the prettiest girls in London. Pity they're also some of the primmest.

London was clear and cheerful. The sun was setting behind him as he came up the King's Road, past shops largely undamaged by the German bombing which seemed to be principally confined to the docks and the East End. A few establishments had plywood shutters covering the windows, but he imagined they were removed every morning. He cut up past the museums to Knightsbridge, attracting a few looks from passers-by to whom an old Bentley and a man in black tie were a rare sight these days.

A number of uniformed men, all officers, were loosely gathered on the pavement approaching the Hyde Park hotel. He didn't see anybody he recognized so he stepped up and over the half door of the Bentley, asking the doorman to park it anywhere safe and convenient as he would probably be leaving by midnight. The onlookers, apparently waiting to go into the dance, were giving him a somewhat chilly reception and scarcely leaving him enough room to walk through and up the steps to the lobby. He heard some muttering and thought he could guess at the probable reason for this unfriendliness.

"Wonder where that damn civilian gets the juice to run that guzzler?"

Penn could think of a few retorts but decided the best path lay in silence. Instead of replying he walked straight ahead into the cheerful melee inside the ballroom. These occasions, deb's balls or coming out parties, as they were known, were surely an anachronism; hardly a part of the war scene when people were being subjected to terrifying bombing raids and uncertain of eventual success. On the other hand, it was a typically British attitude, to carry on as before and not let foreigners interfere with ones way of life. Penn considered it a bit like dressing up and having tea in the jungle. Keeping the old traditions alive, regardless. Whatever the reason it did make a nice break from the unpleasantness of war and, crucially from his point of view, a chance to meet some of the best birds in London.

He made his way through the reception line, not meeting anyone he knew. Certainly no top military brass. Good thing too, he thought. Somebody has to be looking after the war. For his part he was going to look after the girls and with any luck find the rare but willing debutante who had a flat nearby and who thought she should help the war effort in her own way. God bless them all, he thought, as he scanned the crowd.

Most men present were in their twenties, some in black tie and even a few in tails but, for the most part, dressed in uniform representing all the services. He looked around for someone from his old RAF squadron, Fighter Group 11. He would enjoy seeing Keith Park, he thought. Park was the man Penn had cajoled into allowing him back into active service, just in time for the Battle of Britain. Not likely he'd be here, he supposed, but he might possibly see some of the lads from 65 Squadron at Hornchurch, where he'd done most of his fighting. And wouldn't it be marvellous to come across old Squadron Leader Leithhard. Geoffrey smiled to himself, remembering the man who had actually landed a Miles Master on the beach near Calais and picked up his squadron commander who'd been shot down that day. Picked him up and took off again from the beach, right under the noses and guns of the Jerries. What a chap, he thought; I'd love to hear his version first-hand.

By this time he'd manoeuvred into a spot near the bar and been given, in his estimation, a pretty piss-poor excuse for a drink. From this position he could easily scan the available femininity and obtain refreshment from time to time while so doing. He was just considering how best to approach a long, languid blonde when he felt a gentle tap on his arm. Turning, he looked again into the most amazing deep green eyes he had ever seen. He was unable to believe that the girl he'd thought about for the past several years was in front of him and, what's more, apparently alone. He glanced past her and could see that she had disengaged herself from a group of uniformed officers in order to approach him. He fervently hoped she had recognized him and wanted to renew their acquaintance. His sudden glow was promptly squelched by her opening remark.

"Hello, you looked a bit lonely, so I thought I'd leave that horrid gang arguing about which one was going to dance with me, and come talk to a nice, safe civilian. By the way, I'm called Clarissa, what about you? And will you dance with me away from that group please?"

Chastened, but nonetheless grateful for her attention, Geoffrey immediately spun her into the frenzy of noise and dancing. The music and people's voices made the room so loud that he couldn't actually talk, or indeed hear anything Clarissa said, though she seemed to be babbling on regardless, not waiting for, or perhaps wanting, a response. Never mind, he thought, who cares about conversation when she feels this good? Black hair that smells great, black knit dress; God, she's fantastically curvy. Noting several envious glances from various lads both on and off the floor he decided to try and manoeuvre her out of there before the ravening pack closed in.

May be my day, he thought. Just standing still in an old suit, I've scooped the pool! Clarissa has to be the best looking girl here, a bit scatty perhaps, but what a shape, and those eyes! He carefully steered her over towards the window which usually looked out over Hyde Park but was covered with heavy black-out curtains, and asked her if she'd like to step out for some air.

"If that's all you have in mind, OK, but what did you say your name was? Didn't I meet you before somewhere? Was it at Farringdon's shoot?"

"Geoffrey Penn," he replied, secretly delighted that she had actually recognized him, but deciding to play it cool with this clearly rather popular girl. They stepped onto a wide balcony and gazed out over a dark and quiet London.

"I don't *think* we've met," he continued. "Where did you say?"

"What do you do?" Clarissa started chattering while trying to absorb the fact that here was a man who hadn't remembered her. That certainly made a change. "Thought you were a pilot. I'm sure I've seen you. It's so rare but rather nice to see anyone at one of these balls in civvies. Practically everyone's in uniform."

"Well, I suppose pilot would describe me," replied Geoffrey. "I work down in Southampton for Vickers, helping develop aeroplanes."

"Well, that sounds frightfully important, and it certainly is refreshing to hear of someone doing something other than endless heroic exploits, like that lot in there. Are you staying the night in town or driving all the way back tonight?"

Geoffrey, hardly daring to think that this might be a hint, thought he'd throw out a line anyway: never up, never in, he reckoned.

"I had planned to go back but I'd gladly change plans if..." He wasn't given the chance to finish the sentence.

"Don't even think about it," said Clarissa. "You're as bad as the rest, but I *will* let you drive me home. My father insists I'm in not long after twelve. You do have a car don't you? It gives me a good answer for those other twerps too."

Geoffrey guessed that classed him as a twerp also, but there wasn't any chance he was going to turn down an opportunity like this. He quickly agreed and apparently just in time too, for a big rugged face appeared round the doors to the balcony.

"Clarissa, it's about time you gave the flyers some time. My dance, please, as promised."

All this was said as a large uniformed arm circled her and practically lifted her back into the room. As she was being carried off she looked back over her shoulder at Geoffrey.

"Twelve o'clock, *please*" she mouthed.

The rest of the evening was a bit of a tiresome waltz in Geoffrey's mind. He did dance with Martha Turnbull, a girl he had known, very well come to think of it, but he couldn't manage to get the normally erotic memories of Martha to take his mind off Clarissa. There was great femininity there that he felt was matched by a sense of vitality, the combination of which, in spite of the rather typical debutante scattiness, made Clarissa the most attractive woman he'd ever seen. Yes, he decided, she was definitely now more woman than girl. When he had his arms around her as they slowly danced, he had felt such an ecstatic sensation that he wondered if this was what was meant by love. That word had always perplexed him and, in spite of his reputation as a swordsman, he had never before experienced anything like this with any of the women who had given themselves for King, Country and Geoffrey. He had, indeed, never forgotten Clarissa Smythe.

As midnight finally arrived he found himself hovering near the ladies' cloakroom, presuming that Clarissa would at last emerge from the crowd somewhere near there to retrieve her coat and hopefully meet her ride home. He wondered if she had been serious. Undoubtedly she'd get lots of offers and probably better ones too. He could hardly stand it, wondering what he'd do if she didn't appear. He knew he was not going to get over that ever so brief but electrifying encounter. He knew he'd never find another woman as desirable; he was certain of it and was beginning to make himself miserable about the whole affair when she again suddenly appeared from behind, with a gentle tap on his elbow.

Geoffrey, who spent a lot of his time looking around and behind him every day in aeroplanes, reflected that he obviously only had forward vision as far as Clarissa was concerned.

"Ready?" she said, pulling her fox collar up around her neck, for it was still chilly in the evenings.

Surprised and relieved, the normally highly articulate Geoffrey simply led her to the door, asking the doorman for his keys and where he'd parked the Bentley.

"Ah, a Bentley," said Clarissa. "I did pick an important boffin."

"I'm afraid not, Clarissa. It's an old machine and a bit tired like its owner, but it has never yet let me down, which is more than I can say for many machines."

The car was exactly where Geoffrey had left it. There's value in being a bit late, thought Geoffrey, as he held the door open for Clarissa.

"Do you want me to put the top up?" he enquired, trying not to let her notice his glance at the lovely bit of thigh she exposed climbing into the rather awkward front bucket seat.

"Absolutely not, this is delicious. It's been ages since I've been driven through London in an open car. By the way, we're going to Eaton Square. Do let's get away before I get any more stick for leaving with an older man in civvies."

Christ, he thought, only twenty-nine and 'old' and technically I suppose I am a civilian. That's a poor start at best.

Clarissa chatted away, though he could scarcely hear her over the engine noise. She occasionally turned to him to give directions. He in turn was trying to drive reasonably well while shooting covert glances at her legs, so well outlined in the tight knit dress. I can't believe I've found her again, he thought. What a glorious creature she is. I do hope I don't mess this up.

They pulled up in front of a tall narrow building on Eaton Square. Posh, very, *very* posh, he thought as he walked Clarissa to the door.

"Do come in for a drink," insisted Clarissa. "You can't possibly drive all the way home without one. I doubt Daddy's awake and even if he is his bark is worse than his bite. Mind you, I should warn you that he does bark rather a lot!"

The heavy black-painted door swung open to reveal a large marble floored hallway. Geoffrey and Clarissa walked in and past an impressive high-chandeliered dining room into what seemed a very small and insignificant kitchen for such a sumptuous house. Typical, thought Geoffrey, not to worry how your staff prepares food as long as it gets there and someone else has cooked it. Clarissa seemed to know her way around and was soon pressing a glass of whisky into Geoffrey's hand. Not many English homes would be burning coal in these times and at this hour, Geoffrey mused, aware of the heat emanating from the permanently hot Aga. He sat back in the kitchen chair, swirling his whiskey around the glass and admiring Clarissa who was now leaning back against the counter, hip bones showing slightly through the knit. He could see gentle curves formed by what he figured had to be lovely thighs.

His pleasantly erotic reverie was rudely interrupted by the door bursting open to admit a large, mustached and obviously irritated man. His bulk threatened to overfill the already crowded kitchen.

"That your car outside, young man? Better not leave it there long; big cars aren't very popular around here these days. Bentley, isn't it? Nice one, too, I'll give you that. Archibald Smythe, by the way, Clarissa's father."

Who bloody else would you be, thought Penn, already recognizing his invitation to bail out, and at too low an altitude too.

"How do you do, sir, Penn's my name, Geoffrey Penn. I'm delighted to have been able to bring your daughter home, but I really should be getting back to my own."

"Where's that then?" asked Sir Archibald. Geoffrey had by now recognized the rather well known tycoon's face. Steel or coal or something of that order, he thought.

"Southampton, sir."

"Bloody long way to come for a dance, isn't it?" demanded Sir Archibald. "And what do you do down there, may I ask?"

"I'm with Vickers, sir, and yes, it is a long drive, but rather nice to get away from work. Also, if I may say so, to have the chance to meet someone as charming as your daughter."

"Hmm, got a charming son too, a flyer. He's home tonight, Clarissa. Pop in and wish him goodnight."

Taking the hint and realizing he had pushed his chance re-acquaintance as far as he could, Geoffrey excused himself and let Clarissa lead him to the door.

"Don't take Daddy too seriously: he has a bit of a thing about anybody not in uniform these days. Wishes he were in it himself. He's terribly proud of my brother Robert who's just been commissioned. Daddy thinks I should only go out with officers, the higher-ranking the better. His idea of helping the war effort, I guess! Though I'm sure he has pretty strict limits on how much help!" she added mischievously.

A quick word of thanks, a peck on the cheek and Geoffrey was alone on the stone step, reeling with emotion. I think I might be in love, he thought, astonished, if it's possible to fall in love in what has probably been less than thirty minutes actual conversation and with a totally unknown person. I suppose that what's known as chemistry, he mused, and why not, he continued, as his faithful Bentley purred down through Chelsea. After all, he recalled, he'd been involved in an extremely violent and intense dog fight with a Messerschmitt pilot not so long ago. The fight hadn't lasted more than a few minutes but had been so fierce that he'd actually seen his entire life pass in review. And I never even *met* that chap, he thought, so maybe sometimes a particular thirty minutes of someone's life is a lot. I only hope that my pretending not to have met her will at least be different than all the chaps who must be pursuing her. Oh God, perhaps it was a bad gamble.

Clarissa held up the whisky bottle and looked at her father with an enquiring expression. He rather pointedly looked at the kitchen clock. Putting the bottle back in the cupboard she explained how she had met Geoffrey who was, she said, very good-looking even though not in uniform, which, she continued, and if he didn't mind her saying so, made some very plain men look a lot better than they normally would. She didn't bother to tell him that she thought that he too had seen Geoffrey Penn before. She was upset and more than a little embarrassed that he didn't even remember her. Sir Archibald, about to release his usual lecture on the importance of military morale and so on, was himself interrupted by his son Robert, who it seemed had heard the marvellous sound of the Bentley driving off and had come down to see who Clarissa possibly knew with a car like that.

"A very nice man called Geoffrey Penn," she stated defensively, expecting the same sort of reception her father had delivered; not exactly impolite but frosty.

"Good heavens," said Robert. "How'd you ever meet *him*?"

"Do you know the chap? Is he all right?" demanded Sir Archibald.

"Oh, more than all right, Dad, he's only one of the greatest pilots in Britain. *Everyone* who flies has heard of him. He was the second man to fly the Spitfire, after Mutt Summers, and he has been the chief test pilot at Vickers for years. I believe that a lot of the improvements in the Spit came from his experiences when he left Vickers and fought in the Battle of Britain; he shot down several planes before going back to Vickers. He's got more air time in Spits than anyone in the world. I've also heard that when we try and sell the Allies some of our planes, he puts on a demonstration that's hard to believe. I'm really impressed, Clarissa, how did an ordinary-looking bird like you ever bag such a catch?"

"Well, well, well," muttered Sir Archibald as he shuffled off to bed. "Well, well indeed!"

TEN

London was dark, quiet and faintly surreal as Geoffrey headed away from Eaton Square and down the King's Road to Putney Bridge. He drove as if on auto pilot. Thoughts of Clarissa filled his head and he was beginning to accept that something special had happened to him in those few precious moments. Christ, he realized, I've never even kissed her. That peck on the cheek she administered as I left certainly didn't count. Most likely a thank you for the lift home. And what a scary father! I'd rather dead stick land a Spit than spend a night having to chat with him, though he's probably a decent enough sort of chap. Rather over-protective of that beautiful and enchanting daughter. Green eyes, he recalled. Yes, British Racing Green, though not quite as dark as the Bentley. Signor Bugatti once said that Mr Bentley 'built the fastest lorries in Europe'. Well, Clarissa is the absolute opposite of a lorry! Whoa, bloody hell, nearly missed that curve at Ripley. Thank God for those big iron gates, they always remind me. Even this lorry might get a bit bruised trying to go straight through them. Surprised they haven't been pulled down and melted yet; hardly ever see gates or railings now.

The moon was nearly full and the road needed little light, so the Bentley's side lights and his own remarkable eyesight soon brought Geoffrey under the half hour from Eastleigh. The closer he got the more his thoughts left Clarissa and moved to the following day's testing. It was nearly two in the morning and he knew the weather forecast was good. He'd need to be up and on the flight line by eight if he hoped to get through the day's testing quota, even with the help of his other pilots. This brought on a bout of worrying thoughts about the Spit and its alarming new German rival. Ever since the Jerry had bombed Wolston factory just assembling the pieces at Eastleigh was proving to be an incredibly difficult job to administer and co-ordinate.

We really need The Beaver here to organize it himself, he thought, not just suggest it. Spitfire parts were now being manufactured in twenty-eight different locations in the Southampton area, ranging from the Sunlight laundry, Shorts garage, to the Hants and Dorset garage plus several stores converted either for storage, assembly or manufacture. It always amused Geoffrey that the accounts records were kept somewhere called Sleepy Hollow Barn.

Well, at least the headquarters are impressive, he thought. In December 1940 the Supermarine administration and design sections had moved to Hursley Park, the beautiful mansion that had belonged to Lady Cooper. Geoffrey still called it Hursley Park in spite of the now rather formal name of Supermarine Works of Vickers Armstrong Limited. Joe Smith, he thought, is a great chap and a bloody talented design chief, but what a tragedy Reggie Mitchell had to die, only forty-two years old and already having designed the perfect lady. He'd have been amazed to see how many Spits were being turned out each day. Bloody well need them too, as do our so-called Allies who keep on begging for more.

As Geoffrey rolled into Bursledon and towards his digs his mind was churning so much he doubted he could sleep. Nevertheless, within minutes of buttoning down the tonneau cover over the open Bentley, climbing up the stairs to his flat and falling into bed, still in his dinner jacket, he was fast asleep and gently snoring.

ELEVEN

Penn awoke with a start, the sort of shock that often occurs after a very deep sleep. For a moment he wondered if he were still in London. He grimaced at the sight of his dinner jacket, now badly wrinkled. At least it looks run in, he thought. He swung his legs over the side of the bed and sat up, gazing around at his digs. The flat, rented from a nice old couple whom he seldom saw, amounted to a bedroom and a small sitting room which contained a built-in kitchen sink and electric burner stove. The stove and heating unit ran on a meter which required the regular insertion of shilling coins. As Geoffrey fed in yet another shilling he reflected cheerfully that spring had arrived so life might become a little less expensive.

Geoffrey habitually left the flat early and returned late, often via The Jolly Sailor pub which was beyond his digs and up the hill, past the railway station, then down a narrow path to the Hamble River. After work he sometimes parked in the railway lot and then walked half way up the lane to his place, or carried on straight past to the pub, depending upon his mood or thirst. It wasn't easy to park the big Bentley up the hill and he needed the leg exercise after being uncomfortably cramped in the cockpit of a Spitfire most of the day. He never worried about leaving the car in the lot. His landlady had told him that all the thieves were in the army or, and in her opinion it was more likely, in the group of Commandos who were camped up river and who always seemed to be swarming around The Jolly Sailor.

It'll be the pub tonight for sure, he thought as he finally struggled out of his dinner jacket into flying overalls then into the Bentley and off to Eastleigh. At the control tower he was greeted by an irate Sir Robert McLean, the man in charge at Vickers.

"You're late and you look like hell," said Sir Robert before Geoffrey could say a word. In any event he doubted if he would be able to respond, or that it would make any difference to the one-way conversation he knew was about to ensue. "Anyhow," Sir Robert continued with some disturbing news, "we've got a problem, which means you've got a problem because I certainly can't suggest anything more to do to the Spit. We've just had another call from the Air Ministry moaning that our pilots, especially some of the 1st and 43rd Squadrons up in Tangmere are getting reluctant to escort the bombers passing over Cherbourg on their way to bomb the sub pens at St. Nazaire, La Rochelle and further on down the coast. They claim that the Kraut has a new super-plane that's faster and better armed and generally out-performing us, especially the older Hurricanes. They want to know what we are doing about it and they want to know now. I'm damned sure that Joe Smith at headquarters has had an earful too, though I haven't seen him for a few days. Any ideas? No, I didn't think so, not in the condition you're obviously in. You're letting your fucking interfere with your flying and right now I need you flying. Take the next Spit up for test and don't just certify it to fly! I want you to beat the shit out of it. Try and break it apart. If you and it are still in one piece, come and tell me so that I can tell *them* if there's anything more we can do to this model. Yes, I know the Mark IX is on its way but God only knows if it will be good enough to beat this new German plane. Have you heard anything about it? Call me when you're back down anyhow. And, Geoffrey, for heaven's sake be careful, you look absolutely dreadful." As rapidly as the lecture was delivered, this dynamic man walked off, leaving Geoffrey wondering what more he could do to break a Spit that hadn't already been tried by now, by both new and old pilots, though sadly there weren't very many of the latter still around. Some extremes were tried purposefully to avoid death and sometimes tried inadvertently, finding death.

In any event, ten minutes later he was airborne, breathing oxygen straight away as, in his experience, a good blast of it was the best hangover cure he knew and it was one substance always near to hand.

This Spit took off well, seeming to be almost in trim right from the factory assembly. He headed off, following the railway tracks towards

Fareham and Southampton, flying just above the taller church spires, then south towards the Isle of Wight and climbing rapidly at about two thousand feet per minute to where he would commence the test procedures. He calculated that he could make it back to Eastleigh, or one of the several other fields around Southampton, even if he had an engine failure, providing he got enough height and stayed not far south of the island. He could easily see Southampton from there, especially with the weather as clear as it was. He always felt that, if he went past St. Catherine's Point, he was practically in no-man's land, or air, and too bloody close to Cherbourg in any event if these rumours about the German plane were true. Accordingly he began to orbit over The Needles on the west side of the island. At nine thousand feet he throttled back to idle to let the engine cool a bit then went through the routine testing of instruments, throttle settings and trim balance. The guns, eight 303 calibre Brownings, wouldn't be fitted until later, then armed and test fired on the ground.

Glancing down at the impressively sharp rocks below, he thought he'd better try and bend a few aluminium bits, just to satisfy McLean. As all the basics seemed in order he was sure there wasn't any point in doing much more to this model except to make as many as possible and as fast as possible. Incredible, he thought, how many planes I've tested and how few had real faults, and thank God for that too. He didn't relish the thought of ditching in the Channel if any basic parts fell off; a parachute landing with no dinghy was very bad news, even if he had had the time to get off a radio message that would, hopefully, get passed to the Air Sea Rescue. The Channel was still dangerously cold until very late spring.

He opened the throttle and pulled the stick back into his stomach in full climb, full power and kept it there until the plane seemed to hang on the prop, stagger and stall, but as it did so and started to actually fall back, he pushed the stick full forward, depressing the elevators which began to bite as the plane fell onto its back and then, through gravity alone, regain air speed.

As Geoffrey felt the plane begin to respond to rudder and aileron he continued the roll the manoeuvre had initiated and then dived towards the Isle of Wight at full power with a seventy degree angle, noting as he did so the tendency of the bullet-proof windscreen to ice up as the temperature rapidly changed. He also noticed the annoying Spitfire habit of slightly stalling as the carburettors were temporarily starved of fuel by the sudden dive inertia. Penn was flying flat out doing about four hundred and seventy-five mph and beginning to wonder if the Spit would hold together when he pulled up. At least he knew that the new metal ailerons would be there whereas, by now, the older fabric ones would probably be floating away in space and he with them. At three thousand feet he pulled back as hard as he could to bring the Spit out of the dive which, if continued into the denser air near ground and with the combined force of gravity and Rolls Royce engine at full throttle, would probably pull the wings off and prove only that everything has its limits.

"That should put a few wrinkles in the wing roots and please old McLean," Geoffrey murmured into his oxygen mask. Again he scanned the sky above and around and in the rear view mirror for chance Messerschmitts, only to have his radio crackle into the voice of Clive Donovan telling him that an air raid was warned and the barrage balloons were going up.

"Well, that completes a shitty day." Geoffrey hoped that Clive was the only person on the control tower frequency. Another devastating daylight raid was the last thing they needed now, even though Geoffrey thought the dispersed nature of the Spitfire production would probably protect the flow of the new planes, unless the Germans got a lucky hit on some vital storage or manufacturing point. The way things seemed to be going, he thought it very likely that could happen.

"Damn it!" he cursed. "I can't even shoot one of the bastards down if I see one, which, incidentally, I don't, and right now up here at two thousand feet over the Isle of Wight I can probably see better and further than our radar."

Geoffrey turned back towards his favourite bad weather landmarks more from habit than necessity, for the weather was still perfect. He quickly picked up the familiar shape of the Bursledon Windmill which, without its sails, looked more like a lighthouse than a windmill, standing just in from the coast like a dark and forbidding sentinel. From there he had only to dodge the extremely annoying balloon cables. He proceeded to do this by pulling the Spit into very tight turns which pushed him hard into the seat as the G-forces ebbed and flowed. Fun flying, he called it, but it terrified anyone on the ground watching. He was practically on the ground as he raced back to shoot across the end of the runway, throttled back downwind, did his checks for mixture rich, prop fine, wheels down, a shot of carburettor heat then into the final approach with flaps down and onto the runway, breaking hard both to test the brakes and get the Spit back to park and, hopefully, less likely to be bombed, if indeed this were not just another jumpy false alarm.

The air raid never did materialize, but the scare put paid to more flight testing by Geoffrey or any of his other pilots that day. He therefore busied himself catching up on the dreaded paperwork, in his opinion the bane of any flier's existence. He recalled with satisfaction his Battle of Britain days where all he had to do was keep jumping into his plane, hopefully getting back down without any assistance from his parachute, and then getting a verbal debriefing by some bright young intelligence officer. At times, he remembered, he was even too exhausted to do that and simply dozed in the plane while it was re-armed, re-fuelled and swiftly checked for serious damage. He'd take off his helmet for these naps, counting on his chief mechanic Gordy to wake him up when the plane was ready to take off and fight again. Those were the days, he thought, so tonight, when I'm through with this nonsense, I'm going to The Jolly Sailor to get very sloshed before stumbling back to my sack. Tomorrow has to be a better day. Maybe I'll even try and call Clarissa.

TWELVE

As Geoffrey descended the winding path down to The Jolly Sailor the din which rose to meet him meant only one thing; Group 12 Commando was having a night off, probably given to provide some relief from what Geoffrey presumed must be very tough training, to say nothing of the hazardous missions they were called upon to perform. He had never actually heard specifically what they did, but the rumours were frequent about boats coming and going along the Hamble River, always at night, and with few, if any, lights. Geoffrey thought his own high risk life was probably fairly safe compared to what they most likely got up to, so he didn't begrudge them the odd knees up at the pub. There were a couple of attractive barmaids, but generally the place was pretty much devoid of women. Most females, he was sure, wouldn't dare go near the place, in spite of its reputation for good food and beer.

The location of the pub, too, was fantastic. Right on the outside bend of the river, with many yachts moored around it, up and down across the river, which was probably fifty yards wide at that point. The pub itself was not old by British standards, in fact, almost new at fifty years or so, constructed of brick with a red tile roof. Inside it boasted a fairly nautical decor with deck-like floors and simulated mast going up through the rather low ceiling, or perhaps it was a real mast, Geoffrey couldn't decide. Getting down the hill to the pub was a cinch but, as Geoffrey recalled, getting back up some nights was a real pig. Tonight might be one of those. He needed to get the Kraut Ghost plane, and Clarissa, out of his head and just plain relax.

With keen anticipation Geoffrey pushed open the rear door, the front one being off a short porch facing the river, and forced himself through a gang of already quite pissed Commandos, most of whom begrudgingly gave him room or 'leave to pass'. When he finally reached the bar, Geoffrey decided he would start the night's work with a stiff gin and tonic. He ordered this from the voluptuous barmaid, Ada, who had on previous evenings given Geoffrey the idea that she would be pleased to exhibit to him even more of her cleavage than showed as she bent over to pick a tonic bottle from under the bar. You get a better view with a gin and tonic, thought Geoffrey, than when she pulls a pint. Well worth the extra money.

"I wish this one was on me," she cooed to Geoffrey, "but the boss insists I collect two and sixpence please."

"'I wish I was on you too, sweetie," a tough-looking corporal remarked. Jerking his head towards Geoffrey, he added, "and if I thought you were giving it to this little piss-pot civilian I'd break your arse as well as his balls."

This really was the last thing Geoffrey needed after a bad work day. He was well aware that the place was full of fighting fit Commandos, so he tried to back quietly away, but there was no room; just a rugby-like scrum of uniforms, some of whom were obviously amused by the corporal's behaviour and curious to see where it led.

"If you don't mind, Corporal, this is my pub too, and I'd quite like to simply walk out quietly and enjoy my drink."

"Well I do mind, you sweet-talking tight-arsed poofter. Why don't you just get out and stay out, while fighting men drink?"

The corporal was drunk and belligerent. He had started moving ominously towards Geoffrey, beer mug in hand, when a large arm suddenly appeared over Geoffrey's shoulder and, before anyone could react, a hugely powerful figure moved like lightening around Geoffrey, one hand grabbing the Commando by the shirt front, and the other by what must have been his balls judging by the sound he let out. The corporal was lifted off the floor, almost hitting his head on the ceiling, and carried bodily through the pack of uniforms which seemed to part like the Red Sea, leaving a clear passage to the open front door through which the corporal, still yelping, was carried and then tossed over the brick wall into the river a couple of yards below.

"I know every one of you bastards can swim, so get out and clear out, and I'll see you at seven am tomorrow morning to try and find out just how tough you are. You'd better be tough 'cause you're sure as hell stupid."

"Yes, Captain," came faintly up from the water as Geoffrey's benefactor stooped slightly to re-enter the pub. The raucous laughter inside the bar subsided, whether through fear or respect Geoffrey wasn't sure.

"Sorry about that, Penn. I'm Philip Quigley, Captain of 12 Commando, stationed just up the river. Usually my lads are a good lot, a bit long on guts but short on marbles, which makes a good Commando but a lousy social drinker. Can I buy you another?"

"Thanks, Captain, I needed that help. I seem to have a propensity for pissing people off these days, even without opening my mouth. By the way, how'd you know my name?"

"Ada told me. I do wish they'd put ugly barmaids in here. The lads are bad enough with anything in skirts, but she seems to inspire riots, and she obviously likes you. I asked her one night who you were when I saw you here, and she told me you were a famous pilot, or so she'd heard. Used to be RAF and now testing Spits at Eastleigh, is that right? I figured it would be a serious loss to have you put out of the game by some drunken jealous corporal and isn't this war a mighty fine game too? Believe me, after tomorrow he'll lick your shoes and kiss your arse next time he sees you, or the reverse, if you wish."

By this time the other Commandos had backed off, giving Quigley, who seemed to be the highest ranking officer there, in fact probably the only officer in this part of the bar, lots of room. He needed it too, thought Geoffrey. What a great rugby forward prop he must have been; could have used him back in my days as fly half.

As they chatted Geoffrey learned a little more about 12 Commando which, as he knew, had been camped for some time up the river at Cricket Camp, where he supposed they trained for amphibious manoeuvres and action. Apparently, this night out had been designed to take some pressure off, as the training had been hard and there had been no missions for a while. Geoffrey thought of that as good news but, apparently, if you wanted to be a Commando in the first place, a lack of missions was seriously bad.

"How's the testing going?" asked Philip who, after another whisky and a gin and tonic for Geoffrey, had suggested to Geoffrey that 'Captain' was a little too formal for The Jolly Sailor.

"Not bad, not bad," said Geoffrey. "It's amazing how well put together the planes are. It's almost getting routine to trim them, certify them and send them off, but every now and then somebody in a factory somewhere makes a cock-up. Then, as you can imagine, my lads get that adrenaline shot which you Commandos seem to like so much. Quite frankly I can do without it."

"Well, we kicked Heinz's arse but well and truly with the Battle of Britain, so I'm told," said Philip. "Does that mean the bombing will stop and eventually we can land in Europe and chase the bastards home?"

"I wish I could say that," said Geoffrey in a slightly slurred, four gins and tonic voice, "but the bloody Germans are anything but dumb. Their best plane, the ME109, is a little long in the tooth; early versions were around in '36. But word has it they've got a hot new job. I've never seen it, and haven't even talked to anyone who has but, and for God's sake don't repeat this, I'm worried and so it seems are some big, big-wigs in Whitehall."

The discussions about the war, Ada's breasts, Geoffrey's Bentley and the quality of fish and chips they had eaten, pretty well carried them through the evening. Philip, who was probably not more than two years older than Geoffrey, seemed to have adopted a rather paternal feeling about him, realizing perhaps that Commandos come and go, but there couldn't be many other men like Geoffrey Penn about. Having promised to meet again the next evening, Philip left by boat for camp up-river and Geoffrey staggered up the hill to the road and then the few hundred yards back down to his digs.

THIRTEEN

Testing the following day was left to other pilots since Geoffrey had to spend most of the day at Hursley Park talking to Joe Smith, the man who had taken over from Mitchell as big chief of the Spitfire design group. Geoffrey flew up there from Eastleigh in a Spit, giving it the routine test procedures en route, then landed at Worthy Down, another airfield just north of Winchester, where they also tested but without the added hazard of barrage balloons. The meeting, attended by a few boffins from the design group, along with Geoffrey and Joe, also included Sir Robert McLean who sporadically popped in between crises which seemed to Geoffrey to be occurring every ten minutes somewhere in the complicated production system.

Having been on oxygen between Eastleigh and Worthy Down, Geoffrey felt somewhat recovered from the previous night's effort with Philip Quigley. His usual hangover cure had been given the chance to work its magic for a little more than the fifteen minutes required to run through the basic test procedures. Just as well, he thought as the meeting started.

Joe Smith opened the batting with a pretty basic question.

"How much is left to do, or can be done, to improve the Mark V, or should we forget it and concentrate only on the Mark IX?"

"Well," answered Geoffrey, "at Sir Robert's invitation I took a V straight from production yesterday and I really beat hell out of It. I think it's a damned good aeroplane; not without some basic problems which we all know about, but I honestly think we'd be smarter to put all our effort into the next best variant, and not tinker with what is already a bloody good fighting machine. We might foul it up in the process."

McLean, uncharacteristically quiet up to this point, replied.

"Geoffrey, I think you and the others here should know that Headquarters are desperately worried about this new German plane. So far it has apparently outclassed the V, even when flown by some of our better lads.

We're getting more pressure than you can imagine to either tweak the hell out of the V or accelerate the introduction of the IX, and how do we know what we've got in the IX will ever equal the Hun plane, let along leap-frog it? You know how long it takes to get from drawing board to production, though as it happens in this case we're way ahead in having the basic airframe, and a bloody good one it is too. Still, I don't like it. Why on earth can't we shoot one of those mysteries down over England and find out what they've done to make it so good? Geoffrey, you've flown the 109 and, as I recall, you didn't think it was so marvellous, in fact nothing like as good as the V, I believe."

"Absolutely right, sir," said Geoffrey, impressed that McLean seemed so genuinely concerned. It was obvious that he was getting real pressure from above and they certainly knew how to deliver it. But it was more than pressure, Geoffrey knew, that drove McLean. In fact, probably no-one could have really pressured him, with the possible exception of Winston himself. Sir Robert had a genuine belief in things British and a deep hatred for any foreign threat to that way of life, or indeed, that way of thinking. Geoffrey thought he would be the last man fighting on the beach if it came down to that, and now, it seemed that he knew, apparently from a reliable source, that McLean's beach was being threatened. It appeared that there was simply no hard data on the new German plane, only a few blurred air-to-air photos. The enemy was probably too nervous about losing the secrecy of their new plane to risk having one crash over Britain and, as far as anyone could ascertain, they only came up to intercept British incursions over France and didn't even venture very far over the Channel.

"This gives them a big advantage," said Joe, following up discussion on that thought, "because they have a full fuel tank, and our lads are spending a lot of time checking to see if they have enough fuel left to fight full throttle and still get home. Ditching in the Channel is no joke any time of the year and it's still cold as brass monkeys out there."

A couple of hours of frustrating conversation with few new ideas left

Geoffrey again feeling somewhat depressed and thinking ahead to The Jolly Sailor, Ada's cleavage, and that nice but rather fearsome Commando who had saved his face from being remodelled by a pint mug. Even some aerial photos taken by a brave and very quick unarmed and stripped down reconnaissance plane hadn't revealed much because the aircraft on the ground in the two or three fields photographed were, for the most part, under camouflage nets or in individual bunkers or hangers. One or two were caught out in the open, however, but didn't seem to possess any unusual features, which depressed everyone even more. The meeting broke up and everyone parted, having agreed to work even harder to accelerate the Mark IX programme and hope for some kind of lucky break.

Flying back to Eastleigh Geoffrey was contacted again by Clive Donovan in the control tower who asked him if he would fly out to the Isle of Wight, going on out to sea for perhaps twenty miles and flying back directly towards the island at six thousand feet altitude, then again at three thousand and lastly at sea level.

"May I ask what on earth for?" demanded Geoffrey. "Is this another crack-pot idea of the Navy?"

"No, my friend," replied Clive. "Please just do it as it might well save your precious backside one day. It's to test a new radio installation at Blackgang."

"Roger that, Clive; see you in twenty minutes or so. Please don't organize another false air raid, *or* a real one come to that."

Back as promised, Geoffrey parked the Spit, made out the usual forms of certification which included a few trim suggestions and noted a small canopy crack which might create a major problem at the wrong moment. He then headed for his Bentley and the road back to Bursledon. He didn't especially want to talk to anyone else that day, especially about aeroplanes, but he did recall that he had promised to meet Quigley at The Jolly Sailor and right now that sounded pretty good. At least the big man liked to talk about women, cars, and rugby, roughly in that order. Geoffrey presumed that Ada not only talked to Philip but probably shagged him rigid as well which, in fact, made him rather envious, even though Ada was not really his kind of girl.

The pub was much less busy than the previous night and the few Commandos there seemed to remember Geoffrey, even smiling a welcome which he thought was an encouraging step in a good direction. He really didn't fancy fighting every time he wanted a drink, and certainly not with a Commando.

Philip was already there, holding forth at the other side of the bar, filling up most of a square-paned bay window which looked out on the lovely, warm late-spring evening river scene. Geoffrey joined the group and was introduced as Penn, a local pilot, which seemed sufficient to secure him due respect, but he suspected Philip had already identified him pretty fully to his chums. In any event, they all gradually wandered back to the bar and other groups to help, Geoffrey thought, raise the noise level.

"Geoffrey, old boy, you're looking a bit worried. Can't take the late nights, or was it a bad day at the office?" asked Philip, while at the same time signalling Ada to bring them a couple more drinks. Even her presence didn't seem to cheer Geoffrey however, but Philip was having none of it.

"Come on lad, tell Uncle Philip your troubles, 12 Commando can fix anything!"

"No," said Geoffrey, "I'll accept that you can break anything, but fix it I doubt, and certainly not *my* problems."

"Well actually, Geoffrey, I think you're wrong. I've been thinking about your problem; I presume it's the dreaded Hun's new plane you were telling me about. In fact, I lay awake most of the night thinking about what you told me. Probably more than you can remember. You said that no-one had actually seen this plane up close, except the guys that had their backsides shot up and lived to boast about it. You also said you had flown most of the German planes we had captured and didn't think they were so great. Maybe this one isn't either: you know how you pilots like to exaggerate. Anyway, I thought so long and hard that I almost forgot to get up and lay out an impossible day's training for that half-assed corporal who wanted to rearrange your pretty face. Now, as a result of all that hard thinking I've got an idea, but it depends on you, not me. First of all, do you think you could actually fly this new plane? Are all planes much the same, or what?"

Startled out of his mood by this train of conversation, actually more of a locomotive of conversation, he thought, Geoffrey could only impart what he believed.

"I don't know, but I imagine they progress their planes much as we do. Nothing too new or complicated in the basics, too hard to convert old pilots over, and they are the ones you usually want to fly new and better aircraft. Yes, I probably could fly it, but only if it were already started. I'd have a hell of a time to get a Spitfire engine running all by myself. Never even tried and don't hope to. Why do you ask, incidentally?"

"Well," said Philip, leaning low and speaking softly, "the plan is that we should steal one!"

"You must be bloody *joking*, Philip!" Geoffrey's response was loud enough to attract the attention of several men in the bar. Philip raised a finger to his lips. Geoffrey, in a softer tone of voice, continued. "*You* may be out of your mind, probably are, but *I'm* sure as hell not, not that far anyhow! I have to admit to being intrigued, however, as to just how you would propose to do it. I'll even buy you another whisky to hear this one."

Waiting until Ada had replaced their empty glasses with fresh drinks and returned to the bar, swishing her hips provocatively, Philip spoke quietly and confidentially, which bothered Geoffrey even more, for he thought that Philip must be serious. Either that or more drunk than he seemed to be.

"I listened to you, and I thought about it a lot, Geoffrey. As I recall you said the planes were on the north French coast. As it happens I've been over there and back a couple of times recently, so why not again? I think I could get you into the seat of a plane and if you can fly the damned thing back everyone will be happy, everybody except the Hun. Piece of cake, as I believe you boys are prone to say."

"You can't be serious."

"Bloody right I am!"

"You'll never get permission."

"Wait and see. I need something to do and this sounds hairy enough to be fun and more worthwhile than the last two trips I took over there."

"I can't believe this, you *are* serious!"

"Don't wimp out on me now Geoffrey: you said you could fly the fucker, or is it Fokker?"

"Jesus!"

"Geoffrey, have another one on me, keep this between thee and me and tomorrow I shall unveil my plan, the Quigley plan. I'll even let you shoot holes in it, if there are any. Not another word now, too crowded. I'll see you tomorrow, sleep well."

FOURTEEN

In fact, Geoffrey scarcely slept at all that night. Every time he dozed off he'd wake up wondering if Philip was really serious; *could* he ever get approval for such a scheme? It would take a full troop of Commandos to storm an airfield and he was sure the attempt would result in enormous losses. And so he fretted through that night and during the following day's testing, where even his ground staff noted that he was more quiet than usual. It worried them if they noticed anything unusual in a test pilot's demeanour. Normally they assumed it was a hang-over, girl trouble or just normal war worries, but what alarmed them was that accidents seemed to happen more frequently when the pilots were less than their normal selves, whatever that normal self happened to be. Penn was seldom detached or distracted and almost invariably polite and pleasant. Seeing him as he appeared this day quite worried his crew. Even Clive Donovan suggested he break off early and sort out whatever was bugging him.

So with that small amount of encouragement, all he needed, Geoffrey set off for The Sailor again, arriving around six o'clock to find Philip waiting for him at the top of the hill; a very excited Philip too.

"Geoffrey, old man," he began, taking hold of Geoffrey's arm and turning him around, "we can't talk down there, but I've got great news. We've got approval from my boss, he's going to forward my plan to Combined Ops to get the first go-ahead, and he's sure they'll buy it. How about that?"

"Wait a minute, wait just a minute my friend."

They were now walking down the road away from the pub, a direction which Geoffrey viewed with almost as much alarm as Philip's words. He was sure he was going to need a stiff drink very badly, very soon.

"First of all I'm not sure I even remember hearing your plan, or if I do remember it, I'm not sure I want to do it. Just take me through it one more time please and then let's go back to the pub and forget all about it."

"Oh, no you don't, Geoffrey, you agreed last night, and if Combined Ops agrees, you and I are going to have a hell of a lot of fun, and you'll get to fly that plane that seems to be worrying you so much."

"What do you mean, *you and I*?" Geoffrey was horrified. "It would take a small army to storm an airfield and keep a plane intact enough to actually be able to fly it."

"Now that's where you're going wrong. You'd never make a Commando, though I guess I'm going to have to try and make you into some semblance of one. No way could a troop make a successful landing on a guarded shore and capture anything. Too bloody obvious. No, the only way is just a few, or in this case, just you and me. We land at night, creep up on the airfield that's chosen, camp out and recce the place, pick our plane, which as you remember you insisted must be running, get you into the seat and away you go before the Boche even know what's happening."

"You must be bloody mad," said Geoffrey, aghast at the idea. "Just the two of us, right under their noses? We'd never even get on shore, much less up to an airfield." He paused for a moment, staring thoughtfully into the distance. "How do you actually reckon we could do it?"

"Ah, you are a little bit intrigued, aren't you, Geoffrey? Listen, if this is as important as you seemed to feel last night, it's worth a go. Never up, never in, as they say in love and golf.

"Well, here is Quigley's plan, modified slightly, it pains me to admit, by my CO, Colonel Harrison, who would actually quite like to do it himself. He even asked me to write it out longhand for submission upwards. He thinks that security has to be absolute to give it any chance at all.

"First we get taken by submarine or Motor Gun Boat, probably the latter, to a chosen spot just off the French coast, maybe a mile or two out. We get into a Folbot: it's a neat little Norwegian kayak which folds up and is easy to assemble, and then paddle ashore at the least guarded beach we can find. We land on a very black, even, with luck, foggy night, bury the boat and leave some false clues as to why we're there in case the boat gets discovered.

"Next step is to head inland towards the airport, but not directly as that route is bound to be well guarded if these planes are still top secret. We'll find a nice spot in a dense wood where we'll camp for three days, 'till we're sure of the routine of the field then, on a chosen day, we'll cut the wire, creep in to the plane and I'll dispatch anyone in or around it. You jump in and we'll see if you really are as good as they tell me. Piece of cake."

Geoffrey was looking doubtful. "Just suppose this actually worked, just for argument's sake now, how do *you* propose to get back? I'm damn sure there'll be no room in the plane."

"Well, Geoffrey, that's my problem, but I did confess to you with all due modesty that I had actually been over to France recently a couple of times and here I am back again, so it is possible. Please don't ask me what I went over for; turned out to be a waste of bloody time and quite a pain in the arse in any event."

"Well," said Geoffrey, "I guess I'm lumbered if Combined Ops actually agrees. As you've been rabbiting on I've actually been thinking whether some bloke could come over here and steal a Spit, and, having thought about it, it would be quite easy at most fields. It's probably the last thing that anyone is thinking about or expects. It would just take balls to walk in and do it. Balls and no brains I might add, and as I'd like to think that I had more of the latter let's find some other truly crazy bastard like you who can also fly and get *him* to go with you!"

"Geoffrey, you know that's not possible. You're undoubtedly the best man to fly it and you'd hate like hell, having thought of it in the first place, to see some other guy pull it off. And pull it off we shall!"

"Don't pull that 'you thought of it' ploy on me, my friend. You bloody thought of it. I simply said what we needed."

By now they had walked a long way down the hill and were at the river's edge when Geoffrey finally managed to convince the highly animated Philip to head up the hill towards the path back to the pub. Geoffrey knew that he was in great need of a drink but, in truth, he found that he was also excited about 'Quigley's Plan', though he couldn't believe it could happen, or even that he'd get the permission to go. Half of him hoped he wouldn't and the other half knew that this, if it worked, was worth doing and could make a hell of a difference to the war. He even cheered up a bit with that thought......

There were so many details which Geoffrey wanted to explore, but the big Commando had firmly said that there wasn't to be a word about it in the pub, not one word. He did however, before they descended, ask Geoffrey to start thinking about any issues relevant to his part of the game, any needs or indeed any snags that might be anticipated before they finalized the operation, which Quigley hoped could take place within a month, or possibly even less. Every day they waited tripled the chance of a leak, he reckoned. Any leak and they could forget it or save a lot of time and government money by committing suicide. This, he added, was something he thought Geoffrey already tried to do each day by testing aeroplanes that some other arseholes had put together.

Back in his digs Geoffrey knew he would have another bad night's sleep. Would he ever sleep soundly again, he wondered? In the event, he started making a list of ideas, problems, alternatives, then promptly tore it up and burned the pieces. Christ, Quigley had really put the wind up him regarding security. The more he thought about it, the more convinced Geoffrey became that getting ashore on a highly fortified, enemy-held coast in the middle of the night was a far worse prospect than even bailing out of a falling plane. He figured that his job was pretty damn safe by comparison. Maybe Combined Ops would think it just as impossible as he did, and with that somewhat comforting thought he did eventually slide off to sleep.

FIFTEEN

Back in London Sir Archibald Smythe was letting himself be convinced by a very serious Clarissa that she was old enough to be doing something more important to help the war effort than knitting and attending deb's balls.

"And just what did you have in mind, my dear?" asked Sir Archibald who, up to this point in life, had never refused his only daughter anything and probably wouldn't start now.

"Well, Daddy," she began, "I've been hearing about a system, apparently quite secret, pretty hush hush, that we use to help our planes get around in bad weather. Two girls I know are already working with it, though they wouldn't or couldn't tell me much about it. I believe they are already being trained and will be in the army and stationed somewhere near the coast and actually operating something that will be very important to the war effort. I want to do that too. It sounds just technical enough to be interesting but not overwhelming, or so the girls say."

"Are you sure, Clarissa, you aren't suggesting this just so that you can get down nearer that Penn fellow? You seem to have been talking about him quite a bit recently. Have you seen him?"

"No, Daddy, but I would like to. He has called several times; I think he likes me. I must admit I *am* rather attracted to him, especially after discovering he is quite a hero in his own right but never even mentioned it. Very different from most of my hangers-on. It did enter my head, Daddy, but I've no idea where I'd be stationed. So, do you think you could you help?"

"Well, I could try. I like the cut of young Penn's jib too, if I can use a naval term to describe a flyer. Your brother certainly idolizes him and that's rare for him. But, if I do help, you must do me one favour first. I promised to go up to Roehampton to a hospital where they fit artificial limbs to casualties, sort of a morale booster *they* say, but I can't believe they want me for that. Rather to help them get some more money I suspect. Well deserved too, and of course

I'll do that anyway but you, my darling, if you think you can handle it, would do anyone's morale a bit of good. Would you go for me? I know they'd welcome you, and I'll give you a large cheque to donate, too, and then they'll be doubly happy."

"Of course I will. I've come across a few men who have lost limbs and I'd be proud to try and cheer them up. They certainly deserve it."

"Thank you, darling. I'll have Briggs drive you up there tomorrow afternoon. A Dr Baldock will show you around. You'll meet some very brave men who deserve a little of the sunshine you radiate."

He knew Clarissa would handle it well and keep her composure; she wasn't his daughter for nothing. He thought how he would miss her around the house if she took on this new job which, he happened to know, was called RDF - radio direction finding - but, yes, she really should have a full-time uniformed job. He would like one too, if they'd only take him, but one war per lifetime was probably enough.

SIXTEEN

It was June twenty-fifth 1942 and Colonel Harrison, Commanding Officer of 12 Commando, had received and read Capt. Quigley's plan and now wished to hear a bit more detail and to throw in a few of his own ideas. He was just as enthusiastic as Quigley, and more than a little jealous that it would be the Captain and not he who would have a go at pulling it off. My God, this will really irritate old Jerry, he thought. Even if it fails it will make him realize how vulnerable he is, just one hundred miles away from an enemy he knows won't quit, unlike our good allies, the Frogs.

"Good morning, Philip." A beaming Harrison welcomed Quigley into the room. "I've slept on your plan for a couple of days and this morning I like it even better than ever. I'm sure we can get you two ashore and, knowing you, I'm even sure you'll get up to the airfield and onto it. But do you think this chap Penn really has the bottle to make it? I know something about him, but sloshing about in canoes in the middle of the night, crawling past Jerry and sleeping wet in your clothes isn't exactly like testing planes, warm beds and pubs at night, is it?"

"No, sir, it certainly isn't, but I've no doubt about Penn. He's quiet but self-assured, and you can't question his balls. I can't imagine taking up a new plane every day and wondering if someone forgot a useful piece and the whole fucking thing's going to go bang any minute, and he does that every day, even *trying* to make them fail sometimes. No, this might be a welcome relief, even though he's dubious about the Folbot; would rather sail I think. He also nearly had a heart attack in the pub when I told him that just the two of us would be making the trip. He had visions of No.12 storming the beach, taking the field, and him strolling over to pick out a nice plane and toddle on back. He's more than willing to go, though, because he's so damn convinced we need to know all about this plane. They think it's called a Focke-Wulf 190. Apparently he can fly anything that can fly, so we've got ourselves the best possible jockey."

"And the meanest bastard in Commando to get him there," ventured the Colonel. "He will be in RAF uniform I should think," he continued, "so *if* he gets caught the Krauts will probably treat him like a hero. You know they even gave an Iron Cross to one RAF chap who had been captured and was lying in a hospital. And look how well they treated Bader until they got tired of him trying to escape, no legs and all. No, he'll be alright, but you're another matter. What do you think is your best route out?"

"Well, sir, the plan is to go by Motor Gun Boat to a couple of miles off-shore, down the east coast of Cherbourg, just south of St. Vaast-la-Hougue. I've requested some aerial surveys to refresh my memory. From there onto shore via the Folbot, then up north through a pretty well-connected series of woods to come in behind the field. I'm assuming that Combined Ops will agree Maupertus as the best choice, though Abbeville would do. Depends, I guess, where we're most sure of finding the Focke-Wulf. We don't need another bloody Messerschmitt!

"But, to answer your question, I have two choices. The first is to recover the boat and paddle back out to some pre-arranged point, meet the MGB again and get back that way. The Navy would like that, but I don't. Too many ifs. *If* the bloody boat is there, and *if* I could re-launch through the surf, *if* I could find the Navy. I could go on....

"No, my plan is to don my peasant's beret and blue overalls and wander into St. Vaast, hang about and borrow a small boat with a sail, and then hopefully motor back this way until the Navy panics, thinking that I'm invading, and picks me up. The timetable will be tough and I don't want a radio on me if I get challenged before I get to sea. So I just have to take my chances. I sure as hell am less likely to get shot by my own people than poor old Penn."

"Well rest easy, Philip, because I did send your scrawled plan up. By special courier, in fact, to preserve the security. Since old Louis Mountbatten is Chief of Combined Ops now, and since he liked what he saw of you and your troop when he visited here, I'm fairly sure he'll give it the go ahead. I'm worried, though, whether they'll be willing to risk Penn, whom I'm told is the living expert on the Spitfire. They'll be quite ready to risk idiots like you and me. That's what we're paid to do, they'll say, and they're right.

"Now, I've some thoughts on the Folbot. They're bloody tippy at best. If you've a lot of chop or tide, and sod's law would guarantee both, you'd better get Penn to put in as much practice as possible. You can do that in the evenings, after dark would be even better, but could make some people wonder what the hell Penn was doing and start getting nosey.

"Incidentally, Top Secret status, no talk in public, no notes. Any equipment requisitions will go through on your signature. No mission name. I'm sure the only way you can pull this off is to make it a complete surprise to our people also, otherwise there's always some bloody leak or rumour. We'd better do it fast, too. Nights will soon start getting shorter and I gather the air war is not going as well as we'd like. In brief, Top Secret - Urgent. Get what you need organized, get Penn trained and clued up on what to expect. And let's say maximum three weeks from today. Report to me in person, no memos. Oh, and another thing, I've an idea to help confuse the Kraut if he finds the Folbot; leave a small official document that they can decipher indicating that you're going south looking for possible landing sites. That will surprise them because they think *they're* about to land on *us*.

"Go and get it done, Philip, and good luck. Oh, I almost forgot, I promised an old doctor pal of mine who works up at Rochampton Hospital, you know, where they fit people with new bits and pieces if they've been blown off, that I would send him up a sample of a fit chap that they could test and measure to see what the maximum stress an artificial limb might be required to take. I couldn't think of anyone who's caused me more stress so I volunteered you for a day. A Dr Baldock. Will you call him and pick out a day you can spare soon? Might be useful for a chap that leads your sort of lifestyle to have a few friends at a place like that."

"Thank you, sir, you've always been good about looking after me. Oh well, perhaps I'll meet some nurses and at least I can avoid smelly Commandos for a day. I'll go right away. The only useful thing I've done recently with my fitness is throw a chap out of The Sailor."

"I know about that, too, but I've forgotten it," replied the Colonel, rising to terminate the meeting with the Commando he most admired and often envied.

SEVENTEEN

Due south and about eighty-eight miles away, there was a much livelier meeting under way. The place was the beautiful chateau of Pepin-Vast, east of Cherbourg and only a few kilometres from Maupertus airfield, which was known by the Germans as Theville. The chateau had recently been appropriated by Major 'Assi' Hahn as headquarters of JG2, known as the Richthofen Gruppen. Assi Hahn was having a birthday party. Most of the pilots there were already high-scoring aces. Some were so-called 'Spaniards' who had learned their basic air warfare in 109s whilst helping Franco. Others had had successes in Poland and now they were doing very well against the stubborn Brits. One reason, they reckoned, was that they now had a plane that was unquestionably the best.

To help Major Hahn celebrate and congratulate the entire group, Hugo Sperrle, who commanded Air Fleet 3 from Paris, of which JG2 was a part, had flown in. Even Hermann Goering, the Commander in Chief of the entire German Air Force, the Luftwaffe, had sent a letter, in part because he was aware of a little unrest amongst the fighter groups who wished to be given more freedom to roam and not to be designated so often to protect bombers.

There were five air fleets in all, each with a separate and fairly independent command. JG3 included Cherbourg, JG2, Abbeville and north up to the French and Belgian coasts, so there was some rivalry for equipment and opportunities. Each group idolized their aces, some of whom had more than a hundred victories, and each Jagdfliegerfuehrer, or Fighter Aircraft Leader (Jafue), wanted his boys to be the best. Hitler knew well how to honour and cater to these talents and egos.

A Geschwader consisted of about a hundred planes and included several Gruppen, designated by roman numerals. A Staffel was a squadron of twelve planes numbered by arabic numbers 1-9. These Staffelen made up a Geschwader, the Jagdfliegerfuehrer being the fighter unit and the

Kampfgeschwader being the bomber unit. A Staffel Kapitaen could command a Gruppe and a Kommadore commanded a Geschwader.

Assi Hahn was a popular leader of his Gruppe, much admired for his aerial skills and also for his joie de vivre, not uncommon amongst pilots who often thought each day could be their last and therefore made each night a memorable one. He also had a great love of animals, had a Great Dane of his own, and had even started a small zoo at Pepin-Vast.

Assi was obviously delighted and impressed that General Hugo Sperrle had flown his own Messerschmitt 108 down to Cherbourg Theville for this party and was using the occasion to butter him up, not for personal gain, but to ensure his Gruppe continued to get the weapons they, or he in particular, wanted - namely the Focke-Wulf.

After a fine and typically French meal, washed down with a considerable amount of Bordeaux wine, Sperrle spoke up.

"Assi, you birthday boy, and you other fighters. You have set a real target for our other Gruppen. Your No.2 and No.26 have already shot down more than seven hundred and fifty Allied planes. Confirmed kills, not maybes or hope-so's like the British claim. You are the masters of the skies which must be controlled if we are to soon invade our enemy. I congratulate you, I salute you, I admire you, and I envy you. Your war here is pretty good, and your life here is pretty damn good. I don't do so badly myself in Paris, but I am not so far as you from Headquarters, and we fighters know that it is not a bad thing to be a little far from Headquarters. Well done, and long may it last," he concluded, raising his glass in a toast.

Major Hahn rose to respond and duly thanked Herr General Field Marshall Sperrle.

"We are honoured to have you here, sir, you who take care of your boys so well. On behalf of all fighter pilots I thank you, but may I say some of these pilots would thank you even more if you could see to it that we got more Fw190s to replace the 109s. I know that Kommadore Galland of JG26 prefers the 109 and has great success with it, but we would be happy to change any 109s we have with him for 190s. I would like to go myself to Bad Eilsen, to the Bad Hotel, and personally thank Kurt Tank for designing so nearly perfect an aeroplane. I am faster, can climb quicker and can shoot better with cannon than machine guns. I even think I can turn better, but I have some arguments with my fellow pilots on that one. Please, sir, send me more and we will clear the skies of Hurricanes and Spitfires. The latter, perhaps a bit more slowly, I'll admit."

He sat down amongst great applause, table thumping and a few more toasts as the party became less and less formal.

"My dear Assi, I will do my best, but you said 'nearly perfect' aeroplane. What is not so perfect?"

"Well, sir, I enjoy lying down in most circumstances, and especially under a French girl, but it is not so much fun in an aeroplane. I know it helps in a tight turn to keep away the blackout but it makes it hard to see behind, even though the rest of the visibility is great once you have survived the take-off."

Again, much revelry, for the Major was also popular for his frankness and willingness to tilt for whatever he thought might help him and his group, or the war for that matter.

"Assi, you know we have examined many Spitfires. The latest they call the Mark V. I believe it is a good plane, but even the 109 can out-dive it and it flies better above ten thousand metres. The Spitfire still has an old-fashioned fuel system, no injection, and if we dive suddenly they lose a little power from the carburettor failing to deliver. A few seconds means a few kilometres and now you with your BMW engine have forty-two litres of power compared with only thirty-nine in the Mark V. Assi, you can lie down and still kick their arses!

"And now, my fighters.......," continued the bear-like Kommandant, who in spite of the drinking and the relative informality of the Luftwaffe compared to the Wehrmacht, commanded great respect from the men,"....my incomparable fighters, my friends, I would indeed see that you had more 190s but, as you know, we are battling on many fronts, some less secure than those guarded by you, and we have been forced to allocate. Your neighbours at Brest have a few of them in order to defend the submarine pens down the coast and, on the other side of you at Abbeville with JG26, we have mostly 109s, but a few 190s to help protect the Seine. You know we had 109s in Spain when I commanded the Condor Legion, so I know they are a little long in the tooth, but Old Willy Messerschmitt has been pretty good at improvements. But, I agree, 190s for you, and make damn sure none of you get shot down over England. If you do, burn the plane or, better still, dump it in the Kanal and swim ashore. So far, our informed sources, I might even say informers, tell us that all they do is bitch about the 190. They have never, and may they never, see one, except on their tail!"

"My Kommandant, sir. May I change the subject and ask a bit about flying in the last war?" asked Oberleutnant Bruno Stolle, another ace pilot with more than twenty victories. "I understand, sir, that General Ernst Udet once had a major dog fight with the great French pilot Georges Guynemer, and when Udet's gun jammed and Guynemer saw his plight, Guynemer saluted him and flew off, a true sign of an honourable airman. My question, sir, is what is wrong with the British? I heard that they are now shooting our Heinkel 59 rescue float planes, even when they are clearly marked and on the water. What manner of beast are we fighting? Have their airmen no code of honour?"

"Well, my friend Bruno, perhaps you have killed too many of their pilots and they wish to revenge themselves on any unfortunate man down. I admit I am surprised. Not what one would expect from them, but perhaps they are as desperate as the Fuhrer believes. We will not lower our principles, however, no matter what they do. You could say that war is not a game, and therefore should have no rules, but I believe that a man from either side who has done his best, shown his honour, and has the misfortune to be in a parachute or down in the sea deserves the chance to fight again. War is there to be fought by men, not cowards. Men of principle. With that, I bid you good night and good hunting. I am very proud of you, my Game Cocks."

Rising to their feet and laughing, the pilots applauded as the large man, who rivalled Goering in bulk and, reputedly, other appetites as well, lumbered from the room. His Game Cock remark would be often repeated, for he referred, of course, to Assi Hahn's insignia on the side of his plane, a cock's head, cock being the meaning in German of Hahn.

The talk carried on for a while, touching especially on the size of the Spitfire in the gun sight: at three hundred metres it filled the sight. Many of the pilots thought this too far, even though cannon did have a longer range than the machine-gun equipped Spitfire. The really high scorers seemed to be the men willing to practically ram the enemy before firing. Flying tactics was one thing all the men had in common, a never-ending subject of interest. Even ahead of sex, since it was generally accepted that, as occupiers of another country, they were by and large not getting a lot of co-operation in that department from the local girls, who looked pretty rural at best.

One thing they all agreed upon was the frustration of not being able to risk losing a plane over England, thus limiting them to escorting bombers to the coast, meeting them coming back and hoping to engage the Brits attacking the bombers. Generally not enough action for a naturally aggressive fighter pilot. Well, perhaps the following day they'd get better orders. At least they'd had a chance to air their grievances to someone pretty high up the chain of command.

EIGHTEEN

Combined Ops meetings were never dull and today an item had been submitted which intrigued them all. A proposal from 12 Commando to steal a German Focke-Wulf aircraft. Before they began to discuss this, however, Mountbatten asked Air Chief Marshal Park to outline the problem the RAF was having with the Fw190 and the current state of development of any plane which might challenge it. Park wasted no words in painting a very grim picture. He was followed by a Colonel Henriques who was there representing the Commandos who were a part of the Army, though many people thought the Commandos acted so independently that they weren't a part of any service.

"Well, sir," Colonel Henriques began, "we received an absolutely audacious proposal a few days ago from one of our chaps and we've been studying its feasibility. In essence, the plan is to steal a Focke-Wulf 190 and fly it back here so that we can really see what it has and how to copy or, better yet, beat its apparently superior performance. Now, before you say no and that you can't allow a naval assault or landing party, let me say that it is proposed that only two men participate, a top quality Commando and an equally capable pilot. We agree with the Commando that probably the only way to pull it off is to have as few people as possible involved. It's just a pity the Commando himself can't fly! We would ask the Navy to put them ashore at a point down the east coast of Cherbourg and from there they would make their way inland by canoe and then bivouac behind the airfield; another clever part, because the tendency of most defences is to face the enemy and not worry much about the rear. The RAF will send a plane or two every morning for a few days to strafe the field, establishing a sort of habit which we're sure will have the Jerry warming up the planes to nail the intruders one morning. Our pilot, a man called Penn, insists the plane must be running for him to have any chance. We think that, after giving him a refresher at Farnborough on captured German planes, he can do it if anybody can."

Relieved to sense that the proposal was not going to require more precious resources to be diverted from one service to another, Mountbatten, who liked solutions rather than problems, asked if anyone thought this plan had any hope of success or, if not, whether they had alternative solutions.

"I think this could work, sir," interjected Park. "I know Penn well; he flew with us during the Battle, shot down a few, and is probably the most knowledgeable man in the world about flying and developing Spitfires, but does it make any sense to risk losing this man? That has to be the question and, having posed it, I think my answer must be yes. Any risk with a chance of success is worth it. That bloody Focke-Wulf could actually change the entire balance of air power, and very quickly too."

"Where is the airfield?" asked Mountbatten, scanning the map laid out on the table in front of him.

"Here, sir. It's called Maupertus by the French, Theville by the Boche. Built in '36 and pretty well situated for this sort of caper. Penn preferred Abbeville: it's nearer to Tangmere, where he would rather fly to, but Abbeville has mostly 109s. Maupertus, on the other hand, has mostly 190s. It's about six miles east of Cherbourg and just a mile or so south of the Channel, and it's only three hundred and seventy five feet above sea level so the flight back from there is quite quick and so is the climb up.

"Admiralty chart No.1106, sir, for your professional interest, shows a low, rocky shoreline. OK for scramble landings at high tide, tides up to ten to eleven feet, gradient one in thirty-three and dangerous tidal streams of four knots. The shoreline around the other side of the point the beach is not easy, so may be less well guarded.

"The airfield defences are something we've got to find out more about, so we'll get a photo Spit to fly recce over there a few times, ostensibly filming the coast. We really need to give these two men all the information we can to avoid any nasty surprises."

"What about the airport at Brest-Guipaven?" asked Park. "Is that any good?"

"Too far and too popular, sir."

"Well, you people seem to have done your homework." Mountbatten again took over. "Personally I like it, and if nobody objects, I say let's have a go. We could use a little morale booster. I'll take it up to Winnie. He loves this sort of thing. It'll really cheer him up, even if it fails. Show the Krauts that they can never count us out and, incidentally, gentlemen, two things. One, if it fails, it never happened, right? No minutes. And second, I've been thinking about Penn; he knows too much to risk, yet he seems the best choice, too. I suggest that he must not be captured. Do I make myself clear?"

"I understand, sir," Colonel Henriques replied. "We plan to try within three weeks and no, we won't alert Air Defence at all, although I doubt they could shoot down a lone Focke-Wulf flying on the deck, anyhow. We'll only inform Air Operations the day before the heist, asking them not to shoot at any single Focke-Wulf coming in that morning. It would be a bloody shame to get the thing all the way back here and then shoot it down ourselves."

"Thank you, gentlemen, consider Operation Airthief under way."

The project now had a name. The meeting adjourned shortly afterwards and Colonel Harrison, who had been pacing the hall outside the meeting room, waiting for a decision, was delighted to see a thumbs up from Colonel Henriques as he emerged.

Harrison had optimistically brought both Penn and Quigley to town for the day, on the chance that he or they might be asked to personally appear. In any event he was sending Quigley over to Roehampton for the next couple of days. As soon as he could get Penn temporarily off duty, he'd have him off to Farnborough for the crash refresher course on captured German aircraft.

As events seldom happen as quickly as hoped or planned, Harrison had to be content with getting some aerial photos arranged and securing all the maps he could locate of the Cherbourg peninsula. No-one could be told the reason these were needed, so he had asked for and received a friendly carte-blanche order from Combined Ops to get what he needed. And it worked. He was not, however, quite prepared for the meeting that was demanded the following morning by Air Chief Marshal Sholto Douglas with himself, Quigley and Penn. Obviously furious that he had not been consulted about the proposal now approved, the meeting took a very bad turn from the word go.

"Are you the author of this hair-brained plan to risk the best test pilot in Britain and if so, why was my office not informed? Surely even the Commandos have some form of common courtesy or do you just feel you can go in there and bugger around with other services personnel at your whim?"

Sholto Douglas's reputation had preceded him, so Harrison was not surprised by the ferocity of his speech. Recognizing that the man was no slight adversary and that it would be much better to have him on their side, he apologized and proceeded meekly.

"Sir, the timing was crucial and we were so sure your support would be available for something this important to the RAF that we didn't want to bother you with it until it seemed likely or possible. I'm afraid events overtook us and it got on the Combined Ops agenda sooner than it should have. Again, my apologies.

"As for Penn, I thought he was out of the RAF and a civilian."

"No, he's not, damn it, he's still in the Reserve and *if* he goes on this caper it had better be in uniform in case he gets captured."

Harrison saw in this sentence that there was some hope that the Senior Air Marshal was going to agree, or at least not oppose a decision already made over his head.

"Good idea, sir. We had considered other pilots but research said Penn was the most likely to not just be able to fly the plane, but to avoid getting shot down in the process. Not to embarrass him, sir, but I understand that he's as good in the air as I think our man Quigley is on the ground. It's the best team we can imagine and we'd like your blessing."

"All right, all right." Douglas flapped his hand impatiently. "Penn, you get down to Farnborough as soon as possible. I'll fix it with McLean. Remember, Top Secret. Make up any reason you want to be there, though you really don't need one, given your job. Harrison, you and Quigley stay on a moment, would you? I'd like to have you take me through some details."

Having not opened his mouth once during this fairly volatile meeting, Penn felt relieved and well out of it. He had plenty to organize at Eastleigh before he could take a week at Farnborough.

After Penn left the room and had closed the door behind him, Douglas addressed the two Commandos again.

"Gentlemen, I don't need any more details about your plan. I'm sure you'll give it your best shot, because you'll only get the one shot. I am, however, very serious about the possible loss of Penn. We can ill afford to lose his knowledge and his rare talent to understand what can and can't be done to develop aircraft, especially the Spitfire. But, more to the point, we cannot risk the enemy having access to that knowledge, and he *is* known to them. Of that, we are certain. Under no circumstances, whatever the loss to us, is he to be captured. Is my meaning clear, Captain Quigley? To lose you would be sad, but to lose Penn to the Boche could be a catastrophe."

"Yes, sir, I understand," answered Quigley, groaning inwardly as he absorbed the implications of what Douglas had ordered.

"Yes, sir," echoed Colonel Harrison, who had now heard the same instruction twice in as many days.

"Very well then. I understand, Quigley, that you are a decisive man who has on occasion had to make difficult decisions quickly. Let's hope that this doesn't become another such situation.

"Gentlemen, I'm sure you're both aware that this conversation never took place."

Thus endeth the lesson, thought Harrison as they took their leave.

NINETEEN

Colonel Harrison had been the man designated by the Chief of Staff to break the news of Penn's mission to McLean. No-one envied him the job as they knew how much violent verbiage and outrage it would incur from the head of Supermarine. He had not disappointed them, Harrison thought, as he left what he considered the most unpleasant interview he had ever experienced. McLean's reservations had gone beyond the possible loss to the country of Penn's expertise and had extended to a much more personal, paternal concern. The Colonel had at last been forced to resort to the argument that Penn was still in the RAF Reserve and as such he was under orders, though he knew that no-one would ever be ordered to perform such a mission as the one his Captain Quigley had proposed.

Once begun there was no way to stop what had now apparently not only been endorsed by Churchill but had become of great interest to him. One of the Chiefs of Staff had said that this was just 'his sort of caper'. In any event it was now definitely on, and as soon as Quigley got back from Roehampton, and Penn from Farnborough, the Folbot training would commence.

Meanwhile Captain Quigley was sweating, quite literally, in one of the weight rooms at Roehampton Hospital, the Centre for Artificial Limbs Research and Fitting. He was clad only in very brief grey cotton shorts, which appeared strained to the point of bursting as his massive thigh muscles pulled against the heavy spring scale, which was in turn hooked to a wide leather belt around his back. The two doctors and one nurse observing his efforts were, he gathered, trying to ascertain how much weight he could lift with his legs and how long he could sustain the pull.

Absorbed as they were in monitoring the large man's impressive efforts, they didn't notice the arrival of the visiting party led by Dr Baldock and including Clarissa Smythe. The visitors opened the door on the observation landing, slightly above the work area, just as a dripping

Quigley, getting more than a little bit testy in his role as guinea pig, swore.

"Jesus Christ, how much longer do I have to pull? This fucking strap is cutting me in half."

Clarissa looked down in absolute fascination, not at the scientific exercise involved or the language, but rather at the most incredibly muscled man she had ever seen. Gleaming with sweat, clad in shorts which barely covered his navel, and straining with an intensity well evidenced by his cursing, he seemed to her to be the most attractive man she had ever seen. Her eyes kept straying to his well-filled shorts. At that moment Philip Quigley felt her gaze and looked up.

"Good morning ma'am, sorry about the language."

Clarissa blushed deeply.

As Dr Baldock explained to his group what was going on, namely an attempt to find the maximum stress that any artificial limbs might be forced to bear, Clarissa found herself totally unable to concentrate. Looking at the powerful, nearly naked man in front of her, she felt that his casual exposure of his body should have unsettled her. It irritated her that he seemed aware and even amused by her discomfort. However he did at least put a towel around his waist as he came forward to be introduced by Dr Baldock.

"Captain Quigley of 12 Commando, Miss Smythe. He's here on loan to find out what levels of performance our prosthetics should attain in order to give as much confidence as possible to the wearers."

Clarissa looked at the glistening arm being extended towards her. She thought his bicep was probably the same size as her waist and, although slightly loath to get sweaty, couldn't prevent herself placing her hand in his. As it disappeared into Philip's great paw she thought she might never see it again, but she felt only a surprisingly gentle grasp as his eyes held hers.

"And where are you to be found, Miss Smythe, when you're not touring hospitals, may I ask?" rumbled Philip.

Oh God, even his voice is sexy, thought Clarissa, still not believing that she was entertaining the sort of thoughts that were causing her to blush so furiously.

Dr Baldock had moved below with the group, looking at the machines that had recently imprisoned Philip, who up to this point had not yet released Clarissa's hand.

"If I may have my hand back, I'll tell you," replied a still ruffled Clarissa, struggling hard for composure. "I'm about to do my bit by training at the Radio Direction Operation. Something to do with locating and directing aircraft. Awfully important, I'm told. I think it's about time I did something more useful than deb dances and teas."

"Well, you seem to be doing something quite useful here," replied Philip with a smile. "You've certainly cheered me up. Just think what you'd do for those who really need it! Would you be willing to cheer me up a bit more by having dinner one day, or even lunch? I suppose that if you're going into RDT you'll be somewhere down around the south coast, near where I am at Warsash? So, how about it?"

"Well, I'm not sure about 'it', but thank you for asking. Who knows, perhaps we shall meet again," said Clarissa, falling now more naturally into her slightly distant debutante way of talking, yet wishing she dared to say something more provocative. She really would like to see this man again, although he was being awfully pushy.

Philip, called away to get more tests scheduled, left Clarissa with a grin and a good view of his back, broad, glistening and looking a bit like a knotted wash-board. She was again conscious of most unladylike thoughts. This surely isn't love, she thought, I imagine it's what one has to call lust. I now know what they mean when they talk about body chemistry; I actually ache.

Philip, too, stimulated by meeting Clarissa, thought that she was the finest looking piece of crumpet that he had ever laid eyes upon, and promptly told Dr Baldock.

"And eyes are the only things that you'll lay upon her, Captain," replied

Dr Baldock briskly. "Her father, Sir Archibald Smythe, keeps her well locked up, I'm told, and 'keeps' is probably just the right word. I doubt that even the 12th Commando could break open that wall."

"Never challenge a Commando, Doctor," retorted Quigley with a grin, although he suspected the doctor was probably right. However, before leaving the hospital he did manage to extract Clarissa's phone number and address from the eagerly helpful receptionist.

The next day Clarissa received her marching orders, as she liked to call them. She was to report to a radio station on the Isle of Wight, called Blackgang. This would work out amazingly well, she thought. In addition to several calls from Geoffrey Penn, she had also received a telephone call from the masterful Commando who had occupied her thoughts for most of the night after leaving Roehampton. Captain Quigley had indeed breached the walls, and had been lucky, as he said to himself, that Clarissa herself had answered the phone, and not the butler or worse yet, her reputedly fearsome father. In any event, the escapade to France was on hold for the time being and Clarissa had agreed to a picnic and an outing in his canoe whilst en route to Blackgang. For her part, she hadn't been strictly accurate when telling her father the exact date she was expected to commence training. She wasn't sure whether it was fear or fascination which dominated her thoughts. She was not afraid of the Commando, but she *was* afraid that her body was taking control over her mind which, up to now, had been almost fully occupied with Geoffrey.

TWENTY

Geoffrey, having been at Farnborough for two days, quickly realized that little new was to be learned, since no further German planes had been captured, nor were there any remarkable changes in any of the types he had previously flown. Nonetheless, he worked hard on the German nomenclature and the feel of all the toggles and knobs so that, even in the dark, he thought he could recognize most; unless, of course, the Fw190 had all new instrumentation and controls, which was an unpleasant thought that he quickly brushed aside.

Still, he felt he was about as well briefed as he could be and to distract himself from thoughts of the mission, from which he really doubted he would ever return, he ought to propose some serious R & R. So, summoning up his courage, he telephoned Clarissa at home and suggested the same.

"Um, just what exactly is R & R?" Clarissa asked nervously.

"Oh," came the casual reply, "just rest and recreation. It's something the Yanks, who like to abbreviate everything, dreamt up! How about tennis?" In truth he was more interested in seeing her in shorts or, better still, a short skirt, than actually playing a game.

"OK, why not? I'm a member at the Hurlingham. I'll book us a court. Then we can have supper at my house; that will give you time to get back to Bursledon before dark, and I'll be able to tell you all about my new job."

Geoffrey, delighted that he would be seeing her again, though subdued by the suggestion that he would be leaving early, thought the phone a poor place for an argument and agreed to meet Clarissa at the Club. He thought it would probably take him only half an hour to drive there from Farnborough.

Managing to cadge some spare petrol from the mechanics, who always had some lying around the airfield which they were happy to pass on to Geoffrey, he topped up the Bentley. His old girl, as he affectionately thought of her. As usual he diluted it with some of his own normal ration. Arriving at the

Hurlingham at 1400 hours (his time)' and a bit earlier than arranged, he wandered around the quiet grounds for a while. Not many mid-week tennis players these days, he thought to himself, before setting off to find his designated locker area. Clarissa had indeed arranged everything, quickly and efficiently. He liked that.

Feeling pale and certain he looked dismally unathletic in white shorts and white V-necked sweater, Geoffrey thought he'd knock a few balls against the practice wall and was busily doing that, in a hopelessly rusty fashion, when he heard Clarissa's voice.

"Not bad, not bad, but I think I can take you on."

If Geoffrey had been smitten before, he knew now that he was finished. She looked fantastic, schoolgirlish and sexy at the same time. How was that possible, he wondered, then realized it was her eyes that were partly responsible, that incredible, deep green that seemed to challenge you as she looked so, so directly into your own.

My God, thought Geoffrey, how I *would* like to have you take me on. Trying to look a good deal calmer than he felt he twirled his raquet around.

"Right, you win, I buy dinner; I win, you cook dinner."

"That's a deal," she said confidently and for the next three hours did her best to beat him. Indeed, she did manage to win one set when he became too preoccupied watching the short skirt swirl above those incredible legs.

"*Geoffrey*, stop looking at my legs and play tennis," Clarissa protested. "They're like a rugby player's anyhow. Too much riding, I suspect!"

Geoffrey was playing to win and her legs were hardly like any rugby player's he'd ever seen. He wanted desperately to be with Clarissa, at home and private, for in the course of the afternoon he'd discovered that Sir Archibald was away for several days. Now or probably never, Geoffrey thought later as he happily drove this delightful creature home, realizing that not once during the entire afternoon had he even thought about an aeroplane, let alone the mission.

Between the engine noise and the wind sound in the open Bentley Geoffrey could scarcely hear Clarissa, but his heart leapt when he did gather that in her new job she might be stationed, at least for training, at Blackgang on the Isle of Wight. Christ, he thought, the very place over which he had flown test flights not more than a few weeks before.

In explaining to Clarissa why he was at Farnborough he decided to tell her he was on a refresher course. Clarissa, fortunately, didn't seem particularly curious about what it was that needed refreshing, but at least they knew a bit more about each other by the time they reached Eaton Square and the remembered kitchen.

Clarissa did not appear to be able to cook much better than Geoffrey himself but, he thought while cheerfully watching her move about the small room, she had to be mediocre at something. She, feeling a bit awkward with his eyes following her around, dispatched him to the cellar to pick out, as she said, any wine he fancied. Surveying the rows of bottles stacked in carefully labeled bins he decided that he 'fancied' just about every one there. Eventually he settled on a 1929 Smith Lafitte, trusting that Sir Archibald probably wouldn't notice its loss as much as the Margaux and Haut Brion that he had stashed away.

Christ, he thought, most men would marry this girl even if she were ugly, just to inherit the wine cellar.

He wasn't quite sure what the main dish was; he thought possibly Spam mixed with potato and egg, but he really didn't care. He knew he was as happy as he had probably ever been. He knew he was indeed deeply in love, so much so that he desperately wanted to feel closer to this woman, yet he felt a curious fear of not wanting to lose the trust she seemed to show in him.

That's bad, he thought. She's comfortable because she feels safe and what I'd like to do is tear her clothes off and just love her to death. During these musings and Clarissa's chatter about radar and whether he understood it, and some banter about the tennis game, the wine slipped down easily.

Both began to feel more comfortable with each other, more relaxed. She teased him about being such a modest hero and he, secretly thrilled to have her consider him a hero, protested that all he did was his job.

Geoffrey dreaded even thinking about returning to Farnborough, although at least it was a bit closer than Southampton. Clarissa seemed content, with the cook away and the butler downstairs in his quarters. Geoffrey was desperately trying to think how to manage to kiss her when, leaning over him to fill his wine glass, he felt her hair fall across his face and suddenly she had kissed him softly on the mouth, then more urgently as he rose from the chair and held her and felt her body move against his. Knowing she could not avoid feeling how aroused he was, he tried to murmur an apology.

"Clarissa, I'm sorry, but I can't help ......"

"Don't talk, darling," she interrupted, laying her fingers against his lips. "Come upstairs. I want you too."

Geoffrey, experienced lover of many women, had expected to have to gently initiate Clarissa to the joys of physical love, but was staggered and overwhelmed by her passion, intensity, noise and apparent real pleasure in his exploration of her and her subsequent examination of him.

"I love you, Clarissa, I really do. I've never said it before to anyone, but I now know what love is. I can't bear to even think about not being with you."

Clarissa lay, naked and beautiful, gazing at the face of the man she had just loved as she had never done before. She wondered guiltily if it were Geoffrey or the memory of the Roehampton Commando that had turned her into somebody that had surprised even herself.

"Geoffrey, I care for you a great deal, I really do. I scarcely know you and yet here I am in bed with you. Is it the war that's made us all crazy? How do I know I'll ever see you again? Yes, I definitely do care for you a lot, but I'm not *sure* I love you. I'm not sure about *anything*, come to that, especially love, but I don't regret this for a minute. You know I've only been to bed with a man twice before: once drunk after a deb's ball and all I can remember was that it was terrible, and once with a soldier I liked very much and never expected to see again. He was listed as missing two weeks after. I don't want to fall in love and have that happen again. But I *do* want to see you again and, maybe, that is a beginning to some sort of love. Now, please go home so I can think and sleep and I promise to call you when I get to Blackgang."

TWENTY ONE

Colonel Harrison, back at 12 Commando at Warsash, had been busy. The handwritten plan, now officially dubbed Operation Airthief, had been formally approved by Combined Operations headquarters in London. Mountbatten, who at age forty-one and still only a captain had replaced the sixty-four year old Admiral Keyes, thoroughly approved of the idea. He recalled being favourably impressed by 12 Commando and Quigley in particular. Harrison had heard that the plan had actually been tumbled upwards to Winston himself, who had approved and, when someone had questioned using a civilian to work with both the Navy and 12 Commando, was brusque in his response.

"Bugger procedures which hamper efficiency. What these chaps are proposing to do is a damn sight more important than petty bureaucracy!"

Anyhow, thought Harrison, Penn was still in the Air Force Reserve and therefore McLean at Vickers had been over-ruled in the matter. Churchill rather enjoyed going around the bureaucrats, and even the military hierarchy, now and then. Besides, the whole purpose of Combined Ops, or Comops as it was sometimes known, was to find ways and means to invade France and keep the Germans nervous by harrassment whenever and wherever possible. This was a sweet plan, he thought, and might even work; if not, it would scare the shit out of the Boche in any event. Churchill thought when the hierarchy got shunted aside this sort of thing kept them humble and even sharpened them up a bit.

Harrison recalled Churchill's use of Professor Lindemann, a Swedish scientist and friend of Churchill's, along with Lindemann's pupil at Oxford, a Professor Reginald Jones, to try and find a way to bend the radio beams that he thought were directing German bombers to night-time London a couple of years before, the Knikerbien beam he believed it was called. Churchill had gone around absolutely everyone on that one. In any event, since the Old Man had given them the go-ahead they were away, and already plans were afoot organizing a Motor Gun Boat, now deemed better than a submarine, to make the initial approach to Cherbourg Peninsula. The decision was based upon water depth at the point they had agreed as the best drop off for Penn and Quigley, alone and at night in their flimsy Folbot. Ever the Commando, Harrison actually envied them the excitement of their mission.

The airfield chosen, after considerable debate, was Maupertus, just eighty-eight air miles from Eastleigh, with the nearest British land being the Isle of Wight. Penn had preferred Abbeville, which was also an Fw190 base, due to its fairly short run back to the UK but he had been overruled. With the bases agreed and the date for the mission swiftly approaching, Harrison called in Penn and Quigley for a final planning session. It was Penn's first visit to the Commando headquarters up the river, though he had seen the fairly basic area from the air countless times. It was known as Cricket Camp and was situated a few miles up the River Hamble. Geoffrey was impressed with the number of landing craft and Motor Gun Boats anchored around the river, concealed by nets and trees where possible. Everything he saw there convinced him how much better it was to fight a war in the air. A few tough looking Commandos admired his Bentley as he rolled up to Harrison's office, still in his grey flying overalls, having been instructed by a very irritated McLean to report immediately to Harrison.

He looks damned near as hard as Quigley, thought Geoffrey, meeting the legendary character for the first time on his home ground.

"Welcome to Quigley's private war, Penn," said Harrison, eyeing the slight figure of Penn with some consternation. To his eyes Penn seemed to be about half the size of Quigley and not at all his idea of what to throw at the Germans, even though he had heard from the Combined Ops people how valuable Penn was and how he was one not to be lost to the Boche.

Using a blackboard, which he himself would wipe clean after the meeting, Harrison proceeded to brief the two men in the room on the mission which to Penn, seemed increasingly unlikely to succeed and even ridiculous.

"Quigley tells me that you can fly anything, providing the engine is running and warmed up, so here's the plan. In brief, the Royal Navy is going to drop you about two miles off Cherbourg, not far from the lighthouse on Cap Levy, three weeks from tonight. They hope the boat will be low enough in the water so that, at that distance, German radar won't pick it up. If they do, we think it's far enough out so that the stop, only to last about three minutes, won't alarm them. They won't expect any landing to be attempted from that far out either, we hope. Quigley tells me you've been practicing in the Folbot a little, but I think you'd better keep it up every night after your normal flying duties. Big as Quigley is, he can't paddle you both in if the wind happens to be against you, as it's apt to be. With a bit of luck you won't get much wind at three am, so you should be ashore within an hour."

"How do we get through the beach guard?" asked Penn. "And what do we do if we're spotted?"

"Strangely enough," said Harrison, "that may be the least of your problems. We've been doing our homework and have had the RAF fly overhead on photo recs. from a few different directions. One reason we picked Maupertus is that the beach areas nearby seem to be fairly sparsely guarded. The field is about three miles inland and I think they have surmised that, because of the shallow water extending out so far, any large boat probably wouldn't land there, and why would a small one? Besides that, they can't guard the entire coastline without leaving a few gaps and through one of them, we hope, is where you'll go, probably passing by just a single patrolling guard.

"The second part of your question is really Quigley's problem. You'll be in an RAF uniform under your black overalls. As you probably know the German mechanics that warm up the planes are called black men because of these outfits, and if you think you've been had, ditch the overalls and you'll be treated as a downed aviator who made it to the shore."

Yes, thought Geoffrey unhappily, and if caught with the overalls on, undoubtedly treated as a spy. "Incidentally," said Harrison, "you'll be Sgt. Peter James and carry all identity to that name. He was killed last week at Tangmere in a strafing attack before he got airborne. If we know you haven't made it, he'll be listed as lost over the Channel just to help verify you. Quigley will have a similar ID but the silly bastard is unlikely to get captured; at least he hasn't managed to so far."

While Geoffrey fretted over this rather worrying information Harrison continued.

"Aerial photos and info from the French Resistance tell us that Maupertus has 190s as well as a few 109s, a few Dornier 215s and a Junkers JU87. The idea is for you two to get around behind the field, creep up and bivouac near enough to pick out your plane and carry on from there. The RAF will strafe the field every morning at about five am, or first light, for three days prior so we're going to be pretty sure the Hun will be wide awake with warmed up planes waiting for the fourth day."

Having seen the expression on Penn's face and anticipating his next question, Quigley broke in at this point to explain to Penn why they should bother to go all the way around to the back of Maupertus in the middle of the night.

"If I may, sir, no enemy expects to be attacked from the rear and we think the majority of the airfield defence will be directed outward towards the Channel and Britain; it's human nature to face your enemy rather than covering your backside. Incidentally, we're going to walk quite close to the Luftwaffe headquarters for this area at Pepin-Vast, again something they probably would think unlikely."

"Right," said Harrison, nodding agreement, "basically it's a sound plan. Quigley here tells me you thought that at least a troop or section would attack the base and hold it until you got away but, believe me, in raids such as this the fewer men involved the more likely you are to pull it off. Besides," he added, clapping Quigley on the back, "Quigley's a platoon in himself, aren't you, Philip?"

With that the meeting ended. Penn and Quigley left the room and walked out into an open area. Quigley never wanted to talk shop, Geoffrey realized, unless he could see three hundred and sixty degrees around him.

"Now listen, Geoffrey, even your boss McLean doesn't know exactly what's up, and he absolutely must not find out. We're going out of here at 0300 hours the night of the fifteenth of July in an MGB and the crew will merely be told that they're going out that night. Only the Captain will know the destination. Hopefully it will be a bit foggy and, of course, no moon. My plan is to paddle in through the oyster beds and pass over the beach into some scrubland between sentry marches, assuming they have them. I do know from rec. photos that they have pill boxes every five hundred yards or so.

"I had thought of us going right through Cherbourg, which is so busy we probably wouldn't attract much attention, but instead we'll go down the east coast to land at Morsalines, skip into the nearest woods and work up to Bois de Brillevast behind the airport. It's about a ten mile walk and should get us pretty well into position before dawn breaks."

"What about the Folbot?" muttered Geoffrey, realizing with increasing alarm that this mission was actually going to proceed and thinking that he'd found himself in the hands of a lunatic who actually enjoyed this sort of thing.

"No problem. Once we're in the scrub behind the beach, which with any luck will be soft and sandy, we'll bury the boat which, incidentally, is going to contain some false papers 'accidentally' left in our haste. These will lead them to think that we're headed south scouting for possible landing sites for use if and when we ever get far enough ahead in this damned war to consider that. Neat, don't you think?

"For your part, Geoffrey, old pal, I'm presuming you *can* find England from there once you're up and running?"

"Well, *old pal*, I've been doing a bit of homework too, just in case you got this ludicrous scheme approved. Maupertus is all right as an airport; it's about eighteen minutes straight flying at three hundred mph in a Spit pointed thirty degrees to Eastleigh, or nearly due north from there to Goodwood, only about eighty-eight air miles if I'm lucky. There's a grass runway at Goodwood and maybe that's a better place to duck in and hide. I hope nobody will have time to take off and follow me. I hope even more that the Spits and Hurricanes at Tangmere, Dunnsfold or Boscombe Down or any other damned place won't have time to scramble either. I plan to fly so low that our radar will miss me and with any luck the coastal gunners will all be asleep, not that they seem to hit anything anyway. Nonetheless, there's a lot of ack-ack around Southampton and Portsmouth and they could get lucky. Incidentally, did you know that the field at Maupertus is at an altitude of about three hundred and seventy-five feet and was first built by the Frogs as Cherbourg airport back in '37. No? Actually, the Germans have improved it since they took over in '40. They would, though, wouldn't they? Two good runways: one hard, a mile and a quarter long, and one grass. Please, for God's sake don't let the RAF bomb the bloody runways; the last thing I need is to dodge rubble and craters on take-off."

"My, my, you are fussy aren't you?" teased Quigley who, for his part and from experience, never expected things to be perfect.

TWENTY TWO

In fact the only perfect thing in Quigley's life so far, at least in his opinion and not counting his spaniel, Cool, was Clarissa, that absolute gem he'd met in Roehampton Hospital. He thought she had shown a glimmer of interest in him. He also thought that in a fair turn of life he should at least get to see as much of her as she'd seen of him. What little he'd seen beat anything he'd set eyes on in his life so far, and so his scheming Commando mind had been working away at a plan.

For Philip to find himself nervous about anything was a strange experience but the truth was, he felt decidedly jittery as he again called Clarissa from a Warsash pay phone. Relieved when the butler answered, he enquired after her and was told, after he had properly identified himself, that the butler would ascertain whether Miss Clarissa would wish to speak with him.

Would she, or indeed should she, thought Clarissa, remembering all too well the muscled, sweaty body. She told the butler to advise Captain Quigley that it would be a minute or so before she'd be available. It's going to take a minute or two to calm my pulse, she thought and, by God, she probably was available for this man.

Quigley's 'Clarissa' plan, which he thought probably had fewer flaws than Operation Airthief, was to follow up his original suggestion and ask Clarissa to come down to Warsash the following Sunday for a picnic, and maybe a stroll through the base to cheer up the Commandos. The walk through was to give her some justification for the visit but the picnic required some planning.

"Why, Captain," Clarissa declared brightly when she eventually came to the telephone, "I certainly do remember you. Didn't we meet at the Roehampton Limb Centre? Since you seemed to be doing some frightfully good work there I'm sure the least I can do is help cheer up some Commandos. Well," she continued coyly, "at least one. Actually my new job is not far from you. I'm being sent next week to Beachy Head near Eastbourne for training, so I can meet you at the station."

"Let's say the nearest train to eleven, shall we?" replied Quigley, scarcely believing the positive notes he hoped he was hearing. He had heard something about the new RDF stations on the south coast. The first one at Bawdsey in Suffolk had a range of about seventy-five miles. What niggled at him was the thought that it was quite likely the Germans had something similar or even better. He'd rather dwell on Clarissa than German radar, however, so, meeting set, this normally intrepid Commando nervously prepared for what he knew would be his last date for some time.

In the period until Sunday he and Penn had to spend at least an hour each night in and around Southampton waters and the River Hamble, in a Folbot. Quigley was amused that Penn, who seemed to everyone who knew him and spoke of him to be fearless, claimed to be terrified of that 'damned wood and canvas contraption'. He considered it had less chance of safely crossing the Channel, or any part of the Channel, than Bleriot's aeroplane. Despite his fears he gamely showed up at the pub every night and, suitably fortified with a couple of gins, reluctantly went off with Quigley for his hated paddle practice.

TWENTY THREE

"Listen, Philip," said Geoffrey as they turned to paddle into shore on the Hamble, trying to make as little noise as possible, "just supposing we do get ashore in this horrible contraption, we've got to carry it up the beach then come back and cover our tracks. I don't see how we can possibly do all that and not be seen."

"My God, Geoffrey, you are such a worrier. Uncle Philip has a plan for that too. We should make shore at ten minutes or so before high tide, which gets us in close. If I get it right, there won't be much beach and the scrub comes very near the sea so, as long as we can pass the sentries, the sea will cover our tracks for us."

"Too many bloody ifs for my liking," muttered Geoffrey, slightly mollified by Philip's apparent planning of detail. So far he hadn't come up with any scenario that Philip hadn't a possible programme for. "So you've done this before then, Philip, have you? Can you tell me where? I might feel more comfortable unless, of course, all this is just bravado and posturing, like most Commandos seem to be doing down at The Jolly Sailor."

"Happy to cheer you up, old man. The answer is yes. Actually the Commandos were formed in June of '40 with the prime purpose of harrassing the Boche, especially on the French coast, partly to test their defences. I was lucky and got in at the beginning, I think because they thought brawn would be more useful than brain. We could pretty much pick our own men at that time, too, so I gathered a section of good, tough bastards from the Berkshire Yeomanry. A guy called Henriques commanded us and then, would you believe it, we were sent off to learn to ski at Chamonix. Great stuff! The idea was that we were going to go help the Finns but, when the Ruskies joined our side, all that was forgotten. At that time old Churchill couldn't seem to decide if he liked small raids or not and then I suppose he got intrigued, for the next thing I knew we were going to raid Pas de Calais. The Old Man cancelled that, but soon after set up a caper called Operation Chess, where we raided Ambleteuse just north of Boulogne. We got spotted, however; lost a couple of men. Damned shame."

"How many did you start out with?" Geoffrey asked.

"Ten men then, but the next op, called Basalt, was on Sark. I had four lads with me for that. Afterwards we went to the Lofoten Islands, off the coast of Norway, that time with a full troop. We stayed a few days, then things got hot and we had to evacuate. You'd scarcely credit it, but I got arrested after that raid for chucking a cameraman's equipment overboard. Should've thrown that bastard over, too. The stupid fart would have endangered every person on the island if the wrong people ever saw that film. It only showed how the islanders had helped us and how much they hated Jerry. Charges dropped, however. Easy to find a cameraman, not so easy to find crazy Commandos!"

Christ, thought Geoffrey, the rumours I've heard about this man are true. He couldn't decide whether this was a comforting thought or not.

They touched shore and stepped out of the Folbot one each side and simultaneously, then lifted the boat and walked inland about thirty feet, before turning back to the river.

"Philip, for God's sake, haven't we got this down pat enough yet? I can't tell you how tired I am of wet feet and trousers every bloody night. Even my landlady's beginning to wonder why I'm so scruffy whereas, you, well, you're noted for being shockingly dirty! My landlady does my laundry and while she sometimes flinches at some of what she suspects might be on my trousers, she does at least understand that pursuit. But she can't really believe the night fishing story I've been peddling." Geoffrey knew he was talking to himself but it made him feel better to have a whinge.

"Poor lamb! But seriously, it won't be long now, Geoffrey, old boy. What you've got to remember is that the Channel, even this close in, is going to be a lot choppier than the river and what a pity it would be to miss all the fun by fucking up this easy part. Come on, chin up; let's paddle a bit more."

After a few moments Geoffrey, not particularly caring about the answer but wishing to get off the subject of Folbots and choppy water, asked,

"What do you use as a weapon?" He presumed all Commandos were walking armouries, but was curious about the confident giant seated behind him in the flimsy, rocking kayak.

"Well, I know you chaps carry a .38 Webley but, frankly, I'd rather throw rocks than try and hit something with one of those. I have a lovely souvenir loaned to me on one of my trips abroad, a Luger. The Hun make good guns as well as aeroplanes, you know. Too bloody good, in fact. Also, helpfully, you can fit a silencer on an automatic whereas you can't on a bloody revolver."

"I'd rather be sitting behind eight Browning 303s and have my target three hundred yards away than thirty feet and me with only a Webley. But even my Brownings aren't a match for what they've got on the Messerschmitt 109s. They've got two cannon *and* two machine guns." Musing, Penn added, "I wonder what the Focke-Wulf has. Hopefully, an armoured back rest like the Spit, because I don't plan on turning around to look back once my backside is off the ground!"

By this time they had been paddling for about two hours, longer than they expected to have to do off Cherbourg. Here in the much more placid waters of the Hamble they thought, or at least Quigley thought, that it was far better to be over-trained.

While Penn had been paddling and worrying, Quigley had been refining the plans for his picnic with Clarissa. It occurred to him that he was definitely more nervous about the forthcoming date than going back to France again. The more he thought about her, the more he fantasized. As they returned to the landing dock, he realized he'd thought of little else but this beautiful society snippet, the very thought of whom managed to give him a hard-on, and that even with his balls resting on the cold canvas on the wooden bottom of the Folbot.

"We're here, mate," Geoffrey nudged him. "Shall we get out, or are you stuck in the seat? What about a sail next Sunday? I could show you a *real* boat, not something you can carry in a back-pack."

"Sorry, old boy, but this lad has a day off and a date; something you ought to do too, just in case you get caught and put in the slammer with your friend, Bader."

This thought had also occurred to Geoffrey and he wondered how the brave and indomitable Douglas Bader was managing, incarcerated in a German prison with no legs and obviously no girls.

"I thought you said this was a piece of cake, unlikely to get captured and so forth," muttered Geoffrey crossly.

"Oh, *I* won't get caught, but *you* might. That's why you'll be in the RAF kit."

Geoffrey found this reply discouraging.

Quigley knew, from his sombre conversations with the people at Combined Ops and Colonel Harrison that, no matter what happened, Penn, the poor bastard, would never be captured. All the more reason, he thought, that Penn should get laid as often as possible before they left.

TWENTY FOUR

It occurred to Clarissa, as the train rattled along the track from Eastbourne to Warnash, that Geoffrey Penn worked at Eastleigh. She remembered him telling her that it wasn't far from Warnash, but however much she cared about the handsome airman, there was something about this Commando that not only quickened her pulse but seemed to set her whole body alight. She felt that an aspect of her life that she had missed up to this point was rushing headlong to collide with her. She felt fluttery and nervous and certain this day and this moment were special.

At Warnash station she couldn't miss Philip, standing about six inches taller than anyone else on the waiting platform. He practically lifted her off the train and then seemed a little nervous about starting a conversation.

"Good trip?" he managed. "Here, let me take your bag. Er, we're lucky with the weather, aren't we?" Irritated with himself he started again. "Damn it, why can't I just say it, you look fantastic. I suppose I'm so used to talking or shouting at dense Commandos, I've forgotten how to talk, much less stop swearing! Anyhow, it *is* a lovely day for our picnic so we're going over to the Officers' Club for a bit, just long enough to show those bastards, sorry, those *chaps* that old Quigley does know at least one very beautiful girl."

With that, he threw her small bag onto the back seat of a Morris sedan, where it promptly disappeared into the general squalor, and headed straight from the station to the base. Sundays at the club were usually quiet and especially so on such a glorious summer day, rare enough in England. The Officers' Club always had a few men in around lunchtime however, and Philip knew that Clarissa would create quite a sensation. For his part, he really wanted to get out on the river, but not until he had managed to get at least two gins into both of them, all part of the plan he had hatched.

In fact, the Club was surprisingly crowded, and even included a few wives and girlfriends. Clarissa's stunning looks and Philip's imposing physical presence created a stir in itself and the throng at the bar parted as people moved back to let them through. So many men wanted to buy Clarissa a drink that the first part of his plan was easy; how to get her out of there was going to be another matter. After two, or was it three, drinks later he extracted her from her group of admirers and they strolled down to the quay where it took some persuading to get Clarissa into the strangest craft she'd ever seen.

Quigley paddled and Clarissa chatted about anything that came to mind: the many military boats in the water, the surprising number of civilian yachts still moored there, the beauty of the day. She desperately wanted to turn and look at Philip but each time she began the kayak starting tipping until she was sure it would capsize. Horrible thing, she thought. I shall be very pleased to be out of it and back on dry land.

They were approaching a small island mid-river, quite overgrown with small trees and rushes, when Clarissa gingerly turned her head to ask Philip to repeat something she hadn't quite heard. Philip, leaning forward and off-centre, supposedly to make himself better heard, flipped the Folbot over, throwing them both in the cool waters of the Hamble. There was nothing else to do but swim the few yards to shore, Philip holding the hawser he just happened to have in his hand when they went over.

"Oh, my God, Clarissa, I'm *so* sorry," apologized Philip as he helped her onto land. "You're *soaked*. Mind you, as luck would have it this is where I've stashed our picnic."

As she squeezed river water out of her hair he quickly set the kayak upright and tied it off before leading a drenched and laughing Clarissa up a narrow, well hidden path and into a small clearing. Clarissa's blouse and trousers were clinging to her like a skin, allowing Philip a good look at the body he had been dreaming about.

"Look, I've got a blanket here and a towel. Get out of your wet things and I'll wring them out, start a fire, and see if we can survive, Commando style."

As he was saying this Philip was already pulling his shirt over his head.

At the sight of his broad and muscular chest Clarissa was hit by another of the physical shocks she'd experienced at Roehampton. This is all part of a plan, she realized, and guess what, I don't care. He's absolutely gorgeous. Slipping off her blouse and then her trousers as Philip stood, transfixed, she grinned at him.

"You bastard," she said, moving into the strong arms held out for her. Philip slowly lowered her onto the blanket, kissing her neck and throat more softly than she thought him capable of, as her hands explored the body she had so admired.

"My God, you don't really think that will fit, do you?" an alarmed yet fascinated Clarissa exclaimed.

"You'll be surprised at just how easy it is," replied Philip, proceeding to show her, to her delight, just how.

The fire came later, she recalled afterwards, laughing to herself as she remembered that she came first, second and maybe even third.

TWENTY FIVE

It was Wednesday morning, the eleventh of July and Geoffrey had been summoned at eight o'clock to McLean's office at the airfield in Eastleigh. McLean looked both furious and worried, a strange combination, thought Geoffrey.

"Geoffrey, for God's sake, how did you get yourself hooked into this madcap idea? I've had a personal Top-Secret hand-delivered note from Comops that I had to read and *burn*, for heaven's sake, right in front of the messenger, telling me that on Sunday night you're going to be gone on a secret mission for possibly a week and that, between now and then, you're not to do anything *dangerous*, like testing bloody aeroplanes, for example, until you return. What in hell is going on?"

"Well, sir, obviously I can't say more, but I *do* believe it's worthwhile, what they've asked me to do, or I wouldn't have agreed. I feel terrible about not telling you but I simply couldn't."

"Of course I understand all of that, Geoffrey, but why *you?* Obviously it has to do with flying; something they want the best man possible to do, but what in hell would be important enough to justify losing somebody who now knows more about the bloody Spit than anyone else in the country? And that probably would include Mitchell, if the poor bugger were here today.

"Geoffrey, do you *really* think that what you're going to do is safe? I know what you've done and what you are doing every day here isn't exactly safe either, but we don't want to lose you. For God's sake, isn't what you're doing *now* enough for them?"

McLean's normally hard face was quivering with emotion. Geoffrey could feel himself getting a bit wound up too, as he realized that McLean was really more than just a demanding boss.

"No, I don't like it and I don't think it's safe. In fact, I think the chances of success are about ten per cent and I'm scared shitless, but I have to say that if we pull it off it will have been worth ten of me. If we don't, well, you'll win the war without me, but it may take longer.

"My biggest regret, believe it or not, would be never again to see the most wonderful human being that God ever created. I've fallen in love; can you believe it, at this time?"

"Well, Geoffrey my boy, good luck. It sounds lame but I know you well enough to know I wouldn't be able to talk you out of it. All I can do, though, is to say God speed. Now go get your arse in that big green bus of yours and see that girl again and I won't even ask where you got the petrol."

They parted, each shaken by the emotional encounter, and doubting they would ever see each other again. This fucking war, thought McLean. Those fucking Germans.

TWENTY SIX

Although Clarissa had started her RAF training in Sussex, Geoffrey persuaded her to come up to London at least once more before Sunday.

"What's so special about Sunday?" demanded Clarissa. "I'm closer to you down here anyway and soon I'll be transferred to the Blackgang station on the Isle of Wight and then you can wave at me each time you fly over!"

Realizing he'd made a mistake by mentioning Sunday, Geoffrey quickly made up a story that he'd been assigned to do some new work up in the Midlands that would keep him away for a few weeks and he didn't want not to see her for that long. Strange, thought Clarissa, for she dimly recalled from her idyllic island Philip saying something about his going away on Sunday for a bit. Two lovers, so different, so special and stationed so near to each other. Life, she surmised, was full of surprise and coincidence.

Geoffrey, so he said, had a meeting on Thursday, somewhere in or near London so they met again at her house. To his dismay, it seemed that the fearsome father was going to have dinner with them. Had he known before he arrived he'd have thought of somewhere else for them to meet, but on reflection he doubted he'd ever get Clarissa into a strange hotel, enticing though the thought was.

Dinner passed well enough, now that Sir Archibald had concluded that Geoffrey was acceptable. He even seemed pleased to have him in the house, although Geoffrey felt sure that their conversation must be excruciatingly boring for Clarissa.

"Tell me, Geoffrey," asked Sir Archibald, spooning some vegetables onto his plate, "how does the Messerschmitt compare to the Spit? I believe you've shot down a few of them. Ever actually fly one?"

"Yes, sir, I have but in my opinion it's not nearly the plane the Spit is, though in certain circumstances it can be better." The wine, a Chateau Latour, was loosening them all up, thought Geoffrey.

"Such as?" queried Clarissa, making a valiant effort to contribute something to the conversation.

"Well, it showed us during the Battle of Britain that we need cannon and not just machine guns, even if they *can* get off a hundred rounds a second. A hit with a cannon shell does a great deal more damage than a lot of machine gun hits, as you could imagine. The Messerschmitt can also out-turn a Spit: it has a radius of about seven hundred and fifty feet versus the Spit's eight hundred and eighty and the Hurricane's eight hundred."

"Doesn't that make it a much better fighter?" asked the older man.

"Not really, sir; the Spit is generally much more manoeuvrable, and a bit faster at most altitudes: we can do about three hundred and seventy mph at twenty thousand feet and three hundred and thirty mph at thirty thousand." He caught sight of Clarissa suppressing a yawn and smiled apologetically at her before continuing. "It also has much better visibility. Interestingly, the Messerschmitt has a gun sight with Spit wings imposed on it, focused for about three hundred and thirty yards convergence. I believe, as do most of our chaps, that one should get a lot closer than that to not just waste ammo."

"Fascinating, fascinating. How do you know so much about the Messerschmitt, anyway? And do they, the Germans, know as much about our aircraft?"

"Well, sir, we have captured a few 109s and I've been lucky enough to fly a couple. I suspect they have a few of our planes too but, as you would know, it takes a long time to build a completely new aircraft - much easier to keep improving what you've already got, which is what we've been doing, especially for the Spitfire. For example," he continued after taking another sip of wine, "in '40 we changed the prop to constant speed and thus added seven thousand feet to the ceiling. We also have better all-round visibility in a Spit than a 109, but actually neither is as good as the Hurricane in that respect."

"Geoffrey, old chap, I'm afraid I'm going to have to push off. I'd love to stay and hear more, this is so much more interesting than pudding and port, but I've got a bridge game waiting for me at my club. Honestly, I think I can make more money there than I can at the office! So, I'd best excuse myself, if you two don't mind?" No, Geoffrey certainly didn't mind and judging by Clarissa's slight smile neither did she.

Clarissa rang for the butler, requested some port for them both and then informed the man that he wouldn't be needed for the rest of the evening. A summary dismissal, Geoffrey thought, as they retreated to the study and the coal fire.

The flames cast a soft glow on Clarissa's lovely face and Geoffrey simply watched her adoringly as she chattered on about her new job. Did Geoffrey understand how this new aircraft detection system worked, she wondered. Geoffrey thought that he couldn't give a bugger about anything to do with aeroplanes at that moment: he was busy imprinting the scene on his mind, not knowing if he would ever see her again. This last thought seemed to focus his mind and, throwing all caution to the wind, he blurted out his feelings.

"Clarissa, darling, I want you so much. I can't forget our last time together; you're all I want and need, more than I can possibly hope to express."

As he spoke she rose and in the curtained and firelit room, moved over to him. Taking his glass of port gently from his hand and placing it on the side table, she slid onto his lap on the leather sofa and began silently to kiss his lips, cheeks, forehead, nose and neck as she undid his tie and started to unbutton his shirt. Amazed at her forward behaviour and yet unable to stop herself, she felt her own arousal as Geoffrey's hands moved under her sweater and skirt. His trousers were scarcely down around his ankles when she pulled him onto her and into her. He could feel the cool leather of the couch contrasting with the warmth of her legs wrapped round his back. Nothing, he thought, could be better than this, absolutely nothing.

Later, as they lay quietly together, Clarissa thought about her two lovers. Each so special, so different but equally pleasing. She thought she might love Philip but be in love with Geoffrey. She'd often wondered how to differentiate those terms; perhaps these two wonderful men provided the explanation.

TWENTY SEVEN

The designated night finally arrived. A driver from 12 Commando picked Geoffrey up at his digs in Bursledon around eight o'clock. Geoffrey had gone to The Jolly Sailor as usual that evening, having done little all day except contemplate writing a will, which he decided against, having concluded that the only worthwhile thing he owned was his Bentley, and he couldn't decide to whom to will it. Clarissa surely wouldn't or couldn't drive it, but he did decide to write her a letter in which he tried, rather lamely, he felt, to express the very deep love he felt for her.

God, he thought, I can make a plane do just about anything but I can't seem to co-ordinate my pen and my brain. In any event he had tried, realizing that it would probably be the last thing anyone ever heard from him and yet not wanting the letter to sound sad, regretful or any other bloody thing. He just wanted to assure the lovely creature who had so captured his heart and mind that nothing else mattered to him as much as seeing her again, hopefully forever.

Entrusting his landlady to mail this and telling her that he would be away up north for a few days, he settled into the car thinking that not only did he wish this insane mission had never been approved, but on a more basic level, wishing he'd had a little more to eat at The Jolly Sailor.

As it didn't get dark until after nine o'clock in July, he and Philip were going to check and recheck their equipment, now stashed in a boathouse next to the dock which, at the moment, had no Motor Gun Boat or any other craft tied up to it. In fact, the place was damn near deserted, Geoffrey realized, and presumed that the ever security-conscious Philip had probably organized that too. Geoffrey thought that Philip was a few gins ahead of him when he arrived, but quickly realized that he was high on adrenaline alone. The fact that he had another opportunity to get himself killed elated him and he couldn't wait to get going.

"This is it, Geoffrey, old boy; a perfect night for a perfect mission. This is the sort of thing we should be all about, a few against many, stealth against power, knowing you can pull off a great caper. Really, Geoffrey, we're bloody lucky they let us do this: could so easily have been scratched by some spineless civil servant or, worse, an over-promoted chair soldier."

"Good God, I think you're serious. I've been praying for days that someone would recognize this for what it is, simply barmy, and lock you up at the same time. If you think this sort of thing is fun you should be committed!"

"Now, now, Geoffrey, this is going to be perfect for both of us. *You* get to do what you like to do, which is fly nice planes, and I get to do what *I* like to do, which is knock off un-nice Hun. What's more, I'll get a decent French meal before I come back whereas you, poor sod, will get nought to eat but what we've got in this little Folbot. Now, that really *is* sad!"

Philip had agreed to Geoffrey wearing his Webley revolver as at least he knew how to use it, even if he'd never had occasion. Philip thought it might be useful to put a wounded aircraft out of its misery but couldn't imagine much else. He had his Luger with its ugly black silencer, a couple of grenades and a very nasty-looking Commando knife.

"I'll carry all the French money, old boy, 'cause you won't need it and I might; besides, you're supposed to be a downed airman if the need arises, which, by the way, I sincerely hope won't! We've got some basic cold rations for four days and two light but bloody useful down sleeping bags. They crush up into a very small bag and are pretty good for June in the woods And, of course, we have our black overalls which will bamboozle the Germans into thinking we're two of their mechanics. I've also got a collapsible shovel-pick which will both speed up burying the boat and dig us into some sort of cover in the woods. Not very useful as a weapon, however, but probably about as good as your Webley."

This equipment was all packed in water-proof bags and stowed in the Folbot which would be carried, fully assembled, on the deck of the MGB. This they could hear just coming alongside the dock.

"We're going to board at 2200 hours," said Philip, "then mosey quietly down the Hamble and out of Southampton harbour. My thinking is that, given a fair wind and no bad luck, we'll be about at the drop-off point in four hours, say 0200. Then an hour to paddle in and find the moment to slip by any sentry and we're off and into the woods and well up toward the airfield before dawn. It will be damn hard to find our final bivouac while it's still pitch black anyway. We want to be close enough to the field to be able to get there quickly but not so close that any perimeter patrol would spot us; hard to judge that sort of thing at night but you'll be amazed how well your eyes adjust after a bit."

"I shall be damned amazed if we're still alive after that, my friend, but, in for a penny...I don't suppose anybody's going to cancel this madness and save us now so, let's go."

Philip opened the boathouse door and the pair of them carried the Folbot and its stowed cargo down the dock to where a couple of sailors wordlessly relieved them of it, lashed it down on deck and motioned them to the wheelhouse where they met the Captain.

"As I don't know your names or your ranks, gentlemen," he began, "I can only address you informally. I understand that I am to ask you to verify and confirm a drop-off point near Cherbourg and that the drop-off should be as near to 0200 as possible. I should also inform you that my orders are to avoid capture at all costs, in other words, to run and not fight but just get ourselves back home. I want you to be aware of my orders in case I have to take that action, my men will not. I should also remind you that, whatever your rank or service, on this boat I am the Captain. If that's understood, gentlemen, let's get underway."

For the next couple of hours Geoffrey lay dozing in a bunk, thinking that he was sure he'd chosen the best service. Who, after all, would want to be tossed around all day and night in one of these smelly diesel tugs? The seas were flat, however, and eventually he went out on deck to get some fresh air leaving Philip still chatting with the Captain; exchanging horror stories,

Geoffrey was quite sure. There was a slight fog, more of a low mist on the water, which obscured the otherwise clear night. This at least kept them invisible to subs and night fighters, thought Geoffrey, so that was a good start. Suddenly there was a dead silence as the engines stopped and the boat slowed until the only sound was the slight wave action against its sides. In the pitch black Geoffrey was suddenly aware of Philip beside him; he'd never even heard him approach.

"Geoff," Philip's voice was a low murmur in his ear, "it seems we have a near neighbour and the Captain's not sure if it's ours or theirs. Makes no difference, he says, since no-one knows he's out here or why, including him, so we're just as liable to get shot by either! Happy days."

Straining his ears, Geoffrey could indeed hear another engine passing by in the fog, quite close. He even thought he could hear voices above the engine throb, but couldn't make out the language being spoken. Christ, he thought, we're not even half way there and my heart's already nearly stopped. How did the Captain pick up the presence of the other boat? He didn't think that sonar, or the still primitive radar, would do that, even if it was part of the boat's equipment. Just great naval sixth sense, perhaps?

Whatever the reason, they restarted after about five minutes and Geoffrey's next reverie was interrupted by another slow-down, this time to a full stop and the sight of Philip shaking the Captain's hand as two burly sailors lowered the Folbot off the lee side. A plank had been suspended there to make it easier for them to board the unstable craft, especially Philip who had trouble getting into it at the best of times. With Geoffrey in the bow and Philip in the stern, they moved away from the MGB and set off on a compass course due west, trusting in the fog that the Navy had indeed dropped them exactly where planned. At this point the fog was a great cover and, as their paddling was nearly silent, they reckoned they would first hear the gentle surf on the beach before they hit it. Ideally they wanted to get a good look at the shore and any fortifications there before they even attempted to land.

Geoffrey figured they must be over the oyster beds when his paddle actually touched bottom, near the shore. He strained his aviator eyes to see through the thinning fog and did suddenly see a light. My God, it can't be more than a hundred yards in front of us, he realized as he frantically motioned Philip to stop paddling and, with their pre-arranged hand signals, guided them to the left but no further in yet.

The mist was just light enough to reveal a blockhouse with a light showing through a gap and a soldier emerging. The glow from the cigarette in his mouth was about all they could see of him as he started down the beach in their direction. Philip and Geoffrey sat motionless in the Folbot, holding it still with their paddles hard on the bottom, hoping no noise would be made as the boat rose and fell in the gentle surf. The guard seemed uninterested in the sea and, from the sound of his footsteps, continued his march down the beach.

When he was out of earshot Geoffrey wanted to make a dash for the beach, but Philip's big hand restrained him. Sure enough, about five minutes later the cigarette glow reappeared as the guard completed his tour and returned towards the blockhouse. Geoffrey's heart hammered against the wall of his chest when the guard turned directly towards them and, flipping his cigarette into the water, unzipped his trousers and peed whilst seemingly looking out to sea right at them.

After what seemed an eternity he turned into the blockhouse and started talking to another guard. Geoffrey felt Philip's powerful paddle thrust almost immediately now that the guard was inside. Three more strokes from each of them and they were on the shingle, standing in the foot-deep water. Silently lifting the Folbot and carrying it five yards into the thick scrub, they found a swampy area where Geoffrey started to dig while Philip returned to erase their tracks. Luckily there weren't many traces of their passage due to the beach being shingle rather than sand. They figured that the guard wouldn't do another patrol for a half hour at least, giving them ten minutes to bury the boat, pack their gear in a haversack, and, as Philip whispered, get their arses out of there. A fifteen minute hike, mostly uphill, would put them into the Bois du Rabey where, Philip assured Geoffrey, he could breathe again.

TWENTY EIGHT

It seemed impossible to Geoffrey that anybody as large as Philip could move so silently, and even politely, he thought, as the big man paused to hold back a branch that would otherwise have snapped in his face. They were nearly out of the low swamp area now and feeling reasonably happy with their progress so far. The Folbot had been buried; Geoffrey hoped he'd never see another one in his life and had actually taken some pleasure in dismantling it and seeing it disappear under muck, ferns and branches. Unlikely to be found, he thought, and Philip hadn't mentioned that he planned to go back in it. Come to think of it, he'd been pretty quiet about how he expected to get back to Britain at all, but he certainly seemed optimistic.

At one point they passed only two hundred yards from a house close to the beach, but saw no signs of life and no noisy French dog, which was one of the hazards they expected to come across at some point. Certainly every French farm had at least one dog, and usually a large and disagreeable one at that. The nearest hamlet was Morsalines, about half a mile from their landing point, if, in fact, they had landed where they'd planned. It was extremely difficult to recognize anything at night, even though both of them had spent hours studying every detailed map they could get of the area. The problem was that they had to work from memory because, if caught with a map, it would be fairly obvious where they were going and even possibly why.

Suddenly they found themselves on a paved road and seemingly exposed. It would be the road between Quettehou and points south running just inland down the coast and could, thought Geoffrey, be regularly patrolled at night. In spite of this, Philip did not immediately cross into cover on the other side but walked boldly down about a hundred yards to the left and then crossed over and through what seemed to be an ancient fort. Built against invasion by us Brits, thought Geoffrey, but, back then we were against the French and not these bastards.

Once past the fort they turned north-northwest and in a few minutes crossed another small lane and then, indeed, they were in the deep woods. At this point Philip paused and whispered.

"So far, so good, old bean. The Navy must have done their job right because I'm sure this is the southern edge of the Bois de Rabey. We won't stay in long, for it's easier walking, especially in the dark, if we skirt the western edge; we can always pop in and take cover if we see or hear anything strange."

Before Geoffrey was able to comment, he was off again; like a bloody shadow, thought Geoffrey. But, sure enough, they found a fairly well defined forest track, probably there for logging purposes, and followed it to the edge of the wood. Here they turned north again and cut across some fields, skirting a farm which elicited one desultory bark, across another road, then back by the edge of the Bois de Rabey again.

"We've got to keep moving, Geoffrey, old boy: it won't be long before morning light and Uncle Philip wants to have you tucked in and resting long before the sun's up! We're right on schedule now. We've just got to cross a couple more fields, keeping the hamlet of Brevolle well to our left, then into another wood, if my memory serves me well. Pretty soon after that we may get our feet wet again, for there's a small stream where I propose we cross. It'll probably be swampy. If we get a shift on and get up there soon enough I may elect to march us over the bridge and right through the middle of a small clump of houses."

By now they had walked, Geoffrey calculated, about five miles at a pretty fast pace and he was feeling in need of a breather. Philip, however, plodded ahead stopping only once to tell Geoffrey that they were only a couple of miles from Pepin-Vast, the chateau that the Luftwaffe had taken over as headquarters for JG2, or Jaggeschwader, Reichthofen, the very group from which they intended to steal a Focke-Wulf. This nugget of information instantly made Geoffrey forget his fatigue and he was sure he could feel the rate of his heartbeat doubling.

"Christ," he whispered to Philip, as though his voice might carry all the way to the enemy, "if it's this easy to get so near, why haven't you chaps come over and popped them all off?"

"Not a bad idea, old boy, I'll put that one up when we get back. Perhaps you'd like to come along too, now that you know your way."

"Not bloody likely," puffed Geoffrey, who was walking as fast as possible to put that dreaded chateau and all it housed as far behind them as possible.

They were, in fact, about to find the stream, having turned due west after emerging from the second lot of woodland. Again, they had passed several houses, but neither a light nor a sound was evident.

"Farmers work hard and sleep well, thank God," muttered Geoffrey, to which Philip only grunted then held up his hand to signal 'stop' and 'silence': they were about to emerge from the wetland and climb up a bank onto another road which, Geoffrey remembered from the maps, would take them over a bridge and north towards the small town of Brillevast. They planned to skirt this town but they were still going to have to walk right between some houses and down a road for over a mile; thank God it was still pretty black and even a bit misty, although Geoffrey felt that it was either getting slightly lighter or his eyes were, actually, adapting to the dark.

They got through the small cluster of houses just over the bridge and had an easy walk up the road, having only once really roused a dog who eventually stopped barking after they passed by. Philip had reached into his pack for the raw meat he carried for just this purpose. He said it contained a drug which would put a big dog to sleep for a couple of hours but, unfortunately, would kill a little one so he hesitated to throw it out unless he had absolutely no option.

"Usually," he said, "dogs will grab the meat, retreat quietly and gulp it down, then give up any chase or quest for more because the drug makes them lethargic so quickly. Mind you, most French farmers don't pay any attention to the barking anyway. They shout at them a bit, or chuck something at them.

Still, I'd prefer not to leave any evidence of our little trek. And now, Geoffrey, my friend, we have almost reached the promised land."

They skirted Brillevast on rural lanes, still heading north toward the airfield. The 'promised land', Geoffrey knew, was the Bois de Blanqueville which they entered slowly and quietly near its centre edge. The top edge of this wood was just a thousand yards from the eastern edge of the main runway and, as the prevailing wind was from the west, the planes would probably be parked and warming up near the eastern end. The main east-west road from Cherbourg to St. Pierre-Eglise and on to Barfleur on the coast lay between them and the field. Philip's theory was that they probably kept their border patrol within this natural boundary and that the fence would certainly be on the other side of this road.

"We're here, lad, we're here! Let's just find a very large hollow under a fallen tree somewhere right here in the middle, settle in for what's left of the night and see what the morrow brings."

After quite a short space of time they found a suitable spot and, as Philip dug out a bit more space as quietly as he could, Geoffrey gathered some fallen branches to give them more cover. In their black overalls they were nearly invisible, tucked down in the root depression, or so Geoffrey fervently hoped as he tried to get into his miniscule sleeping bag, noting, just before his exhausted and nervous body claimed sleep, that Philip had wandered off to do a recce. My God, Geoffrey thought as he felt himself losing consciousness, there's a chance we might actually pull this off!

TWENTY NINE

Geoffrey slept fitfully in spite of being mentally exhausted and physically tired by all that had happened in the past twelve hours. In his life as a test pilot he was used to short half-hour or, at the most, even four hour periods of stress and sometimes they were violent and extreme, but he was not used to spending such long, sustained periods in a highly nervous state. Half-awake, half-asleep, he'd been vaguely aware of Philip moving away from their root cave hide and then silently returning as dawn started to bring streams of filtered light through the pine and scrub oak forest.

"Wake up, old boy," whispered Philip to Geoffrey, who at that moment felt very old indeed and wondering if he would get the chance to get any older. "Time for Uncle Philip's cold breakfast, followed this evening by cold dinner, no French wine, I'm afraid, but lovely English water. No lunch either, but if you're good and quiet and don't moan too much about my cooking skills, or lack thereof, I might let you have a biccie."

"How can you be so bloody cheerful at this hour?" muttered Geoffrey. "Even the Hun are too intelligent to get up before dawn."

"Not true, old boy. Listen carefully and you shall hear what we came for. I got close to the fence on the other side of the road and actually saw a couple of planes which looked a bit different, even to my eye. They were being warmed up by chaps in black overalls, just like ours. So far so very good! I lay back a few yards and saw a ground patrol, two soldiers and a rather lazy dog having a casual sort of stroll right next to the fence. I doubt they do it all day but it doesn't matter as long as we establish the regular time, and being German you can guarantee there *will* be a regular time. We should have plenty of time to cut our way in and get you away well before they complete a circuit. I'm sure as hell they're not even considering the possibility of someone creeping greekwise up their arse."

"How far are we, then, from this fence and does it look like we can cut it? Tell me again: how many days do we have to stay here in this rabbit-hole? Let's just go and do it, or try to do it, and get the hell out of here one way or the other." Geoffrey was feeling sick with anxiety.

"Calm, calm, my friend. We've got to wait two more days while the RAF stirs up the field and then, on the third day, at just about this time, in we go and away you go. Meanwhile, you'll just have to relax and listen to Uncle Philip talk of war and sexual conquests, although perhaps two days won't be quite long enough for that!"

Realizing that he had little option, Geoffrey decided to try and reassure himself as much as he could while he waited.

"I'm simply not good at sitting around doing nothing," he complained. "I'm not used to it. I think waiting around getting more and more wound up about this frankly insane escapade is going to drive me absolutely potty." Hearing a dog bark in the distance he went on, "How do you know that the bloody dog, lazy or not, won't pick up your scent and bring those chaps straight here?"

"Well, first of all," replied Quigley calmly, lying back on his sleeping bag with his arms behind his head, "I don't think that dog behaved like anything other than a pet but, to be on the safe side, as always, old boy, I spread a lot of pepper around where I'd been standing: most dogs hate the stuff and simply move on past it, to greener pastures, as it were. Also, I had to cross the tarmac road which is pretty poor at retaining scent. No, I think that dog is the least of our problems."

Somewhat reassured, Geoffrey tried to settle more comfortably into their temporary quarters, realizing that for the next two days he really didn't have anything to do but talk or, more likely, listen to the big Commando. He eyed the leafy boughs which Philip had artfully placed over their little cave. Quigley, taking up rather too much room, followed his gaze.

"They'd have to fall on us to find us, Geoffrey, my friend. If mother had sent us more rations we could probably wait out the war right here, comfy as can be."

"Tell me, Philip, how did you get into this boy scout Commando stuff in the first place?" Geoffrey thought he might as well relax and learn more about this man he admired and respected more each day.

"Not a long story, really. I'd left St. Neots where I'd done well in sports and hell-raising, but not much else, and lo and behold got into Trinity College, Cambridge, probably to help their rugby prospects because my exam results were deplorable! I really only lived for the holidays when I could shoot and fish for trout on the Avon. Somehow I managed to last a year there, but only because I was hardly ever there - spent most of my time in the Fens shooting birds - then discovered the other kind of bird and started chasing them. Had a flat in Primrose Hill - you would have loved it. It wasn't very large so my flatmate and I had to leave a tie wrapped around the door handle to tell the other when it was in play. Once I kept the poor bastard out for two days! What a goer that girl was, a real yelper; had the neighbours pounding on the wall while I kept pounding on her. Beat the hell out of Cambridge, let me tell you!"

"That's fascinating, Philip," remarked Geoffrey dryly, "but how the hell did that get you into the Commandos? I don't think that fucking is listed as a subject one can read at Cambridge, or am I wrong?"

"Quite right, old boy, but it should be. When we get back I'll write the old school about that and maybe even endow a chair! Well, pressure from the parents pushed work too close so I buggered off to India; had tons of good shooting and climbing in the Himalayas - even got to Tibet - then finally had to come home: I really missed those London popsies. I even got interested in books but only really old ones. In fact, I have a pretty good collection. I'll show you if you manage to fly that plane back."

"You think your journey back is going to be easier than mine, do you?" asked Geoffrey, suddenly brought back to reality.

"Oh, yes. Yes, I've done the land and sea bit before and as far as I'm concerned it's a bloody sight safer than flitting around in a near vacuum.

"Now, about the Commando bit, it's really quite interesting because in

'39 I'd just come back from doing some fishing in Iceland, along with trying to catch as many of those ice-blonde beauties as I could, and somebody told me there was a war started. I thought that was bloody good news, as I was a bit bored, so I joined the Berkshire Yeomanry and they actually gave me a commission! That looked like it wasn't going to be very exciting, too bloody formal, so I resigned my commission and joined what looked likely to be much more fun: a Finnish Expeditionary Force. They even sent me to Chamonix to learn to ski. Never bothered to tell them I was already better than the bloody instructor!

"The whole thing was great. We were going to be sent to help the Finns against the Russians when, lo and behold, because of the Russo-Finnish compromise in the spring of '40, the whole damn thing was cancelled and there went my fun war. Perhaps it's just as well, I met a Finnish soldier once who told me that Finland was great in the winter when you could ski and skate, but in summer the mosquitoes were hell. In fact, he said that there were only two places you could shit in the summer, one was under water and the other over the fire! But then, and now here's the answer to your question, I heard that they were forming the first Commando unit, so I joined up."

Geoffrey thought that as long as Philip was talking, it kept his mind off what he thought was their horribly precarious position. Here they were, two miles from a German Luftwaffe headquarters and about a thousand yards from an enemy airfield which they, a two-man Commando unit, were going to invade to steal an aeroplane. Christ, how ridiculous, he thought, not for the first time. He wanted to keep the confident and reassuring rumble from Philip going.

"So, what was the idea behind forming the Commandos?"

Scratching at an insect bite on his ankle, Quigley replied.

"The original idea was to harass the Germans pretty much anywhere along their extensive coastline. Small scale operations really, but doing enough to learn something ourselves about their defences and keep the Hun on their toes. What I really liked about it was not just having some bloody interesting adventures, but the informality. We have a great chap as CO, Peachy Harrison. You've met him. He once told me he didn't give a shit how scruffy my lot was as long as we were the toughest sods who ever landed anywhere. I don't have a single lad out of the sixty-five in my troop who wouldn't die for Peachy. Incidentally, I was even able to choose my own men - got most of them from the old Berkshire Yeomanry.

"At first it was frustrating as hell, because Churchill didn't think small raids were much use but then, I guess, he got intrigued at the idea of upsetting the over-organized Hun, so we saw some action.

"We made one raid on Ambleteuse, just north of Boulogne; I had ten good chaps with me and the idea was to go ashore, raise hell, maybe capture somebody and get the hell out. Great plan, but we got spotted immediately. Had a good scrap, popped a few of them, lost two of our own and had to get our arses out very smartly. Really shook them up though, that we would even try that sort of stunt.

"Later we actually invaded Sark, four chaps and me. Maybe I told you about that? Again, we didn't stay long but reports from agents verified that these raids really rattled the Boche, so Winnie, I guess, got more enthusiastic and I assume that's why I heard he personally approved this lark! Good thing we met at Bursledon isn't it, or we'd never be having this much fun!"

Geoffrey pulled a face.

The day passed, hot and windless, while Philip's stories of raids, modestly told but terrifying to Geoffrey's ears, filled the hours. Geoffrey even managed a short nap about mid-day, after Philip had allowed him a biscuit and some 'genuine English' water for being a good and polite listener to stories he knew he was repeating.

Philip went out on another recce during Geoffrey's nap and confirmed a second perimeter patrol about five pm, but they still didn't know if the patrols were continuous. Philip doubted it but explained to Penn that it didn't matter anyhow as they would move in right behind the morning patrol, whose time he would confirm on the following two days. They settled in to sleep after a supper of Yankee Ham, or Spam, and English chocolate, all remnants of which were buried. The night being warm they simply lay on the sleeping bags and slept in their clothes, both bodies in the small shelter giving off more than enough heat.

THIRTY

A roar that shattered the pristine stillness of the hide awoke Geoffrey with a shock. Jerking upright from his cramped half-moon position he banged his head on an exposed root and turned, swearing quietly, to look for Philip who had, of course, crept away earlier to check out the patrol guards' time schedule.

The incredible noise, Geoffrey quickly realized, was from what he thought to be British Beaufighters, or perhaps Mosquitos, he wasn't exactly sure. He only caught a glimpse of about half a dozen very low-flying planes which raced over the tree tops and could now be heard shooting up the airfield just beyond the woods.

The entire cacophony of noise, incredibly intense, lasted for only thirty seconds to a minute and was followed by an absolute and eerie silence. About two minutes later he heard the sound of several aircraft revving up and subsequently taking off, presumably in pursuit of what had just violently and briefly attacked their home.

Geoffrey marvelled at how quick the response was and for the first time began to worry about how much head start he could expect if, in fact, he ever got airborne - not a hell of a lot, that was for sure. He doubted if a Spit squadron could get planes off that fast, even if caught at full readiness at five o'clock on a clear July morning. Whatever happens, will happen, he thought. At least the RAF was doing its job and right on schedule too. He was also pleased to note that all he had heard was machine guns and cannon fire; no bombs, thank God, to fuck up the runways.

A few minutes later an exhilarated Philip returned and slid through the concealing branches into their hole.

"Christ, you should have seen the show, Geoffrey: you'd have been proud of your chums; they really shot the shit out of the field. Don't think they actually did much damage, each plane seems pretty well protected by side bunkers, but they certainly had the Boche running all over the place. Looked to me like only a couple of the planes were, in fact, turning over at the time of the attack but even so they did manage to get away in a hurry."

"Even a two minute head start at three hundred mph is pretty useful," Geoffrey calculated. "That gives them a ten mile lead, perhaps even fifteen, by the time Jerry is in the air. He might just catch them by the time they're over our coast where they'll get some help, which they're going to need if the Focke-Wulf is as good as reported. Our boys must have come over just at wave top to have avoided the German radar, which we think can see nearly to our coast."

Geoffrey was already working out what his odds were, maybe better than a Mosquito bomber, he thought, fast as they were. He, at least, would be in a plane as fast as his pursuers, providing he could figure out how to make it go in the first place.

"I was watching the perimeter patrol when the lads came over," laughed Philip. "Scared the guards even more than me! They lay down flat and the dog just barked; the Fuhrer would not have been impressed!"

What neither Philip, Geoffrey, nor the RAF knew, or had any reason to know, was that, had the planes directed their effort against the Chateau Pepin-Vast, they might have reaped an even greater reward, for there, spending a couple of nights to award the Commander of JG2, Richthofen Geschwader, yet another medal, was none other than the Commander of the Luftwaffe, Hermann Goering.

THIRTY ONE

Goering, slumbering in the master bedroom of the chateau, which Assi Hahn always kept prepared for visiting dignitaries, had also been rudely awakened by the roar of the planes. Being an old and experienced airman he knew only too well that these were not his own. He unceremoniously rolled his huge frame off the bed, landing heavily on the floor and, wincing with pain, tried to squeeze as much of his bulk under the bed as he could. His first thoughts were, of course, that there had been some security leak and that the bloody Brits were after him specifically. As the noise of aircraft and shooting disappeared as quickly as it had arrived, he realized no harm was done, at least not here at the chateau, so he sauntered down the hall to where he knew Hahn, the Geschwader leader, slept.

Hahn, perhaps anticipating Goering's arrival, was already up and dressed in spite of the previous evening's plentiful supply of French wine and cognac.

"Assi, my friend," teased Goering, "there will be no more medals for you, no matter how many bloody Brits you shoot down, if I so much as get my arse scratched for merely visiting you to tell you again how much we love you! Even the Fuhrer himself brags about your many victories. You would think he had taught you himself! I told him what a splendid job you did with the antique Messerschmitt 109 and now, with the Focke-Wulf 190, you should easily double your score!"

"Thank you, Herr Reichsmarshal, but please remember that these Brits are not as easy as those untrained Poles and Russians in their dreadful planes. They're getting tougher and smarter but, even so, I must say we are having amazing success. That is probably why they are trying to kill us on the ground instead of man to man in the air. As we discussed once before, they are not as noble or gentlemanly as they would like the world to believe.

"I have called the airfield, however, and there is little damage, only a couple of aeroplanes with repairable holes. Our blackmen do amazing work to keep us in the air."

"Is this the first time they have actually attacked the field?"

"Yes, General, and hopefully the last. We showed them how fast we can be airborne and, in fact, we may even have caught up with them before they got within their own coast; I'll keep you informed.

"Incidentally, sir, I don't really want nor need another medal but, the more 190s you can divert this way, the more good work we can do for you. As far as we can tell, the only thing a Spitfire can do better than us is out-turn us; if we can get them up over ten thousand metres they haven't a chance. Even the 109 is better there. My biggest problem, however, is the fact that we have lost a few of our old comrades. This hurts us because all of these fine fellows had much more experience than the British and generally won their dog fights. But, unquestionably, the enemy is getting better and we need all the Focke-Wulfs we can get."

"Tell me, Assi, were those raiders Fat Dogs or Indians?" asked Goering, making the German aviation distinction between bombers and fighters.

"If they were Fat Dogs we really have a problem, Reichsmarshal, for they seemed to me to be going, as the Americans so charmingly say, like shit off a shovel. From the sound of them I think they were Mosquito fighter-bombers, but I didn't get a good look at them: they left in a big hurry. It was what they call rhubarbs, I think, shooting at targets of opportunity.

"In any event, come and have some fine French breakfast as long as you're up. I can only apologize for the bad manners of the British but, as far as being in danger goes, I don't think you are. I believe they think this chateau is still occupied by French aristocrats and they don't want to antagonize them any more than they naturally do by blowing up such an impressive building. It's a fine place for us, don't you think, sir?"

"Yes, I do, Assi, it's a splendid place, which is one reason I come here so often, not just to give you another well earned medal, or jewel in your Iron

Cross but to get the French food you always serve too! When the war is over we should keep this place just for the use of the Luftwaffe!"

THIRTY TWO

Hunkered down again with no possibility of going back to sleep, Philip and Geoffrey contemplated the long day ahead. They would be limited to doing absolutely nothing except for a brief exit to sort out the body's needs and get a little exercise, which even Philip agreed they had to have. There certainly wasn't much room to move around under the overturned tree stump, even for one person, much less two, particularly when one was the size of Quigley.

"Tell me a bit about yourself, Geoffrey old boy."

Geoffrey suspected that this was just a way to get the long day's conversation going. He figured that Philip would fill in the gaps as he certainly seemed fascinated by the war and all the potential excitement it would provide for him.

"Not a lot to tell."

It had always been difficult to extract anything personal from Geoffrey, who was not only exceedingly modest, but who genuinely felt there wasn't much remarkable about his life, no matter what other people seemed to think.

"I got out of Lancing School and, like you, there wasn't a lot that interested me except sports and girls and I've probably always been better at sports. In any event, I discovered aeroplanes around about '27 and I suppose you could say I'd finally found my thing. I couldn't get enough of them."

"Is that planes you're talking about now, old man, or is it popsies?"

"Planes, unfortunately, but they're probably more reliable although, like women, they're sometimes hard to start. I joined the RAF and got commissioned in '31 after training at Grantham. It was part of something called ADGB - stood for Air Defence of Great Britain. We had a plane called the Siskin. Would you bloody believe it had brakes and no flaps? Perhaps they thought even *that* plane would suffice against the Frogs, supposedly our biggest threat. We switched to Bristol Bulldogs which were much better. They had two 303s firing through the prop. Terrifying thought, but always seemed to work!

"All that got a bit boring so I joined the Met Service in '33. Flew every bloody day, regardless of the conditions, which quite often made it far from boring. Let's see, lots of deb parties in London, then back to Duxford by 0700 to be ready to fly again - oxygen was a big help on those mornings! That sort of flying did have the benefit of forcing one to keep track of steeples and things that might stick up in the fog. Nobody ever needed you up there when the weather was good so it used to be lots of fun trying to remember where the hell the field you started from was. I met some very nice people by ending up landing in their fields or on golf courses, mind you the golfers were never very pleased, funnily enough. I used to tell them they shouldn't play any game which had to be done in such dreadful weather. I had a clue, though, even back then, that the Germans might be more of a threat than the French. In 1935, when a couple of pals and I flew to Germany with some rather sporting young ladies we were jolly impressed by the German airfields and some of the equipment they seemed to have lying around.

"Anyhow, thinking that the war might never happen it seemed like I might be more useful if I joined Supermarine as a test pilot. They didn't have much worth flying at that time, but a great chap called Mitchell had developed a really fine plane, designed to win the Schneider Trophy."

"What the hell is the Schneider Trophy?" interrupted Quigley.

"A race for seaplanes. This plane that Mitchell made did well over three hundred mph, which was stupendously fast compared with anything the RAF had. Anyway, the next thing I knew I got the chance to take up the second flight in what is now the Spitfire. Mitchell never liked the name incidentally, thought it frightfully silly.

"That was the Spit I; we're now on version V and, for my money, it's a damn sight better than the Messerschmitt 109, though the Germans had lots of time to test the 109 out in Spain before Poland and Czechoslovakia. Don't get me wrong, it's a damn fine plane too, but the main reason they do so well against us is the fact that *their* pilots have real air war experience while we're still throwing up boys with very few actual hours in a Spit - and even less time actually shooting at anybody. Flying is one thing, but flying while some bastard is trying to kill you is quite another."

"Rumour has it you've bagged a few yourself, Geoffrey. I imagine it's a bit like grouse shooting, having to give a lead, swing through and all that. How long could you actually expect to be on the target?"

"Oh, perhaps two or three seconds in all, but that can put out nearly three hundred bullets from the eight machine guns. That's plenty to knock pieces off or perhaps kill a fighter, but to knock down a bomber usually takes much more. Also, if you hang about too long in one spot, either the bomber gunners get honed in on you or some bastard you can't see comes up from behind. The trick is to get in and out quickly and turn the way they don't expect. The Poles we've got flying for us now are bonkers though, they'll practically ram the chap they're shooting at. I'd hate like hell to be a rear gunner looking at one of those coming at me. Actually, I'd hate being a rear gunner at all: those poor bastards don't last long on either side."

"So how'd you get from Supermarine back into the RAF? You must have, to have flown in the Battle of Britain, mustn't you?"

"Well, it seemed to me that to really see what modifications the Spit needed to be more effective, against the 109 in particular, I needed to actually fly one against them. It's one way to learn in a hurry. Of course, we had a couple of 109s we'd captured and I'd flown them, but it's not the same as having some chap busting a gut to get on your tail and kill you. Makes for a steep learning curve!"

"Is it true, Geoffrey, what I heard about you sometimes going up with no guns at all? I can't begin to imagine why on earth you would want to do that, seems absolutely barking to me."

"Easy answer, Philip: with no guns or ammo the Spit is very light, close to six thousand pounds and nimble as a pussycat. So, if I threw the thing around enough, I figured that nobody was liable to hit me and I could really see and feel if we were going the right way with the development. Believe me, though, I didn't do that too often."

"Jesus, that sounds like sending a Commando out with a Boy Scout knife - not for me!"

Geoffrey had always felt self-conscious talking about himself, but it helped pass the time and kept his mind off the forthcoming tasks. He was continually reminded of these for they could hear planes taking off and landing through most of the day. From their position, however, they seldom saw the planes unless the wind shifted from the usual westerly and they changed circuit. Then they would occasionally get a glimpse of the grey-green sleek monoplane which Geoffrey presumed to be the Fw190.

"Philip, just how the hell are you going to get back after I leave you holding off the whole German airforce with your Luger?"

Quigley tapped the side of his nose with a finger and grinned at Geoffrey.

"Uncle Philip has a plan, let me assure you. I do plan to get back you know. Lately we have become aware of something called Hitler's Commando Law, not sure if that's what the Boche call it but it seems our little forays into the Fortress of Europe have not only rattled our friend but seriously pissed him off. He's made up his own Geneva Convention rules of war and we Commandos have been classified as resistance fighters or Maquis, as is the case with the French, so we can't expect them to play nicely with us. Suits me all right, though: I never did believe in Rules of War. Seems bloody idiotic for a bunch of old farts to sit around a table and actually make rules on what are fair ways to kill each other, especially when they're deciding on it in a neutral place like Switzerland, where those fat burghers like to see the rest of the world fucked up so they can make money. It's idiotic - lead bullets are OK, wooden or dum-dum are not! Good God, how stupid can humans be? Perhaps war will become less popular if we make it more and more ghastly, instead of giving it rules like some sport."

"For God's sake, Philip, don't get so excited: you'll have everybody at the airfield over here. I had no idea you could be so noisy. I do agree, however. War is a dreadful business and might just as well be conducted that way; but you know, pilots still believe, as in World War I, that one should never shoot a chap in a parachute, just not fair game, old boy. If you think about it, that's mad too if the bastard's going to be back tomorrow to kill you.

"But, to get back to my question, just how the hell are you planning to get back?"

"Oh, that, well, I'm assuming that for a minute or two, in all the excitement of your take-off, I'll be just another mechanic and I'll try to move back to our entry hole and slip out unseen. Whatever the case, that's where I exit. I'll cross the road near Gommeville church, a few yards away, again hoping that the road won't carry my scent very well, just in case those dogs are better than I think they are. I'm going right back this way until the Saire, then walk upstream in the water until the bridge at Hameau Valognes, stuff my overalls under the bridge and emerge as a peasant complete with beret!

"After that it will be on back towards the airfield. Same tactic, old boy, they always think you'll run away instead of towards them. My German's pretty poor, but if I come across any Hun, my French will fool them! There's a safe house in St. Vaast-la-Hougue, a town on the coast just the opposite side of the field from here. I plan to walk over to there on the road; if I can find the house, and it's OK, I'll try to organize a ride on a fishing boat to England or, failing that, steal one after convincing the captain that it's in his best interests to take me there.

"I do keep remembering though, as you reminded me, that as recently as '33 we seriously considered that our greatest threat of war was once again with the Frogs. I never really trust the buggers, so Uncle Philip always proceeds with caution."

The huge Commando and slightly built pilot talked on through most of the morning, emerging from the cave twice to stretch and once even moving to the edge of the woods. Philip pointed out their path towards the field up to the point where they would, for a few seconds, be quite exposed as they crossed the road. They discussed for a while where they could hide on the side yet still observe when the foot patrol went by so they could creep up behind them and cut through the fence. Philip was still guarding his wire cutters with nearly as much concern as his silenced Luger. He thought they might have a chance without the gun but the plan would never succeed without the cutters.

Geoffrey watched, fascinated, as several Fw190s took off. The acceleration on the ground and rapid rate of climb were hugely impressive.

"Bloody hell, Philip, that is one fast ship," he concluded. "It'll be a lightning trip home if you can really get me into one. I shall be down in The Jolly Sailor ogling Big Ada and thinking of you, still bobbing around in the water."

"You could more than ogle her you know, she really fancies you, old man. Christ knows why, when she could take her pick of 12 Commando, *me* in other words. But as we know, it's well nigh impossible to figure women out."

"You keep her, Philip, she'd probably suffocate me anyhow, but you know, I've always thought that women like Ada and the odd posh popsie would do for me, at least until the bloody war was over; but then, right out of the blue, I met the most incredibly perfect girl, so well built that she could have been designed by Mitchell! I think I've fallen in love. Never thought it could happen to me: fly, fuck, and forget was kind of my motto. The bad luck was that it all happened just about the time you came up with this crazy scheme of yours. It's occurred to me that all I may ever have of her is memories and that even they may be cut short, which, if you think about it, is really rather depressing."

By this time they had crept back into their hide again with Philip, as usual, carefully covering any signs of passage that he could discern and scattering some pepper around. Geoffrey couldn't imagine where he kept his seemingly endless supply.

"How'd you meet this dream child, Geoffrey? I'd just as soon listen to your ribald love life as talk about bloody aeroplanes."

"Well, by chance really. I'd gone down to a deb ball in London. Don't really like those things, getting all tarted up in a dinner jacket and looking like a poofter in the midst of a bunch of uniforms, but they're useful for meeting a sweet young thing who thinks she ought to do something for the war effort. I've always been very keen on encouraging such sentiments!"

At this point Philip really startled Geoffrey.

"I quite like poofters, you know."

"Oh Lord, no," muttered Geoffrey, feeling his body instinctively drawing away from Philip. "I had *no* idea; you'd be the *last* person I'd ever suspect."

"No, no," said Philip, laughing at the expression on Geoffrey's face. "I only like them because of the unique service they render the likes of me. Have you ever thought of them this way: the more poofters there are, the more popsies for me?"

"Ah, yes I see. Well, thank God for that," breathed Geoffrey, relieved.

"More about this bird who's clipped your wings please, Mr Fly Boy. She must be quite something."

"Something and everything, Philip. I even think she may love me, though I can scarcely believe my luck. She's really the only reason that I desperately want to survive this war and get back to England. She's going to be stationed near me soon, too, operating a radio-positioning system on the Isle of Wight."

Philip felt the slightest shiver of apprehension. Surely there was no way the gods of chance could have them both in love with the same girl.

"What's her name then, old boy, so I can look her up just in case I get back and you end up in some tall tower over here?"

"Clarissa."

For once the breath was completely knocked out of the Commando.

THIRTY THREE

Back in London at the RAF underground operations room at Bentley Priory, Air Marshal Sholto Douglas was in discussion with his top level staff.

"Tell me again now, when exactly is Penn supposed to attempt this steal, presuming the lunatics actually got there safely? God knows, I hope this thing works: we could really use some information on that German plane. It's kicking hell out of our lads, some are even avoiding flying over that part of France. If we could actually get our hands on one of them I'm sure the boys down at Eastleigh could figure out what we have to do to the Spit to at least equal things up a bit. We really don't have anything coming along in development that looks better than what Penn and the others tell us can still be done to upgrade our planes."

"We've got two more days strafing planned, sir. This morning went well; we got six Mosquitos over the field at just about 0500 hours; might even have damaged a couple of Focke-Wulfs but debriefing says they were in and out so fast that it's hard to assess any damage. What *is* a worry though, is the fact that the Germans got a couple of planes into the air almost immediately and only gave up the chase as they got close to our coast. If Penn gets off the ground it means they'll be right on his tail."

"Understood, but what can we do to help him? I don't want to alert the coastal defence yet and tell them not to shoot at anything, let's say between 0500 and 0800 two days from now. It's still possible for somebody to suspect something and leak it and for the bloody Germans to tighten up all their security. No, we've got to wait on that."

Keith Park, head of Fighter Group 11 covering all of south-east England, interrupted at that point.

"Well, we're assuming that Penn will fly to the nearest possible RAF field, which will likely be Manston, CharlieThree or Hawkinge. But maybe he'll pick up what he knows best and come right to Eastleigh; a lot will depend upon pursuit. He plans to keep it right on the deck to save time and to avoid pick up by either our radar or theirs. A bit dangerous, though, because there's bound to be a Spit or two out on patrol who could spot him and dive fast enough to catch up. Can we possibly also alert the fighter squadrons along this coast to let any single German plane through during that same time frame?"

"Yes, I don't see why not," answered Douglas. "Let's get hold of Ronald Adams. He's down at Hornchurch where Harry Broadhurst's in command; all the lads seem to trust him and know his voice. He's a damned sight better at being a flight controller than he was an actor, in my opinion! He could be briefed on this and he'll know enough to keep his mouth shut until it's needed. He could come out on all channels and I'm confident that he could shut everybody down for that period."

"Good idea, sir, I'll do that. We'll just have to assume that if Penn's not over England by 1000 at the latest on Thursday, that's two days from today, he won't ever be. He might well try Eastleigh because they put those balloons up and down very quickly and he flies through them pretty often. Somehow I doubt anyone else could manage that."

"If he comes that way Blackgang RAF station would, or at least could pick him up and we could try and keep our planes and ack-ack quiet in that area. I don't believe we can get the word to every single gun and aeroplane, those nuts on the ground are just as likely to shoot at one of ours as theirs. Luckily they can't hit shit, or so Penn once told me.

"The Fighter Controllers are damned good, though, and if the radar at Blackgang can pick up Penn, they'll probably be able to work out exactly where he's headed and then Adams, though he won't be able to contact Penn, will at least be able to talk to any pilot who's spotted the Focke-Wulf and talk him out of trying to be a hero. I can only imagine that some of the lads would be only too bloody pleased to be told to stay away from one of those!"

Sholto Douglas left after a few more minutes of planning talk about how best to get Penn back into England. His very presence in the room made Park and the others realize how critically important this mission was. There was no way for them to know that as they talked, two men lay huddled together under the base of an overturned tree thinking not of a Focke-Wulf at all, but solely of one woman.

THIRTY FOUR

Devastated, Philip knew that his Clarissa, the only woman who had ever truly touched his large but hitherto remote heart was, indeed, the same Clarissa that Geoffrey loved. He really didn't know what to say or do. Whatever else, he could not and must not let Geoffrey know he too loved Clarissa, or in any other way distract him from their mission. What they were trying to do was simply too important. Combined Ops would never let him risk upsetting Geoffrey during this operation, particularly after they had quietly told him that Penn was never to be captured. He, Quigley, was the temporary custodian of a national asset who was of vital importance to the overall war effort, which meant that this mission and its potential reward must be enormously significant. For all Philip's apparently casual attitude and love of adventure it would have been difficult to find any other person with as strong a sense of patriotism or greater determination to win the war, single-handedly if necessary. He knew he had to put this dreadful coincidence out of his mind, at least until they had either accomplished their task or died in the attempt.

Hoping to get both their minds off Clarissa he tried to steer the conversation back onto safer ground, any other ground.

"What are you planning to do with your life after this war, Geoffrey?"

"Well, if by any bloody miracle I survive this, I suppose I'll stay in aviation, it's probably the only thing I can do well enough to earn a living. What about you?"

"I don't really expect to survive it, even though it's cracking good fun. Where else could I spend other people's money blowing things up and travelling to lovely places? In fact, *if* I survive, I think the world will be a lot less interesting than I currently find it, so I'll probably bugger off to the Himalayas to live a quiet life with an obliging woman and a good book collection!

"Did you know, there's an old Tibetan theory that when you die you'll spend the rest of your reincarnation doing what you were doing at the moment you died, which is why I spend as much of my life fucking as I can!"

"You probably *will* get your arse blown off, Philip, you spend so much of your time testing the limits. I don't understand why you're still alive now. Tell me, honestly, did you ever think we could really get away with this?"

"Well no, not really, then you told me how bloody easy it would be to walk onto a Spitfire base and, providing the plane was running, get in and get away. At that point I thought, why the hell not, and what a lark to try! I suppose, though, in stud poker terms I would have said, odds against but possible. Now that we're here I'd say it's fifty-fifty."

"Strangely enough, Philip, now that I've met Miss Magic, fifty-fifty doesn't seem good enough. I want better odds than that." He paused and then said, "They do say that love replaces logic in your brain, so maybe we'd better run through our routine again."

Keen to stop Geoffrey talking any more about Clarissa, Philip was only too happy to get back to the mission. How the hell would he or could he stand another day of listening to Geoffrey rhapsodizing about the very woman he loved. He seriously doubted he could bear it. He knew damn well that, if Geoffrey didn't make it back and he did, he was going to pursue this girl; all's fair in love and war, that sort of thing. Maybe even if they both made it back. He knew that whatever Geoffrey said, Clarissa had felt something for him too: no response such as he had experienced could be purely physical. God, he'd better stop thinking about her too.

"Well, Geoffrey," he answered, pulling his mind back to the task in hand, "we'll set off as planned at first light. I'll go through the wire first; it doesn't seem to be alarmed or even barbed wire at the base, just chain link. And if I can get through the hole, there won't be any problem squeezing you through. In our black overalls we should be able to walk directly to the bunker area to the plane I've chosen. I'll climb up as though to talk to the chap warming it up, assuming there is a chap and he *is* warming it up, then I'll pop him and yank him out. If there's another blackman there I'll have to shoot him too, but with luck no-one else will see it going on. At this point you climb in."

Geoffrey nodded, visualizing the sequence of events.

"Right, I'll want as much time as possible to acquaint myself with the controls and system before I signal you to pull out the accumulator plug which, if you remember, will be hooked up to the plane to start it. You'll also have to pull the chocks, again on my signal. It's damn lucky for us that the Germans are so methodical, I suspect that the systems will be very much like the Messerschmitt."

"How so?"

"Well, for example, water lines green, air lines blue, fuel yellow, oil brown and so forth."

"That prompts me to remind you of the old Commando saying that the colour of fear is brown!"

"Very funny, Philip. Fact is, I'm already scared shitless."

Suddenly shooting out an arm Philip clamped his hand over Geoffrey's mouth while raising a finger to his own lips. Geoffrey's eyes widened and, heart hammering, he listened to the barking of a dog as it approached their hide. As they peered through the branches and roots they could see two figures a few yards behind the dog, one holding a gun. There was no way the approaching patrol could possibly miss them. Geoffrey could feel Philip move ever so slightly as he eased the Luger from the holster behind his back and again as he slipped back the cocking mechanism.

The dog seemed to have heard even that faint noise and stopped, pointing directly at them but no longer barking. The still indistinct figures had stopped also. Geoffrey didn't dare breathe, although he did notice that Philip, crouching slightly behind him, was breathing calmly. What Geoffrey could not see was that Philip, while focusing intently on what was outside the hide, had the Luger pointed directly at the back of Geoffrey's head.

The Commando was clearly and methodically assessing the situation. He knew he could probably kill both of the enemy and the dog before they themselves started shooting, but what if he didn't? Could he afford to let Penn get captured? No, he could not, but they'd made it this far. Could he take the patrol out and then they attempt the snatch now? It seemed to him that he had about forty seconds left in which to make up his mind. Killing Penn was not an option, not yet, he decided, and even then it would be the last thing he ever did.

As he slowly shifted the pistol away from Geoffrey he let out an almost audible sigh of relief. He could hear the approaching duo speaking French; a couple of hunters probably looking to supplement their evening meal. But, how to avoid getting shot if he stepped out? They would be seen as soon as the dog homed in.

"Achtung!" he roared, leaping through the branches, Luger in hand. Geoffrey was not sure whether he or the two Frenchmen were more frightened but both of them threw their hands in the air.

"Non! Non!" Even the dog cowered in the face of this gun-wielding giant in black overalls appearing out of nowhere.

Geoffrey, whose heart was beating as hard as it had the last time he had bailed out of a spinning aeroplane, stayed put as Philip approached the terrified Frenchmen. It was now clear that they were a farmer and a boy, not a German patrol. He could see that Philip had lowered his gun and was now talking French rapidly to the farmer who, though white-faced and obviously shaken, was at least nodding his head. After some minutes they all calmed down and he even saw Philip clap the man on the back, gently he hoped: Philip stood a good foot taller than the Frenchman.

As Philip returned to the hide, the pair and dog retraced their way back through the wood, which was at least in the opposite direction to the field.

"What in the hell did you tell them, Philip? I thought the older man was going to faint when you lunged out at him."

"Surprise is a great asset. They thought, of course, that I was a German and that scared them a lot more than what I subsequently told them, which was that a shot-down British pilot needed Underground help to get back home.

I don't think they ever saw you so I just said I was alone. They said the Germans let them hunt in the woods but they, the Hun, sometimes come in here too, so we were lucky it was the Frogs. The old man said he had contact with the Underground and that he'd come back tomorrow with some food and advice. I'll fill you in later but right now I'm going to follow them and find out just where the farm is. It could be useful later. You stay put and I'll be back shortly."

With that he was gone, again moving almost silently through the woods in the direction the pair had taken. Geoffrey was still wondering how much more of this he could take when, just as silently as he had left an hour or so before, Philip returned and squeezed into the hole.

"What's the plan?" Penn asked. "Is it really a good idea to have them come back tomorrow? I wouldn't mind a nice bit of food but I must admit that I'm already a nervous wreck and don't really think that having two Frenchmen around is going to help much. Seems to me that the more movement in the woods, the more likely it is that somebody is going to get interested."

"I'll make a Commando of you yet, old boy. Now listen, all plans have changed; you're off tomorrow morning instead of the day after."

"What? Why?" Penn felt panic rising in his throat. "Does that make sense, Philip? Much as I'd like to get out of this horrible hole, we have a scheduled strafe early tomorrow. There's also the question of the RAF and the shore batteries. They will have been alerted not to shoot down a lone Focke-Wulf on Thursday morning but tomorrow, for God's sake, tomorrow, they'll shoot at anything with a swastika."

"I know, and I'm sorry, Geoffrey, but any good plan has to be flexible and at this point I'm still in charge, so there it is."

"But why, in heaven's name, change at this point? Everything has gone so well up 'till now."

"Quite true, old boy, but Uncle Philip's sixth sense, which has kept me alive so far, tells me that any Frog who has permission to hunt and keep a gun can't be regarded as worrisome to the Germans; ergo, he must be quite worrisome to us. Therefore, it seems to me that we can't jeopardize what has gone so well thus far. Are we certain the old man would contact the Underground and not the Germans? We simply can't take the chance."

"So...what happened back there, then, Philip? What are you telling me? What's making us change the plan?"

"I'm afraid they've become casualties of war, the dog too, and as I didn't have much time to hide the bodies in the barn, somebody is bound to look for them, find them and then the balloon will go up. We're probably all right until tomorrow morning, but not much longer than that."

"Oh God, he was just a boy, that lad."

"Geoffrey, try to think of it this way. What you're going to do tomorrow will probably save a lot more fine lads. As you said the other day, war is not a nice game, and I agree it was rotten bad luck they wandered by here, but you also agreed that the French are not always on our side, even now, and I'm pretty certain that old chap was not. The boy was, I'm afraid, just another of the many sons who have been and will be killed in this war. Now, let's stop pissing and moaning and get on with our war. Maybe the weather won't let the RAF come over tomorrow; one bit of bad luck often brings a bit of good."

And with that the Commando turned and stared out through the branches at the darkening wood.

THIRTY FIVE

The take-off had gone unbelievably well, practically no-one about and only the mechanic in the next bunker seeming to notice Geoffrey taxi-ing. He had nosed the plane into the wind and suddenly opened the throttle and was now looking good, flying fifty feet off the water on course for England. Geoffrey was just thinking how incredibly easy it had been when suddenly he felt his blood chill and heart race. Christ, a string of water-spouts getting closer by the second. Somebody was above him and on his tail and in an instant he would be hit. He couldn't care less if it were friend or foe but right now somebody was about to shoot him into the sea!

He feinted a quick turn to the right, toward the incoming fire, then suddenly pulled the control stick hard to the left together with full rudder and, already at full power, the Focke-Wulf slammed into a high speed turn which nearly caused Geoffrey to faint for lack of blood in his head due to the incredible G-force exerted. As he felt the plane start to shudder he realized he might have over-cooked it by turning too tight, though he thought a Spit could have done it. The waves were terrifyingly close and then, oh shit, the port wing tip just touched a wave and in seconds he was cart-wheeling on the surface before coming to rest upside down. Geoffrey felt the water coming into the cockpit and knew it was all over. Oh God, to have come this far and get this close. How could he have stalled?

"Philip," he cried out. "Philip, we tried. We did try."

"Geoffrey! Geoffrey! Wake up and for God's sake shut up," he heard as he fought for breath against the huge hand clamped over his mouth. "You've had a bad dream and you're making enough noise to alert the Boche! Apparently things weren't going well. Anyway, it's four o'clock, you might as well wake up; in an hour we'll approach the field. Is it safe to take my hand away now?"

"Good God, Philip, I dreamt I'd gone in and was drowning. Ghastly. Must have been your fat hand suffocating me; worse than bloody drowning

I should imagine. Not that I think today is going to be any better than that dream. I feel absolutely exhausted and the day has hardly started."

"Let's eat what we've got left," suggested Quigley as he unwrapped some rations. "It could be the last meal for a while and I suggest you try having a good crap too, if you haven't already, that is. You scared me good and proper, bellowing like that."

As they ate dry biscuits and a couple of chocolate bars, washing it down with water, Geoffrey listened to Philip go over the entry plan again. Geoffrey was to follow Philip and, as the big man firmly reiterated, make absolutely *no* noise. Once inside the perimeter fence they would stand up and casually walk towards the chosen plane, hoping to make whomever was there warming it up think they were there to ask a question. As Philip approached the mechanic, who would probably be in the cockpit, Geoffrey would walk over to the starter accumulator assembly and, if he thought the plane was ticking over warmly enough, he would disengage the apparatus himself. As soon as the mechanic was dead and on the ground Geoffrey would climb in, look quickly at the set up then signal Philip to pull the chocks when he thought he had located the essential controls, in particular the all-important throttle. All this was to be done with hand signals on the assumption that the engine would drown out any conversation.

"Philip, we've got to go as early as we can to try and be away before the RAF comes over to strafe. The last thing I need is to be taking off just as those lads arrive. Nothing would please them more than to pop a 190 on take-off, a sitting duck in their minds! If the RAF have been asked to let a single German plane go through at dawn, it's dawn *tomorrow* they have in mind, not today. Are you absolutely sure we shouldn't wait a day, in spite of the risk of an alarm being raised?"

Quigley shook his head.

"I think the odds are a little better this way. I can never stand waiting for something which might happen; I prefer to make it happen. Now, from what

I've heard about you, you should be able to keep out of everyone's way, and you tell me it's only about twenty minutes to get you home."

"Well, you're probably right. I'm not sure either my brain or my body could stand another night in that hole just thinking about what was coming. Surprise must be the biggest element on our side right now. But wouldn't it be just bloody awful to get the prize all the way back to Merry Olde and then get shot down by one of ours? Bad enough to have the Huns pissed off and on my arse but to be greeted by Spits and Hurricanes and ack-ack is not a cheery thought. *If* I actually do get the plane back there I'm going to put it down on the first piece of English green I see that's flat and five hundred yards long, get out and run like hell!"

"Hmm, yes, I've been thinking about that, Geoffrey, and it poses a bit of a problem. Now, tell me if my maths is wrong. You say it takes approximately twenty minutes to fly about ninety miles?"

"That's the most it should take, figuring slower take-off and landing speeds and assuming that this plane is at least as fast as a Spit, which it is purported to be, maybe even faster."

"OK. And how long can one of these fighters stay in the air before they're out of juice?"

"As long as a piece of string in some respects, because it varies all over the place depending on speed, altitude, attitude, armament load and so on. But in a Spit, for example, at cruise you can get a couple of hours and cover over five hundred miles; the Messerschmitt 109 we tested has less range. A big advantage was fighting over our own land and over our own airfields because the Krauts often had to break off engagements and piss off home for more fuel. To get up to twenty-five thousand feet takes a Spit about ten minutes, same for the 109, so that alone uses up nearly twenty percent of the fuel. Now, if you have a dog-fight in this period, at full throttle and especially on super-charger boost, the fuel consumption goes up enormously. What's all this in aid of, anyway?"

"Well, old chap, if the Boche gets off the ground and chases you, and you saw how quickly they can do that when those Mosquitos came over, you'll both be going flat out. But it's occurred to me that when they get to England, if you actually get to land the plane they'll try and make damn sure that it's shot up and hopefully burned, and what better place for that than on the ground? What a pity to get it there only to watch it go up in smoke. So, I think you'd better play cat and mouse until you can at least see home and they'll be running low on fuel. And by that time they'll probably have to deal with the RAF too."

"Philip, my friend, though actually I don't know why I should call you a friend considering what you've got me into, I think you're right. I'm not going to be able to just drop in on some friendly field for the reasons you say. I've got to stay up and avoid them while they burn up their fuel. Then, when *they're* gone, I'll have to avoid the RAF as well, who will no doubt be wondering what in hell's going on. I'm going to run out of fuel too, but a bit later because they'll have to keep twenty minutes-worth on board to get back to France. It's going to be a merry old time for one and all. I'm hoping though, if I *do* get away and they *do* catch up, I can make it so confusing for them that they allow me to escape. One thing is certain, it's not going to be boring!"

Their final plans were as complete as they could make them. A great deal of time had been spent discussing various scenarios and how they might be dealt with, but few had any obvious solutions. It was going to be a situation to be played by ear, but each man felt confident of his ability, if only they could get far enough to do it.

At dawn, quietly wishing each other good luck and briefly shaking hands, they left the hide and moved slowly through the gradually lightening wood, towards the field. The northernmost end of the wood, the Bois de Blanqueville, ended about four hundred yards from the road they had to cross. There was then a similar distance to the actual field and runway. The perimeter fence at this point, where they planned to cut through, was only just off the road and the nearest to the field at any point. The plan was to lie low in the wood until after the morning guard went by, which they hoped would be soon after they arrived, then make their way across the road to the fence. As it seemed to take the guard just under an hour to make a full circuit of the fence, they calculated that it probably had a perimeter of about three miles.

Even moving at their slowest and most cautious pace it only required about fifteen minutes for them to reach their position at the end of the wood, where Philip had previously hidden and watched the planes and guards. Some lights were already on at the field and Geoffrey was delighted to hear the unmistakable sound of a large engine being turned over by its accumulator starter, then catch and rev up on its own. He thought he heard two, then at least three, start ups as they waited for the perimeter guards to appear.

"Christ," muttered Quigley, "I hope we haven't just missed the bastards. If so, we'll have to sit tight for at least another half an hour."

"Agreed," whispered Geoffrey, who was calculating that the mechanics would only warm up the planes for about ten minutes. After they were checked out and declared ready to fly they would then be turned off. The absolute requirement in his mind had always been that the plane would be running and ready, otherwise the whole plan was a no-hoper.

The sky was still quite dark although streaks of colour from the rising sun were beginning to appear on the horizon to their right. A beautiful morning, Geoffrey thought, gazing at the sky, to be almost anywhere but here.

A jab in the ribs brought his attention sharply back to the present. Philip was pointing to the left where two troopers strolled along the fence, a playful dog cavorting with morning energy a few yards in front of them. They were at least six hundred yards away so neither man worried too much about being spotted. It was up to Philip to decide when the guards had gone far enough past their position to allow them to pass behind, unseen. As the guards turned the corner at the runway end on the north leg of their patrol, Philip motioned for Geoffrey to follow him and they quickly crossed the road to lie low in the tall grass on the other side before starting a slow crawl towards the fence.

After five minutes on their hands and knees they reached the perimeter fence where Philip quickly started cutting through the chain-mail fencing, having first carefully looked for electric wires. Geoffrey's only thought at this point, while listening to the reassuring roar of plane engines, was that their mission to date had already been more trouble than in his dream. In fact, he felt as though he was still dreaming but knew he was not as Philip pushed away a flap big enough for them to pass through. Carefully pushing it back again after Geoffrey had crawled through, he scattered some more of his faithful pepper all around the area.

"Remember, this may be my way out," he half-mimed, half-whispered, "and let's hope I can get away before the boys come around again! Okay, move it. Stand up now and follow me towards that earth bunker. There's our baby and she's ticking over nicely!"

THIRTY SIX

The very evening before Philip and Geoffrey were strolling, as casually as adrenaline would allow, towards the dark rumbling silhouette, several events had been taking place in England which would heavily influence their chances of success.

At Blackgang, Clarissa was being instructed for her first full day of manning the Radio Detection equipment. Blackgang had become increasingly important as more German raiders made both bomber and fighter attacks on the vital Portsmouth naval area and the production facilities of Southampton. Clarissa's job, and that of her colleagues, was to try and pick up the direction and number of any incoming aircraft and pass this information back to Fighter Command Headquarters, via the Filter Room at Bentley Priory. There, the reports would be sorted and combined with reports from the other stations, thereby providing the information necessary for controllers to determine how many fighters to put up to intercept and, more importantly, where they should go to intercept. Ideally the pilots wanted enough notice to get airborne and above the enemy in order to attack in the classic 'out of the sun' position. Once the enemy had passed the coast it was up to the Observer Corps to identify and, by telephone line, advise the control centre of the number, type and direction of the threat. Thus it was especially important that the Radio Direction Finders at stations such as Blackgang provide as much early warning as possible, particularly for places such as Southampton and Portsmouth where the target was on the coast.

To become aware of the enemy at the time they arrived was, in fact, far too late. Recently there had been a number of raids by as few as two fighter aircraft, sometimes carrying bombs as well. They seldom stayed in the area long, but rather seemed designed to be a sort of harassment aimed at picking up any stray British aircraft which happened to be in the vicinity. These raids also served to keep the local population unnerved.

Clarissa learned that friendly aircraft had an identifying signal transmitted at regular intervals, called a pip-squeak or, more formally, IFF, Identification Friend or Foe, which quickly sorted out friend or foe, at least until any battle started, after which point it became totally confusing. The system worked fairly well for aircraft flying below fifteen thousand feet, but grew steadily less reliable above twenty thousand feet, where many air battles took place. The most important thing was to give as much warning time as possible to the Fighter Defence Units. Clarissa felt excited at being entrusted with such a vital job and was looking forward to discussing her new work with Geoffrey. She wanted to tell him that she'd even met Keith Park, who was in charge of all fighter units in the south-east of England and who had visited Blackgang, giving a little pep talk about how important and necessary their work was.

At Fighter Command Headquarters in Uxbridge, Park was discussing with his staff the planned strafing of the Cherbourg airport, Maupertus. This time it was to be done at daybreak with three Blenheims accompanied by six Spitfires. The reason for the extra support for the bombers was because of their relatively slow speed as compared with the Mosquito. He hoped that a fast in and out run would get them away and almost home before the Focke-Wulfs could get airborne. Again, they were to come in at wave top, actually having to rise up a few feet to clear the shore at the airport and avoid Radar Detection whilst en route. He knew it would be a disaster if the Germans detected them in advance and the Focke-Wulfs were airborne high and waiting to attack.

"Gentlemen," Sir Keith was saying, "a few of you know what this mission is all about but, for those who don't, I'll summarize quickly. The day after tomorrow, at dawn and all being well, we will have two men about to enter the German airfield at Cherbourg. They have been hiding in a wood nearby for these past two days. We trust and pray that they got there and that they're still alive. Their mission, gentlemen, is to steal a Focke-Wulf aircraft, the one that, quite frankly, has been giving us such a pasting lately, and fly it back here for evaluation."

There were some gasps from the assembled men. Park nodded gravely and continued.

"Our pilot needs a running aircraft, so we're strafing the field each morning at the same time to try and ensure that they'll have at least a few planes warmed up and ready to give chase. This morning we're going to escort the Blenheims, sending them in from just off Calais where they will turn south at sea level and attempt to sneak in over the field undetected. Six Spits will accompany them. I had to promise that to Bomber Command before they would approve the use of the Blenheims. Naturally I was not able to provide them with any details of this mission. At this stage I would like to remind you that none of this information should leave this room.

"I've asked Roland Adams to join us here today because he will be key to making sure we don't shoot down our own man should he, by some miracle, actually pull this off. Roland has the best-known voice of any of our controllers and, as we know, is the most respected. If his voice is heard, it's my belief our chaps will believe that what they're hearing is true and not some German stunt. We have far too many incidents of shooting down our own planes as it is, without claiming this very special one. No solo German plane en route this way is to be shot at between 0500 and 1000 hours the day after tomorrow. No reasons need be given and do not issue this order until tomorrow pm. Is that clear? Good.

"There's a plane standing by at Denham to take Roland back to Hornchurch immediately, and the rest of you can get back to your jobs. Let's pray this caper works because we're using a lot of resources to make it happen, and I have a feeling my old friend, Leigh-Mallory, would love to see me stub my toe on this one!

"Right, gentlemen, off you go and let's keep our fingers crossed."

THIRTY SEVEN

Sauntering casually across the field toward the powerfully throbbing plane, Geoffrey and Philip could see two blackmen at work. As they approached the bunkered area Geoffrey's feverishly working mind deduced that the earthworks on either side of the plane were open on two ends to allow the planes to be taxied in rather than pushed in backwards. Another German efficiency, he mused, but that did mean leaving two ends exposed to bomb shrapnel or strafing, rather than one. He also noticed that the accumulator's umbilical was still attached to the plane, standing solidly on its wheel-base, markedly wider than either the Spit or the Gustav, as the ME109 was called. Another great improvement, thought Geoffrey as they strolled towards the mechanic on the ground.

The other blackman was inside the plane, absorbed in the instruments and unaware of their approach. The noise from the engine made conversation impossible. Philip started gesticulating to the man on the ground while he continued to move forward. Geoffrey suddenly saw the mechanic's expression change from friendly enquiry to one of shock, pain and disbelief as he grabbed his chest and slumped forward.

Geoffrey hadn't heard the silenced Luger and was himself shocked at seeing the dead mechanic at their feet but Philip, in one fluid motion, was past Geoffrey and on the side of the plane, one foot on the step and a hand on the side of the open cockpit. The second mechanic poked his head up to see who had arrived, just in time to get a round from the Luger in the forehead. Geoffrey watched from below as Philip calmly pocketed the automatic and, with two massive arms, lifted the mechanic's body right out of the cockpit and let it drop to the ground, narrowly missing the horrified Geoffrey.

As quickly as Philip descended, Geoffrey was up and into a brand new but thankfully familiar environment, an aeroplane rather than a foxhole. He looked over at Philip who had pulled the two bodies out of the way and, having quickly checked forward of the bunker, gave Geoffrey a thumbs up sign and even a big smile. Unbelievable, the bugger is actually enjoying this, thought Geoffrey as he turned back to the instrument panel to see how this plane might differ from any other German craft he'd flown.

His eye immediately noted the throttle on the left and it looked like the radio equipment was on that side too, which was the opposite of the Messerschmitt, not that he'd be able to use the radio, he thought. Throttle, compass, flaps, supercharger, that's all he really needed to get up and away, and then, with luck, time to sort out a bit more. Like getting the wheels up, he thought anxiously. Fuel gauge would be bloody important too, and how on earth would he change tanks if he had to?

As his eyes darted around the well organized cockpit his right hand instinctively moved to the control stick which he manoeuvred forward and back, left and right, ensuring no overnight locking devices had been inserted in the tail-plane or elevators. No, thank God, everything moved like silk. He was sure he'd spotted the under-carriage electric switch too, not far from where he knew it was to be found on the 109. He'd hate like hell to try and fly, let alone fight, with the wheels down all the way home.

The thought of home made him turn and look down at Philip who was waving frantically and pointing, of all places, upwards! Christ! The RAF had arrived and was overhead shooting up the field. Looking forward, Geoffrey could see people sprinting towards the planes, including his. He shouted and waved at Philip to pull the accumulator hose free and then the chocks. He'd give himself twenty seconds for Philip to do this then take off, over the chocks if he had to and even pull loose from the hose, but he was fairly sure Philip would take care of it, even if they were the last things he ever did.

A quick glance over the right shoulder down at Philip produced another grin, another thumbs-up. Geoffrey shoved the throttle forward giving compensating right rudder to avoid the tail moving off line due to the enormous engine torque. He practically ran over the approaching pilot who looked totally bewildered as Geoffrey shot past, concentrating on nothing except trying to find a space to take off and avoid hitting anything en route. He could see the ground being chewed up by bullets from the planes overhead; it seemed like bedlam, which was fine by him for it would mean, at least for a few vital seconds, that the Germans would assume he was just a very quick pilot who had got airborne ahead of the rest. He imagined that Philip, thoroughly enjoying himself, had beckoned the confused pilot towards him, ostensibly to explain why some other pilot had taken his plane, and then shot him before walking calmly back towards his entry hole in the fence. Geoffrey had begun to believe that the Commando was either fearless or insane and quite possibly both. All these thoughts shot through his mind as he taxied as fast as he dared toward the north end of the runway where he could get the longest run possible to take off. He thought he might have to get airborne without flaps as he hadn't had time to locate where to activate these, though he suspected the switch or lever would be very near the under-carriage button. The Focke-Wulf felt good on the ground, showing no tendency to ground-loop, but Geoffrey, with no parachute under him, was a bit low in the laid- back seat and was forced to sit upright and keep swinging the tail in order to see ahead.

As he arrived at the end of the longest runway, from what he remembered of the photos, he could see ground personnel shouting and waving. He wasn't sure whether he'd been rumbled or whether they were encouraging him to get up there and give the Tommies hell. No matter, all he wanted to do was to get off. He'd tighten his safety harness later but right now he pushed on the left rudder pedal and what he presumed to be the brake and pushed the throttle slowly forward as he turned and pointed the grey-green aeroplane down the unlit runway. Then, full throttle, the plane seemed to leap ahead, requiring quite a lot of torque correction and thrilling Geoffrey with the astonishing acceleration. As he shot down the runway he could feel the plane trying to lift off the ground. The slipstream in his face reminded him to close the canopy which seemed to be operated by a wheel and handle on his right.

As he looked at this he could see on the low eastern horizon three Spitfires making a wide, wide turn, obviously planning to knock him down just as he became airborne.

"Not bloody likely," he yelled at them, heart pounding and adrenaline surging, "not having got this far."

He was airborne now, after what seemed like no time at all and, pushing the under-carriage button he'd found on his left, he felt the speed build up again as the wheels came up and the inboard indicators signalled that all was flush. He was still climbing at about two hundred and fifty kilometers per hour, which felt pretty good, when he again spotted the Spits ahead and off to the right turning in towards him. Because he was still climbing they had the speed advantage, so Geoffrey knew the best option would be to do the unexpected. He looked around and saw no-one behind him; the cockpit visibility was excellent, but there seemed to be no rear-view mirror so he turned back in his seat to face the rapidly on-coming Spits who, at about five hundred yards, had started shooting, the gun flashes very clear in the dawn light.

While climbing and relatively slow, he presented a prime target, but he believed they had started shooting much too far away. He suddenly dropped the nose and, still at full throttle, drove directly at and below the startled Spitfires who broke away into tight turns to try and follow. I'm well away from you, my lads, thought Geoffrey, again at wave top and now, flying at well over four hundred kilometres per hour, he thought he could try and climb again. So far the plane was extraordinary: he already felt united with it, as though it was a fine race horse, anticipating his next move.

As he turned north and east, back towards England, he passed nearby the airfield and looking down to his right he could see all sorts of activity. The Blenheim bombers were making a second pass, probably on their way home, and several Focke-Wulfs were airborne trying to avoid the Spits who were furiously protecting the bombers. For a moment Geoffrey wondered if he could just break for home and hope to get there before the Germans rumbled him, but immediately realized this couldn't happen. The Focke-Wulfs were ignoring the Spitfires and were heading directly upwards towards him. They were onto him and they were angry.

Geoffrey had surmised more or less correctly: the RAF attack had occurred slightly before the Germans were ready, for their radar had not picked up the incoming flight until they rose up at the coast near Calais and turned south towards Maupertus. At this point all the fighter fields down the coast as far as Cherbourg had been put on alert to get some defenders airborne. They, of course, did not know which airfields might be targeted, but suspected the goal was one of the fields with Focke-Wulfs, those being, the Germans knew, a very nasty thorn in the British lion's paw. In Maupertus the pilots were just heading towards their aircraft when the Brits appeared overhead and had Geoffrey and Philip been even a few minutes later their plan would have gone terribly wrong. In war there is probably as much good luck as bad and so far the luck for the mission was good. But at this point things began to dramatically change.

Philip had indeed seen the approaching pilot duck as his own plane nearly ran him over, then run towards Philip, shouting.

"Auf was das Bumsen geht?"

Philip assumed this could be roughly translated as, 'What the fuck is going on?' As the pilot approached the end of the bunker he saw the two bodies on the ground with the large man looming over them. Swiftly realizing that, as the best turn in the air was a hundred and eighty degrees, he'd better do the same on the ground; he turned, ran and dived just as Philip shot. Philip took a look, saw no movement, and thought it would be a good time to amble, or perhaps run, back to the escape hole and play soldier no longer. Moving away from the chaotic field, Philip failed to notice the wounded pilot struggle to his feet and stagger into the next plane bunker to alert the field.

Major Assi Hahn was already at the field and to him the news of this act of piracy was worse than any strafing, especially with Hermann Goering asleep not twelve kilometres away. "My God," he shouted at a hapless junior officer, "what could be more horrendous than this?"

The full alert against the air raid was quickly converted to an order to shoot down that Focke-Wulf at all and any cost. Immediately after the order had been amended Assi knew that as a first-rate and loyal officer he had to call his supreme commander to give him the news, no matter how bad.

Goering's reaction was much as Hahn had expected: three minutes of shouting, screaming, threatening and then cool, precise planning.

"Assi, this is an unmitigated disaster. We will discuss later how to reprimand security and punish those responsible, even if that includes you. Meanwhile, call Galland at Abbeville and tell him to get airborne, along with anybody else he can muster, and follow the bastard all the way to England. Kill him and make damn sure there is nothing left of the plane. Be sure to tell him the plane's number. I'm sure the bastard is British, that's just the sort of trick they like to pull. Who else would do it anyway? If the French stole it they'd still have to fly it to England. Just get him - I don't care how. The British *must not* get the plane. Assi, do you understand me? Good! Now get going and keep me informed. I do not - I repeat do *not* - want to have to bother the Fuhrer about this matter. I am confident you will resolve this."

Ashen-faced, Assi Hahn did as he was told. He had in fact already done all he could in identifying the plane. It had a large number seven clearly visible on its side. All his planes capable of flying were airborne and in chase, with unambiguous orders, even the instruction to ram it if they couldn't shoot it down. He felt sure that any one of his ace pilots could oblige. He hadn't thought of informing Galland, however, and he had to admit that was a good idea. Abbeville had mostly 109s, but they were also warmed up and even closer to England than Maupetus. Though if Galland himself claimed the victory, thought Hahn with a grimace, that would really get up my nose. That would really sting.

THIRTY EIGHT

Philip turned and walked as casually as he could back to his hole in the wire. Behind him the field was in uproar. At the moment it appeared as though all the energy was being directed towards the renegade plane, but Philip figured there would soon be a full scale search, especially if the pilot he'd shot was not dead and could remember much of what had happened. All this meant he had to get out of his black overalls as soon as possible, into French clothes and under a beret. It was quite light by now and his huge form would be all too easily noticed if seen walking away in a German blackman's clothes.

He found the hole in the fence without difficulty and turned for the first time to look back. So far, so good, just a lot of chaotic running and shouting. He lay down in the tall grass and tore off the overalls before crawling to the hole from which he emerged looking something akin to a French farmer, albeit an unusually large one. His next move was to walk a few yards up to the road where he stopped, hands on hips, looking up at the violent fight going on overhead, just as he was sure any local peasant would do in the circumstances.

And, by God, what a fight. He hadn't a clue which plane Geoffrey was flying, but it was clear that there was one hell of a ruck going on not too far above the field out towards the sea.

"Well done, Geoffrey, you clever old bugger," he chuckled, then thought, right, no more English for the next few days, even to myself. He needed to hide the overalls as soon as possible. He wanted to give himself some time, if challenged, to explain who he was and where he was going. There was no hope of that if he still carrying such an incriminating piece of evidence, and not with the Luger either, but at least that was hidden in a back holster. He was sure the Germans would work out that it took two or more men to pull off this stunt, even if there were no living witnesses. Being German, they would immediately start a highly intensive search.

He'd given a lot of thought about walking to Cherbourg where he also knew of a safe house, this one only seven miles away as well as being in a much bigger town than St. Vaast-la-Hougue. But he presumed that was just what the Germans would expect so opted for the smaller town where, though he would stand out if seen, he could probably stay holed up until he could get his hands on a boat. He therefore turned and ambled east down the road.

A truck full of soldiers came roaring towards him; far too many to handle if they stopped, but they ignored him and sped on past towards the field. By this time the aerial dog fight had moved further out to sea and Philip could not see any British planes. German aircraft continued to take-off from the field, now half a mile behind him. He'd keep the overalls under his shirt until he got to Hameau Valognes, the same little hamlet which he and Geoffrey had passed through at night only three nights before.

As he walked through, the same dog barked again. Philip would never know that as he sat down by the bridge, ostensibly to rest, he was only a mile from where Hermann Goering was anxiously awaiting news from Assi Hahn. Had he known, Philip would very likely have changed his plans and had a go at Goering. Instead, after taking a quick but careful look around he removed the overalls from under his shirt and stuffed them up under a beam in the bridge before moving on. He went unchallenged on these small roads, the verges of which were crowded with wild flowers giving off their heady scent. In such glorious and peaceful surroundings it was hard to believe a significant war event was taking place. Ever practical, the scent in the air reminded Philip to thank himself for once again throwing lots of pepper around his escape hole in the wire. He'd also initially turned the opposite way to his destination when he'd come back through the fence, and started to walk towards Cherbourg before looping back, hoping to fool any dogs that were in any case likely to lose the scent on the tarmac. The one farmer Philip met asked him, in a conversational way, where he was headed. Hoping his accent wouldn't betray him, Philip told him he was from Cherbourg and going to St. Vaast-la-Hougue, looking for a job. This had apparently been enough to satisfy the farmer and he continued his walk, finally reaching the edge of the small fishing village about half past eight that eventful morning. The house he sought was down near the port - 18 Rue de Rois.

His six foot-four frame standing outside a strange door was enough to intimidate anyone, so he stood well back and down off the step after he knocked, hoping that any nosey neighbours were otherwise occupied. Not having any idea of what to expect, he was pleased to be greeted by a tall and attractive dark-haired Frenchwoman who appeared to be somewhere between thirty-five and forty years old.

In his best, but doubtless curious-sounding French accent, Philip asked if this were the residence of Henri Dominic and, if so, did he have any oysters to sell?

"I am Madame Dominic and please, come in quickly, for oysters go off quickly in the sun."

"Thank you, Madame. That information about the oysters reassures me that I have reached the right house, and I very much need your husband's help. May I speak with him please?"

"You can, of course, but not until late tonight, as he's away fishing. You'd better stay here until he returns; there are not many French here who look like you, I must say. Can you tell me what you need and when and, if not, perhaps why?"

"I certainly can tell you some of the answers, but may I say that I'm pleased to find a person here as charming as you. It's a pleasant surprise for a wandering Englishman! I'm sure you'll soon hear that there has been a problem at Maupertus airport and the Boche are very annoyed. What I would like is to get out of your house quickly, so as not to jeopardize you and your husband's safety, and find a means to get back to England. A boat would probably be best. Hopefully Henri can help. He has come highly recommended and is much admired for all he has already done."

"We will do anything to get the pigs out of our country. I'm sure Henri will help you, as he has others. Meanwhile, let's decide where best to hide you if we have to. You know there is a garrison stationed here, primarily to patrol the coastline?"

"Yes, I managed to avoid them coming here and I just hope it's as easy leaving."

Philip was beginning to relax now that he was safely off the road and in the company of this lovely Frenchwoman. For once, he thought, the intelligence service had got it right. Pity about there being a husband, though.

The afternoon passed pleasantly and Philip even had a short nap, something unusual for him, though he calculated he hadn't had more than four hours sleep a night since they'd landed in France. He knew that by this time Geoffrey was either home and safe or, and this was sadly more likely, dead.

"Bloody good effort in any event," he muttered, half awake.

"Qu'est-ce que vous avez dit?"

"Rien. J'espère que mon ami est rentre sauf en Angleterre, c'est tout."

Marie had the sense not to ask further questions. These days, and especially in her circumstances, often the less you knew the better. She only knew she and her patriot husband would help this big, amiable Englishman all they could. Whatever he had done must have been worth some risk. They would take theirs.

Two huge bowls of garlic soup and half a French loaf later, Philip began to feel his old self. Comfortable as he now was he could not stay long in this small town, much less walk about. A stranger in a town this size was news, especially one with an odd accent and towering a foot above most of the sturdy villagers.

"What time do you expect your husband back?"

"Towards dark," Marie replied over her shoulder. She rinsed the last plate and set it to dry in the rack before continuing. "That's probably half past ten at this time of year. He usually stops in the bar for a brandy with his friends after he's put the boat to bed. Sometimes I think he prefers the bar and the boat to me!"

"Not bloody likely," came Philip's indignant retort. "He's a lucky man."

"I wasn't fishing! He is the one that does that."

Their quiet laughter was suddenly interrupted by a knock on the door. Instantly, Philip was on his feet, Luger drawn. Marie was calm and pointed towards the rear of the cottage.

"Probably only a neighbour to keep me company," she whispered. "Just go into the bed chamber to the right of the fireplace. I'll handle this."

Philip knew she would not have had an opportunity to betray him, but possibly he had been seen entering the house, quiet as the street had seemed. He thought about how inquisitive small town neighbours are and wondered if he should have gone to Cherbourg after all.

"Entrez, Angelique."

Philip relaxed slightly, but listened carefully with his ear to the bedroom door. Angelique's voice was low and urgent.

"Marie, something has happened to the Germans at the airport, something that has got them into a dreadful state and they're starting to search every house in the village. I thought I'd better tell you in case you had something lying around you'd rather they didn't see."

Marie wondered if perhaps Angelique was aware of their sympathies, or even her guest.

"Merci, Angelique, you are indeed well named, though I can't imagine what they'd find interesting here. They did this before, some months back, but at least they were polite."

"I must get home to the children now, Marie, a bientôt. Sometimes I think you're lucky not to have any children to grow up in this nasty world. Do you think it will ever end?"

Philip heard the front door close. He put his head around the bedroom door and saw Marie looking anxious.

"Do you have a good place for me to hide or shall I leave now?"

"You can't possibly leave now: it's full light and you're far too conspicuous.

We've got a good hide behind the bedroom closet, but it's pretty small for a man your size and a thorough search might well turn it up."

"Trouble is, Marie, if I'm found here and manage to shoot my way out, that means you're blown too, and where the hell could you hide?"

"That's *my* problem. Our job is to get as many of you back to Britain as possible. At least we can fight by proxy that way. I'm afraid a lot of our compatriots have decided to roll over and let our country disappear. I can't even stand the thought."

Marie stepped towards the window and glanced carefully up and down the street then quickly stepped back, hand to throat.

"My God, three soldiers have just gone into Angelique's house. We're next."

"Show me the hide, I'll try to squeeze in."

"There's no time. I've another idea. The Germans are very polite and discreet about some things. Quick, take off all your clothes; just pile them on the chair and get into bed."

An astonished Philip quickly stripped, while managing to keep an admiring eye on Marie's lovely figure as she did the same. Just as she dived into bed and, incidentally, into Philip's waiting arms, there was a loud rap on the door.

"Un moment, s'il vous plait. Qui est-il?"

A guttural reply left no doubt. Marie rose from the bed and draped a negligee around herself, ruffled up her hair, then opened the door to three soldiers who were rather taken-aback at the sight of her. As attractive as this Frenchwoman was, they knew the strict rules of the Wehrmacht against any fraternization, much less aggressive behaviour towards the French women.

"We must search your house, madam."

Badly spoken French, thought Marie, but French all the same. She sighed irritably.

"All right, if you must, but my husband is in bed, as indeed I was.

He's not fishing today and we thought we'd enjoy a little privacy, and now this. What on earth are you looking for?"

"That I cannot tell you, madam, but we will be brief. I'm sorry to intrude, especially as it seems to be a bad time."

The German allowed himself a smirk as he brushed past Marie and quickly scanned the room. He crossed to the bedroom door and opened it to find Philip, naked and sitting up in bed with only his lower parts and his Luger covered. In rapid and excellent French, certainly excellent to any German soldier's ear, Philip berated the now quite embarrassed soldier.

"Merde, what in hell is this, barging into my house and my bedroom. Have you people no honour, no respect? My God, can't a man have some private time even in his own home?" he ranted as the now thoroughly flustered corporal backed quietly and politely out of the door, and then the house.

A smiling Marie appeared in the doorway.

"You see, they *are* polite. They get very nervous if they think they'll get a complaint from a woman. Remarkable, when they're such pigs about everything else."

Philip, having briefly felt the long, soft body against his own was not about to let this situation develop the wrong way.

"Marie," he said, pulling the bedcovers aside, "you'd best climb back into bed right now: they just might return to see if you were being honest. Let's not make you a liar."

Without a moment's hesitation, and still smiling, Marie slipped in beside him.

Night was falling and, after a supper of soup, sausage and bread, Philip felt hugely satisfied with his life. Taking occasional sips from their glasses of wine and talking quietly, they waited for Henri. When he arrived he clasped Philip's arm and greeted him warmly.

"It is good to have you in our house, my friend. I suspect you are one of those who raised so much hell at Maupertus airport this morning. Down at the bar they are all talking about it. No-one has ever seen the Boche so upset. What did you do? No, on second thoughts don't tell me. I'll learn soon enough from some of the villagers who work there." Turning to his wife he asked, "Did they search our house, Marie?"

"They did, but Angelique warned us in time and our friend here was just able to squeeze into the hide. Luckily the soldiers didn't look too hard."

Hearing the lie Philip felt ashamed that he had, in an Englishman's terms, taken advantage of this kind man's wife, but quickly recovered with his normal thought, well, that's the way things go in war! He addressed the Frenchman.

"I must try and leave your home tomorrow if I can. I'm too bloody big to hide in a small cottage for very long, nice as it would be to stay, and I'm very conscious of the danger to the two of you, hiding me here."

Henri shot a quick glance at his wife who seemed to be blushing slightly. He took another, more thoughtful, look at the giant in front of him and decided it would be no bad thing to move him along quickly.

"Do you want to move inland and further north to try to get back, or try from here?"

"What do you think we could manage from here? I'd rather not have to trek all the way back down the peninsula and then back to the coast again. Do you have any ideas?"

"Yes," Henri nodded. "A good one, I think. Marcel Christian is an old man with a good boat and he fishes most days if the weather's not bad. I think you should hide in the boat, tonight even, and when he 'discovers' you in the early morning, you will force him to sail you out to the fishing grounds, then on to England."

"Can he be trusted? I'm sorry, that was a foolish question - I take it back."

"Yes, of course he can and he'll be delighted to spend the rest of the war in England. He has no relatives to speak of and hates the occupiers. If you get stopped, have him tied up, and whatever happens to you, at least he'll be safe. What do you think?"

"Let's do it," Philip said decisively. "Do you need to alert him?"

"No, but better if I slip over tonight after getting you into the boat. Got to make sure he's fishing and advise him how to drift away from the fleet; he often does, so nobody pays much attention. All the Germans do is occasionally count the boats in port to make sure none are missing."

"It would be a bit too late to go tonight, but we wouldn't have much time if they did their count tomorrow night, would we? They'd be very likely to send out planes to shoot up the boat if they could find it."

"As you say, *if* they could find it. In the sixteen hours before the fleet returns, you can have gone nearly one hundred and thirty kilometers. At eight kilometres per hour, that's pretty damn near England. Worth a go, I'd say.

"Tonight it is then. Let's have some wine, then down to the docks after midnight; we'll all be sailing at dawn. Bonne chance, mon ami, et merci pour tout."

Well, perhaps not for all, thought Philip. It was he, he reckoned, who should be the most grateful.

As dawn broke, Philip felt the diesel engines start as the small boat came to life. The old man had not even bothered to look for Philip, who had levered himself into the tiny head.

Now there's a cool one, he thought. I think I'm going to like this man. Can't wait to get out of this smelly pissoir and say hello, but I guess I'll leave that to him. Philip dozed in the small space as the boat throbbed on. For the first time in about a week Philip thought he might actually get home too. What a fine caper this has been, he thought sleepily. Just hope old Geffers made it as well.

THIRTY NINE

It was agonizing for Geoffrey to realize, as he shot over Maupertus airfield, that if he just made a sharp turn to port he would be over England in under twenty minutes. Somewhere below, or so he hoped, Philip would be walking down a French lane looking upward at all the aerial activity just like any other bemused peasant farmer. At this point, seeing the swarm of German aircraft heading up towards him and several Spitfires roaming around as well, Geoffrey wasn't sure he didn't almost envy Philip. He knew their plan was correct, however. He must somehow exhaust the Germans' fuel while being still able himself to make it to some British field. It also dawned on him that he had no parachute and no oxygen, so any flying he was going to do would be limited to maybe eighteen thousand feet in any event. His early weather flying experience would help him here, for then he often flew well over the 'O2 over ten' formula, that is, oxygen over ten thousand feet, simply because he preferred not to breathe the stuff if he didn't have to. He knew it was a great cure for hangovers but, in his case, too much of it seemed to bring one on. In any event, he wasn't sure at what altitude this beauty performed best. He did know that, so far, it seemed to be a wonderful aircraft and it made him all the more determined to get it back to England.

Geoffrey did a tight orbit, a three hundred and sixty degree turn, to check out what was happening below and behind, as well as to get a feel of how tight he could turn and not stall. The turn was neat but possibly not as tight as he could hold a Spitfire. He'd better remember that for when the Spits came after him, which was bound to happen when he got near the British coast. This German plane had also impressed him mightily when he dived at and below the Spitfires: the speed into the dive and the subsequent acceleration was breathtaking.

This short, concentrated bout of thinking was interrupted by the glint of something off his left shoulder. Bloody hell, a Focke-Wulf! How did he get up here so fast? Must have a power boost I haven't found yet. Again, turn right into him, fly at him, roll hard right then a tight left turn, God, there's another! Well, at least it's getting confusing which might be to my advantage.

Geoffrey realized that, even during these violent evasive manoeuvres, he was edging his plane closer and closer across the Channel towards England. What seemed like an eternity of jerking his head around and constantly changing the position of his plane was probably taking only a few minutes. He wondered how long he could keep this up before somebody, clever or just plain lucky, got him in their gun sight. At least the Spits seemed to have gone home. They must have been wondering why the Focke-Wulfs hadn't chased them, and were probably mightily relieved, Geoffrey surmised.

Wham! A shot slammed into Geoffrey's plane as he was half way around another tight turn; he rolled out of it and threw the plane into another dive. My God, he thought, this plane is so responsive to a roll and dive; faster than anything I've ever flown. Too bad the other chaps can do the same thing. At this point Geoffrey was resorting to every flying trick he ever knew, trying at all times to do the unlikely or unexpected. There seemed to be about eight or nine planes in the air around him at the moment. The more the merrier, he thought as he flew right into the middle of them. Whoa, that bastard nearly rammed me. Was that a cock-up or did he deliberately try? Are they that desperate?

Wherever he'd been hit, his plane didn't seem to have suffered any serious damage. He thought the shot had gone just behind him, perhaps a shell that went straight through without exploding. He could certainly use a bit of that sort of luck.

The fight had now risen to an altitude of about five thousand feet. Geoffrey wanted to get even higher, just in case his engine got hit or failed, in which case he might be able to glide home or at least to belly in over land if he had to. What a fat target I'd make gliding, though. Christ, even the coastal anti-aircraft guns might hit me then, though, as I keep saying, they can't hit shit in an outhouse and thank God for it, they've taken potshots at me more than once!

He could faintly make out the Isle of Wight now, to his north, emerging in the bright morning light. It was suicide to fly in any one direction or altitude for more than a few seconds and thus far his great aerobatic skills had paid off. Two Focke-Wulfs had nearly collided and he was sure he'd seen one actually shoot at another. He wished he could hear their radio, even though he wouldn't understand it. He'd even thought of taking a shot himself: the trigger was right on the stick and he presumed he was fully loaded. Next bastard near me I'll have a go; that might keep them away, even if I miss. God knows, I'm not a great shot even in a plane I know well.

At least twenty more fighters suddenly appeared, coming up at him from below and to his right. Geoffrey's heart sank; another base must have been alerted. They looked like ME109s as well as a few Focke-Wulfs. How in hell could he possibly evade all of them? Well, he thought, my last tactic worked. He turned, rolled and dived directly into the oncoming swarm causing what had been a well-ordered formation to split apart violently; he even saw a collision.

"Yes!" he shouted. "Two down."

He wondered if he could count them as victories, if he actually made it home. He zoomed up and, after an aileron turn, headed right back into the melee, determined to create as much confusion as possible. Somebody coming right at him, shooting. Another hit, this time on the windscreen, glanced off, up and over. Oh, thank God for good tough, sloping German glass - hope nothing hit the engine. He shot past the oncoming fighter, the two planes belly to belly as they each turned away, then pressed the firing mechanism as a lone Messerschmitt crossed parallel in front of him; no time to look if he hit it. Sharp roll to the right, climb and suddenly push the stick all the way forward into a bunt: almost a somersault into an outside loop. Sea below and upside down, roll off at the bottom, hard down stick to the left, start to climb and jink again; that seemed to puzzle a few and for a second or two he saw no-one near him then, suddenly, he had three around him only a thousand feet above the water.

Geoffrey assumed they'd expect him to climb again and be a slower target in the process so instead he stayed at the same altitude, throwing the Focke-Wulf all over the sky, feeling more familiar with it by the minute and hugely grateful for its really tight aileron turns and amazing acceleration. The rate of roll was electrifying and must make him hard to hit. As far as he knew he'd only been hit twice and he was sure the Germans had shot down at least a couple of their own. Still, the numbers painted on the side of all the planes were pretty big and he was sure they knew his, even if he didn't. Ergo, he reasoned, the best plan was to keep right in with them as close as possible, and never give them a decent shot. A quick glance at the fuel gauge seemed to show about half; he thought it meant all tanks but he hadn't time to properly check the fuel situation.

Damn that French farmer for showing up, he cursed, and damn Philip for shooting the man and making this whole thing happen a day early. He thought he might have had a hope if it was only the Germans trying to kill him. Any second now he was sure he would see a squadron of British aircraft come up and join the fray. They would certainly wonder what was going on but at least they would attract a few of the Hun away from him, or so he hoped.

At Blackgang radar station the level of excitement was sky high, especially for the group of new trainees, which included Clarissa. They could now see for themselves what a mass of incoming raiders looked like on the radar screens. What confused them was the apparent lack of direction of the group, which now looked to number over fifty aircraft. It appeared that the group seemed to be headed towards the Isle of Wight itself but now and again seemed to veer off towards Dover and even back towards France. In any event it was heady stuff to Clarissa who now could feel that her job really could mean something for the war effort. She couldn't wait to tell Geoffrey and her father; she was sure they'd both be pleased and impressed.

Telephone calls had been made to Air Defence Command and appropriate messages were being sent out to fighter bases, but they were a bit vague as to the actual direction of the incoming enemy. Air Defence Command monitored German radio whenever they could and today were able to pick up garbled messages and shouts which puzzled them greatly, as they were neither orderly nor precise, contrary to most German fighter pilot aerial communication. There seemed to be a great deal of swearing and frantic shouting.

"Get the bastard!"

"There he is!"

"Watch out, watch out!"

"Christ, did you see that?"

It was certainly not the usual radio silence connected to an incoming attack. Something strange was happening but at that point either no-one knew of Penn's plane theft or, if they were privy to that top secret operation, connected it to what was happening today.

Roland Adams, controller at Hornchurch, did, however, know about Operation Airthief and was at that moment launching a defensive squadron of Spitfires to head off whatever attack seemed to be coming in. Blackgang had given a good early warning and the Spits should be able to intercept some twenty miles before the attacking force reached British shores. That would be good news, thought Roland, who felt that normally his planes got airborne too late to prevent at least some bomb damage, even from fighters who dropped their five hundred pound bombs and then ran for home before anybody was the wiser.

"Tally-ho."

His group of fighters had spotted the melee and was suddenly in the middle of what seemed to be an incredible dog fight. He heard complete uproar: noise, radio advice, oaths, yells of triumph and shouts.

"Shit, they're Focke-Wulfs!"

"Dive, dive, there's one on your back!"

"Jesus, look at that bastard fly! Unbelievable, I think Jerry's shooting at *him*. What the fuck is going on?"

That one caught his ear. Roland could only imagine the chaos of fifty or sixty fighter planes hurtling around the sky trying to line up another to shoot whilst, at the same time, never presenting themselves as a target. He didn't know how anybody could do this day after day. Thinking furiously he wondered if perhaps something had happened in France a day early and that maybe Penn had actually got a plane and got away. He was fairly sure that what he'd heard from the Spitfire pilots' radio chatter told him just that. Nobody but Penn and a very few others could fly in such a manner as to cause another pilot to express awe; and why would one German plane shoot at another, even though accidents did sometimes happen in the heat of aerial battle.

Roland spoke in a clear voice, so well known to so many pilots.

"Flight Leader Group 56, this is Hornchurch. Please confirm unusual German behaviour shooting at their own plane. Important. Over."

"Hornchurch, this is Johnson, Flight 56, confirm shooting. Looks like some Hun's gone berserk. Everybody's chasing and shooting at him, including us. Enemy starting to break off and head home. Over."

"Johnson, this is Adams, Hornchurch. Break off and do not shoot at crazy German pilot. I repeat *do not shoot* at crazy German pilot. If this plane survives and heads for England give escort. I repeat, give escort. Advise all flight in case this message has not reached all. Over and out."

With this Adams put out a frantic call to Air Defence advising them of his decision. He prayed he was right. He then learned from them about the strange German radio chatter and the behaviour of the incoming flight; no fighters had come within ten miles of Britain thus far. They agreed it was likely that Adams was correct and that it had to be Penn. They would try and alert all coastal defences not to shoot at anything for the next hour and also for no planes to attack any lone German plane entering British air space. But, would the orders get out in time and would they reach everyone? Roland Adams fervently hoped they would and help to save this man he so liked and admired and who seemed to be about to achieve a miracle.

FORTY

Geoffrey, still doing incredible aerobatics all over the sky, saw a few German planes break off and head back towards France, fuel low, he presumed. He also saw a whole horde of Spitfires entering the fray which, by now, was absolute pandemonium. He was sure no one could tell who was who as far as the Germans were concerned, but he was still fair game for the Spitfires and if any pilot like Johnny Johnson or Ginger Lacey were in their group heading his way he doubted like hell he'd be able to dodge them. He had no idea that he had actually been evading German pilots who had chalked up over fifty aerial victories, including no less a figure than General Galland, possibly Germany's top ace at that time. He did know, however, that he too was running low on fuel and that the frantic and violent manoeuvres and acceleration demands he was putting on this BMW engine were beyond anything he had ever attempted or asked of a piece of machinery.

He thanked God for the methodical Germans who had put most things in the cockpit right where they should be and dutifully colour-coded by function, just like the Messerschmitt 109, only a hell of a lot better in every respect. He rolled right, then pulled into a very tight turn only to break it off half way through and dive right, pushing stick and rudder right hard over and down. Christ, that would take the wings off most planes, he thought as he felt the plane juddering, but he was still intact, at least, the plane was, he was not at all sure about himself. My God, there's a Spit on my right side; how in hell did he get there? He started to jerk left, planning to follow the fake turn with another hard turn right into the Spit, when he realized how close the Spit was, and the pilot was raising his hand to him, or was it two fingers? Still, in that moment he hesitated, looked left then back again at the Spit and realized it had not changed position and, in fact, was simply flying parallel to him. Could it be - *could* it be? He turned again in his narrow seat and noted that most of the sky he could see was clear of German planes and there were only about ten Spits, two of whom were in a serious dog fight with a 109; no Fw190s in sight. Now had to be the time to head for the English coast clearly visible only a few miles ahead.

The accompanying Spit turned towards what Geoffrey thought must be Biggin Hill and it seemed a prudent idea to peacefully follow. He did just that and, moments later, the English coast flashed by just a few hundred feet below.

"My God," he gasped, "I may actually make it!" There, just ahead, lay Biggin Hill. The two planes roared directly over the field at about three hundred mph then broke left to enter a down-wind leg, far too fast but both anxious to get down. Geoffrey was knocking off speed as rapidly as he could, throttle way back, a bit of pitch and yaw and a hard turn into final with wheels down at what he guessed to be about a hundred and sixty mph. Too fast, he reckoned, but would surely slow him down. He found the flap actuator, pulled full flap and the 190 settled smoothly onto the long, hard surface runway.

Overhead, six Spitfires seemed to be patrolling, whereas the pilot who had guided Geoffrey in had landed almost parallel to him on the grass. With still no way to communicate with the tower, Geoffrey turned in toward that building and a row of hangers then suddenly saw a small Austin 7 with a "Follow Me' sign on its back come racing towards him, causing him to brake and stop as a figure jumped out and ran around the side beckoning him to open the canopy.

All Geoffrey wanted to do was park the bloody plane, get out of it and kiss the ground. He was totally spent, as exhausted as he'd ever been, but his natural good manners prevailed and he actuated the canopy slide.

"Mr Penn, Mr Penn!" The slight figure from the Austin 7 was poking his head over the cockpit side and shouting. Geoffrey was still frantically scanning the sky but could only see Spitfires so he turned back to this sergeant who somehow knew his name.

"Mr Penn, sir, a message from Mr Adams at Hornchurch. He said, 'Great job, but don't stop here! The Jerry spotted you landing and we suspect they'll be right back. Turn around and fly to Goodwood. They'll be waiting for you and will hide the plane.' Go right now please, sir; there are absolutely no German planes over England at this moment. Goodwood heading from here is two hundred degrees...."

"I know where the fuck Goodwood is," shouted an exhausted Geoffrey, all manners deserting him as he glanced at the near empty fuel tank gauge, then started to turn around and head back up the runway. The sergeant jumped back and hurriedly moved the diminutive Austin truck out of the way.

Oh God, thought Geoffrey, this is insane, but I know Roland is right. Here I am at who knows what time in the morning, sitting in a German plane on an English runway, about to take off again and try another field. I don't bloody believe it. This time, though, he felt he knew the plane better and, if the juice held out and he didn't hit a tree, he'd get the beast into Goodwood and hopefully under wraps. Then all he wanted was to sleep and after that all he wanted was Clarissa.

As he roared down the runway he caught sight of what was probably the entire base, standing outside watching and waving. For the first time he felt a rush of joy instead of the clammy cold of fear. He was back and those were *his* people; *his* England. Yes, it had been worth it, but now he had to try not to overshoot Goodwood, an easy thing to do, flying in at treetop level and just as fast as he could. He probably had fifteen minutes fuel left and that should, he hoped, do it, if he didn't miss the tiny and secluded field just fifty airmiles away. While accelerating down the runway he worked out that, factoring in take-off and landing he'd hope to average two hundred and fifty mph, meaning the journey would take twelve minutes. Doesn't leave much petrol for farting around, he thought, trying to avoid somebody or even missing my first approach, but I'm off now and if I fly at two hundred degrees I should hit Goodwood on the head, and from there it's only twenty-five minutes by car to home and bed.

The clearly marked German plane roared just off the ground and over a few startled farmers and postmen on early rounds. Not many other people saw it, the passage was so swift, but the noise woke several who wondered what new drama was unfolding overhead.

Goodwood and Tangmere were not far apart but Goodwood had been a private field belonging to the Duke of Richmond until he had, naturally, turned it over to the RAF. Tangmere, only a few miles away, was a base for a couple of Hurricane squadrons. They'll get a shock, thought Geoffrey with a smile, as he had to turn virtually right over their field in order to get into position for a right hand circuit at Goodwood so that he could land into the prevailing south-east wind.

There! There it was and without any attempt to signal the tower, Geoffrey turned downwind, quickly onto final approach and safely landed his prize. Home, he thought with a rush of emotion, truly home.

FORTY ONE

Geoffrey cranked the canopy lever and inhaled the crisp English morning air as he taxied towards one of the few buildings. Already there were several people running towards the plane, dragging a large, green tarpaulin to cover it as soon as it came to a stop. Geoffrey brought the plane to a standstill and sat motionless for an instant, overcome with feelings of relief and amazement. He found it hard to believe that he had made it. He felt like leaping from the plane and kissing the ground. God, how he hoped Philip had made it back safely too. He was sure the big Commando would never allow himself to be captured alive.

Jack Hutchinson, the aerodrome adjutant whom Geoffrey knew well, ran out to where Geoffrey now stood and actually hugged him, rather embarrassing Geoffrey who, as a staid and proper gentleman, wasn't used to such effusive behaviour. He had in fact only once before been embraced by a man and that had been a Polish general who had been carried away by Geoffrey's demonstration of the Spitfire.

"Jack," said Geoffrey, disengaging himself with an awkward chuckle, "can you get me transport to Bursledon, please? All I want is to get to bed. Please call Combined Ops, though, anybody, and just tell them the plane's here and, yes, it's fantastic, even if it does have a few holes in it."

"Geoffrey, they already know! I've had no less than Park on the phone whose actual words were, 'Let the poor bastard sleep until tomorrow,' then up to his office, please, for a debrief."

Geoffrey barely heard these words as he staggered, already half asleep, into a waiting Morris Minor which set off immediately for his digs in Bursledon. His last thought but one was whether he should call Colonel Harrison at 12 Commando but then he felt sure somebody had already done so. His final thought before falling into a dreamless sleep was of Clarissa, as indeed was his first thought nearly twenty-fours later, when he woke having absolutely no memory of how he got up the stairs into his flat or into bed. Actually, he thought, looking at his wrinkled overalls, *onto* the bed and fully clothed too. He supposed it was the phone ringing that had woken him and wondered eagerly if it might be Clarissa.

To his disappointment it was not, but rather an operator from Combined Ops telling him that she had been calling since eight o'clock and it was now nearly eleven o'clock and would he please get himself up to London as soon as possible. Air Marshal Sir Keith Park, no less, would like to see him.

A later call to Clarissa's house had elicited from the butler, who had now accepted Mr Penn as 'cleared' by Sir Archibald, a number on the Isle of Wight for Clarissa. He also gave him the information that she would, in fact, be in London that night for a debutante's ball and, yes, he did think she had a date or was at least being picked up. Perhaps Mr Penn could go directly to The Hyde Park Hotel? Yes, sir, black tie of course, sir, and he was sure that Mr Penn would be admitted as he would personally contact Miss Smythe. Yes, sir, she would be advised to be on the lookout for him.

Geoffrey took a taxi to Eastleigh where his Bentley had been hangered during his absence. McLean was waiting to greet him and again he was overwhelmed by the elder man's reaction. He must never have expected to see me back, thought Geoffrey who realized that he cared very much about this abrasive but deeply emotional man.

"Geoffrey, Geoffrey, my boy, you pulled it off! I can't, *we* can't, believe it. It's an absolute triumph and I want to hear every detail as soon as you are able, but I know that you've to get up to London, so it'll have to wait. Incidentally, don't let them even think of talking you into another of these hare-brained escapades: you've done more than your share!"

"No sir, I can absolutely guarantee that, never again. I'm not sure I ever want to even go to France again and I certainly don't want to camp if I do, it's the George Cinq for me or nothing, and no bloody Commandos in my bed either! No, I'll just tell them all I've found out so far about the Focke-Wulf.

It's marvellous, by the way, a really terrific plane, but I do think our next Spit development will match it. Right now, I'd give it a jolly wide berth, if I came upon one.

"But tonight, I'm going to go to a dance and, if I can work it, I'm going to steal a special girl away. With any luck it'll be easier than pinching an aeroplane! Good afternoon, sir - it's very, *very* good to see you too!"

FORTY TWO

Geoffrey was ushered into the hallowed interior of Combined Ops Headquarters, where a group of at least thirty people was waiting to hear all about the aeroplane as well as the details of how the entire escapade had been managed. Apparently, experts from Farnborough and Supermarine were already at Goodwood poring over the plane which, he was told, had taken quite a pounding from at least one cannon shot and several machine gun hits, none of which had damaged much except the radio, which Geoffrey hadn't known how to work anyhow. They were impressed that he had managed to fire a few shots himself but quite understood when he said he hadn't had time to see if he'd hit anything, and doubted he had, unless by accident.

As Geoffrey related his story he modestly insisted that he truly could never have achieved anything relating to this steal without Philip Quigley's involvement. In fact, one officer remarked later that to hear Penn's version, the Commando all but flew the plane back. Geoffrey's humility and quiet, clear debriefing had impressed each man there enormously. They were aware that they were listening to a remarkable man tell an even more remarkable story and they knew just how much the combined effort of those two men had done to strengthen Britain's war effort.

At last, out of a meeting that Geoffrey had found somewhat embarrassing, except for the technical details, he fairly raced the faithful old Bentley into London to a friend's flat where he parked, bathed and changed into what he called his monkey suit, gradually feeling more civilized and relaxed. He was so looking forward to seeing Clarissa at the dance he even felt he could ignore the usual civvie suit jibes his non-uniform dress always seemed to elicit.

At the door of The Hyde Park Hotel the dance receptionist assured him that Clarissa Smythe had indeed informed them that he would be arriving.

"Please go right in. I imagine you'll find her in the middle of a pack of uniforms!"

True enough, he thought as he spotted her dark hair and flashing smile across the dance floor and he had started moving towards her when a shout went up.

"Penn, that's Geoffrey Penn!" A number of heads turned towards the shouting man and then to Geoffrey as more and more men took up the shout, "Penn! Penn!" They were all RAF chaps who suddenly abandoned their confused dates and streamed towards a hideously embarrassed Geoffrey who was trying, on his part, to get to an equally baffled Clarissa. He found himself surrounded by men in RAF uniforms pounding his back, shaking his hand and generally drowning out the band which at someone's behest started to play 'For he's a Jolly Good Fellow'. The crowd parted just enough to let Clarissa in next to the horrified and red-faced Geoffrey who wanted none of what he knew must be a celebration of his exploit. News certainly gets around the RAF quickly, he thought, panicking slightly. All he wanted was Clarissa. He grabbed her by the arm and amongst all the shouting and singing, whispered imploringly in her ear.

"Please let's get out of here, *now!*"

They managed, hand in hand, to get through the crowd who seemed willing to let Geoffrey leave with his trophy, no doubt feeling, even those who didn't know exactly what, that he must have done something to deserve such a prize.

Once out of the hubbub and in the car Clarissa couldn't contain herself any longer.

"Geoffrey, darling, what *was* that all about? Where have you been and what in God's name have you been doing?"

"Just my job, darling, just my job. But I absolutely don't want to talk about all that, I want to talk about you. I missed you so much. I'm desperately in love with you, you know that, don't you? All I want on this earth right now is to take you somewhere, your home, my friend's flat, even this cramped old car, and make love to you forever. You have *no* idea how I've missed you!"

"You can, Geoffrey, you can, but please not here in this car. Let's go home. When Daddy heard from James that you were going to meet me at the dance he, rather thoughtfully for him, decided to go to his club for cards. He likes you, you know, and so do I, darling. In fact, I think I love you. But you've simply got to tell me *something* about all that fuss. I thought you were up north doing something. What on earth was it? Those men were treating you like some sort of hero! Surely, if all those men know what you did you can tell *me*, and if you don't," she pouted so prettily that Geoffrey suddenly couldn't breathe, "I won't let you take me home."

"That's blackmail, blackmail of the worst sort, Clarissa, and I shall have to think up a suitable punishment. But before I do I will tell you a bit, very quickly, because I have certain other things on my mind. I played a modest part in an adventure which will help the RAF and that's what those chaps were all on about; making a bit much of it, I'm afraid, but these days we need a few things to cheer us up."

"Yes, but what did you actually *do*, Geoffrey, and *where?*"

"Well, another chap, a very brave man, without whom none of this could have happened, and I got ourselves over to Cherbourg and pinched a German plane which I flew back to England yesterday. The word seemed to get around pretty quickly, no secrets last long these days."

"My God, Geoffrey, if you were there too you must be just as brave. If you flew back together, why didn't you bring him to the dance too?"

"I wish I could have, darling, but this Commando, the toughest man I've ever met, incidentally, wouldn't fit in the plane. But, in any event, his plan, and it really *was* his plan, was to stay behind and find his own way back. Poor bugger really had no choice. One day I'll tell you all about him. I hope to God he does survive, the Germans are absolutely furious about this affair. I was told they attacked Biggin Hill today with a vengeance."

"A big Commando, you say? Are you allowed to tell me his name?"

"Yes, I don't see why not. Captain Philip Quigley."

"Oh! Oh my God! . . . ."

The End

AUTHOR'S NOTE

This book is, of course, a novel and as such I have taken the liberty of ascribing words and thoughts to the characters within, most of whom actually existed. The two principal characters in this book are based upon real people who did, indeed, conspire to steal a Focke-Wulf. That they did not attempt this extraordinary mission is simply the result of a confused (or very smart!) German pilot who actually landed his Focke-Wulf 190 at a startled Welsh airfield. Oberleutnant Arnim Faber had apparently, in the heat of battle and exultant over having just shot down another Spitfire, mistaken the Bristol Channel for the English Channel and presumed that he was landing back in France. The need to implement such a risky plan was therefore obviated.

Philip Pinckney, the real name of the Commando, was dismayed by this turn of events, exclaiming to Jeffrey Quill, his co-conspirator, 'We've been robbed,' whereas Jeffrey himself was delighted.

Jeffrey Quill was my neighbour in Churt, Surrey, England where he resided while working for British Aviation. I first met him at a dinner party where I was proclaiming the problems I had with all the regulations relating to my humble efforts at private flying within UK airspace. He remarked that he, too, had once had a pilot's licence which had lapsed and he wasn't sure if he'd bother to renew it for similar reasons.

A few weeks later I met him again at a Goodwood Vintage Rolls Royce and Bentley rally in southern England. At this event the owners of cars with Rolls engines gathered for a pasture picnic in the rolling hills of the Earl of Richmond's estate. As we ate we were suddenly startled by the unmistakable roar - at least to those who had lived in England during World War II - of a Spitfire and a Hurricane coming across the fields at what seemed more barbed wire than tree top height. Just before reaching us they pulled up into a vertical climb until they finally lost power and tumbled and spun towards earth, only to pull out again and engage in a mock dog fight, displaying the most incredible flying I'd ever seen before or since. At the end of this breathtaking show they landed on the grass and taxied up towards us. When the hatch went back on the Spitfire out stepped my neighbour, silver-haired and wearing an old blue pullover. This modest man had indeed renewed his licence in order to demonstrate to the club members another great use of Rolls Royce engines. I was later told, and in fact read in a book by Alex Henshaw, another famous test pilot who worked with Jeffrey at Vickers Supermarine, that Jeffrey Quill was perhaps the greatest aerobatic pilot of that time.

When I got to know him much better and happened to discover the existence of Operation Airthief it was with great difficulty that I was able to extract any information about it from him, such was his modesty. 'But it never actually took place, old man, did it - so I really didn't risk anything!'

I had, in fact, learned about this proposed exploit from a relative of his lovely wife, Claire. He, my wife and I were all dining together with the Quills. This man had just returned from a meeting with the 'stoker' on his motor torpedo boat who had kept him afloat in the water after the raid on the submarine pens at St. Nazaire where his boat had been sunk. He had been captured and hospitalized by the Germans. Upon my remarking what a great story that would make he replied that I really should talk to Jeffrey about his crazy plan to steal a German plane. 'Now that really is some story.'

So that is what I have tried to tell - as I imagined it might have happened - for there is no question that these two men were prepared to risk their lives in the effort. Philip Pinckney's hand-written top secret memo outlining the plan and proposing it to Combined Operations is held at the Public Records Office at Kew, England.

Sadly, both these remarkable men are gone. Jeffrey died aged 83, highly acclaimed as one of the most important and best-loved names in British aviation's history. Honoured, but surprisingly not knighted by a country which seems willing to ennoble supermarket owners and pop musicians but which, in my judgement, owed much more to this man. He is survived by two daughters from a previous marriage. Sadly the lovely Claire, who was indeed a radar operator, is now also deceased.

Philip Pinckney died in Italy during September, 1943, having parachuted in to perform another heroic act - this time a plan to blow up the Brenner Pass. At the time he was nursing a possibly broken back. Sadly he did not survive this mission and is now buried in Florence in the British Cemetery. Of Philip, Jeffrey once told me, 'If there had been no war, one would have to have been created for him somewhere,' such was his fearless love of adventure and his country.

I hope I have done these great men justice.

SOURCES

'Spitfire' – a test pilot's story by Jeffrey Quill;
'Fighter Pilot' by Edward H. Sims;
'Fighter' by Len Deighton;
'Jagdgeschwader II Richthofen';
'F.W. 190 in Action' by Brian Filley;
'Warplanes of the Luftwaffe' by David Donald.
'Aeroplane' magazine – various issues.

ACKNOWLEDGEMENTS

Eleanor 'Red' Shively - my wife, who patiently listened to me talk about writing this book for far too many years.

Meredith Shively who tirelessly edited the text.

Kent Shively who took care of the production.

Jeffrey Quill O.B.E., who provided me with much help before he died.

Capt. Eric Brown C.B.E., R.N. who gave me invaluable advice as one of the few people to have actually flown both aircraft, the 109 and the 190.

Heinz Schmidt - a genuine 190 pilot from World War II - who kindly gave me much good advice on this 'wonderful' aeroplane.

Luc Dufour, Manager of the Aeroport du Cherbourg, Maupertus.

R.A.Knight of Warsash, U.K., Collector of Archives 12 Commando.

Kenneth Scott, author of 'H.M.S. Tormentor'.

Dale Snitton, M.B.E., R.A.F. retired - a test pilot.

Gordon Leith, Curator of the Royal Air Force Museum.

Richard Riding, Editor 'Aeroplane' magazine.

"